D0050618

BY JANET EVANOVICH

THE STEPHANIE PLUM NOVELS

One for the Money

Two for the Dough

Three to Get Deadly

Four to Score

High Five

Hot Six

Seven Up

Hard Eight

To the Nines

Ten Big Ones

Eleven on Top

Twelve Sharp

Lean Mean Thirteen

Fearless Fourteen

Finger Lickin' Fifteen

Sizzling Sixteen

Smokin' Seventeen

Explosive Eighteen

Notorious Nineteen

Takedown Twenty

Top Secret Twenty-One

Tricky Twenty-Two

Turbo Twenty-Three

Hardcore Twenty-Four

Look Alive Twenty-Five

Twisted Twenty-Six

Fortune and Glory
(Tantalizing Twenty-Seven)

THE BOUNTY

JANET EVANOVICH

AND

STEVE HAMILTON

A FOX AND O'HARE NOVEL

THE

BOUNTY

ATRIA BOOKS

New York   London   Toronto   Sydney   New Delhi

ATRIA
BOOKS

An Imprint of Simon & Schuster, Inc.
1230 Avenue of the Americas
New York, NY 10020

First Atria Books hardcover edition March 2021

ATRIA BOOKS and colophon are trademarks of Simon & Schuster, Inc.

For information about special discounts for bulk purchases, please contact Simon & Schuster Special Sales at 1-866-506-1949 or business@simonandschuster.com.

The Simon & Schuster Speakers Bureau can bring authors to your live event. For more information, or to book an event, contact the Simon & Schuster Speakers Bureau at 1-866-248-3049 or visit our website at www.simonspeakers.com.

Interior design by Jill Putorti

Manufactured in the United States of America

1 3 5 7 9 10 8 6 4 2

Library of Congress Cataloging-in-Publication Data has been applied for.

ISBN 978-1-9821-5713-5
ISBN 978-1-9821-5715-9 (ebook)

CHAPTER ONE

"The target is approaching the Vatican."

It was something Agent Kate O'Hare never thought she'd hear, at least not outside a movie theater.

As she stared at the video monitor, Nick Fox leaned down next to her, so close she could feel his breath on her neck. Cologne, hair product, pheromones. Whatever the combination, it tried to have its usual effect on her, but she kept her focus.

"Do you really think this guy is as good as I am?" Nick asked.

"Maybe better," Kate said. "You're the one who got caught."

Nick laughed that off. Even if he was "retired" from the business, he was still loving every minute of this trip to Italy, especially this chance to watch a master thief at work. He had once been a world-class thief himself, and had barely avoided a lifetime stay in the federal ADX Supermax prison. He bartered for his freedom by agreeing to help the FBI run semilegal cons and takedowns on the worst-of-the-worst, technically out-of-reach criminals. Kate tracked him for years and finally brought him down, only to be told by the deputy director himself that her next assignment was to be Nick's full-time handler, minder, wrangler, manager, baby-sitter, whatever you wanted to call it. Nick didn't go to prison in leg irons. He accepted the full-time shadow employment offer from the United States Department of Justice.

Nick was six feet tall, with soft brown hair, intelligent brown eyes, and a boyish grin that brought out the laugh lines around his eyes. He had the agile body of a tennis pro, lean and firm. He was smart, sexy, and playful, and if Nick had once been a world-class thief, he was still and always would be a galaxy-class kisser. From the beginning, it was all Kate could do to keep a professional distance. It was a goal she had thrown out the window on more than one occasion, and even now she wasn't sure what to call their official "status." In Facebook terms, it would have to be "It's complicated."

Tonight, Kate was six thousand miles from her Los Angeles cubicle, officially on loan to Interpol. She was part of a small international task force assisting the Vatican Gendarmerie's *Gruppo Intervento Rapido,* the Rapid Intervention Group, who were acting on dark web intel that the museum complex was being targeted for a nighttime break-in. Her job was to provide Nick Fox's expertise to the RIG, and make sure he acted like an angel. As exciting as that assignment might sound, she actually felt more like the trainer who brings the gorilla onto the movie set for the big action scene. No one even notices the trainer until the gorilla starts tearing everything up and stealing all of the food from the catering table.

Nick had been on his best behavior so far. He generously led the team through every phase of a high-level professional infiltration, taking them step by step through everything *he* would do if he were in the mood to break into the Vatican City Museum and steal something incredibly rare and incredibly valuable. The inspector general of the Vatican Gendarmerie was a serious, no-nonsense man named Lorenzo Vitali, a former commander from the Italian Carabinieri. He was essentially half policeman and half soldier, who had answered a higher calling to take over security at the Vatican. He'd been skeptical of everything Nick Fox said, until Nick walked him around the city's perimeter, pointing out every possible point of "surreptitious entry."

"You have just over six hundred full-time residents living in this city," Nick had said. "Yet every day, you open the gates and admit how many people?"

"On a busy day," Vitali had said, "over twenty thousand."

"Signore Inspector, you are tempting me back into a life of sin."

"We have one of the most advanced security systems in the world, Mr. Fox."

Nick had smiled. "That's an interesting first response, Signore Inspector. You didn't say you have a hundred highly trained and heavily armed guards. You didn't say you have a sniper positioned on every roof. You said you have a *system*." Nick leaned in closer to the inspector and said, "I spent my entire professional career absolutely in *love* with *systems*."

Nick and Kate were now stationed in a small room on the

third floor of the museum complex, in front of a large bank of video surveillance screens. As a precaution, Pope Francis had been taken by helicopter to the summer residence at Castel Gandolfo, twenty miles away. Forty-two members of the combined Gendarmerie/Interpol force were closely watching every inch of the museum. Kate was the only woman on the team, and if she felt at all uncomfortable working in a city where women were required to cover their arms and knees, at least she was wearing her favorite outfit, a blue windbreaker with the letters "FBI" written across the back, with a black T-shirt under a black Kevlar vest. Her chestnut-brown hair was tied up in her usual all-business ponytail. She had her Glock 9mm handgun tucked into her belt, and her Ontario MK 3 Navy SEAL knife strapped to her leg. Both were technically forbidden here, but Inspector Vitali, who tonight was personally commanding the Rapid Intervention Group, had seen Kate sliding her Glock under her windbreaker. If he was going to object, that would have been the time, but he had done nothing other than raise one eyebrow in appreciation.

The radio on the table squawked again. "The target is climbing the north wall, near the Cortile del Belvedere."

Nick and Kate watched the video screen directed at the north wall. The image flickered for a moment, then was restored. There was nobody to see.

"He looped the camera feed," Nick said. "Very smooth. Couldn't have done it better myself."

"The target is moving through the Pigna Courtyard," the radio voice said, "toward the north side of the museum."

As they stared at another screen, they saw nothing but the brief movement of a single shadow.

"No security guard would ever catch that," Nick said, nodding in appreciation. "I'm watching a master at work."

"Don't get too attached to him," Kate said. "He's going to be in handcuffs in about five minutes."

"You don't have him yet."

"We've lost visual," the radio voice said. "Last seen a hundred feet from the Command Center."

They sat in silence as a full minute ticked by. They waited to pick him up again, but then every video screen went black.

"He took them all offline," Nick said. "It's a gutsy move. Makes us blind, but at the same time announces that he's on the grounds. He's going to have to move fast now."

"We've got the backup cameras," Kate said. "On a separate circuit. The team spent all day yesterday installing them."

She opened a laptop and brought up a multiscreen view.

"There," she said, pointing to a dark figure moving down a hallway.

The resolution wasn't nearly as good as the regular security cameras, but Nick and Kate could make out the figure, maybe six feet tall, moving with speed and efficiency. Like UCLA's beloved basketball coach John Wooden used to say, *Be quick but don't hurry.*

"What is he wearing?" Kate asked. She leaned forward, squinting. The thief was dressed all in black, and he appeared to be wearing a thin backpack.

"I don't get it," Nick said. "If you're going for the ring, you just slip it into your pocket. You don't need a backpack."

The ring was the diamond-encrusted ring that once belonged to Pope Paul VI, the featured piece in a special exhibit of papal jewelry displayed in glass cases throughout the Galleria dei Candelabri. Worth many millions of dollars, it was the kind of ring that the current pope in all his modesty would never wear, but Pope Paul VI hadn't seemed to mind a little bling now and then.

Only this ring was fake. The Vatican officials had refused to leave the real thing vulnerable to theft, or even to being *touched* by an outsider. But this fake ring was so convincing, especially in the semidarkness of the closed museum, the team was sure that the target would take the bait.

They watched as the intruder left one camera's view, then appeared in another. He was in the Galleria dei Candelabri now, where a trap had been set.

Nick and Kate held their breath as the figure approached the display case. All he had to do was lift the glass and the charges would go from simple trespassing and breaking and entering to grand theft and desecration of a holy artifact and a dozen other charges that would put him away for the rest of his life. If the good Catholics around here had their way, for the rest of his afterlife, too.

The figure came closer and closer to the display case. He paused for one moment, the time it took to let out one breath, then kept moving. Nick and Kate both stared at the screen.

"What just happened?" Kate asked.

Nick didn't answer.

"Did he know it was a fake?" Kate asked. "Is that possible? He didn't look at it for more than *one second*."

"I saw them put that ring in the case today," Nick said. "It would have fooled me." He kept staring at the screen. "Maybe we're asking the wrong question. Maybe this was never about stealing the ring."

"What else could he be after?" Kate asked. "What else is as valuable? And as easy to take out of the museum?"

"From the beginning, we've been assuming that he's a world-class *thief*, looking for a big score. But you said it yourself, if he's so good, how come we've never even heard of him? A thief this good just doesn't appear out of nowhere."

"What are you saying?"

"I'm saying, if you're thinking like a thief, you take the easy score that's right in front of you. This guy didn't do that."

"He's still moving south," the radio voice said.

"Don't lose him!" Another voice, the team commander.

"Let's go," Kate said, grabbing the radio and opening the door.

"We're not supposed to leave this room," Nick said.

"You heard the man. He said *don't lose him*!"

Nick ran out the door after Kate and followed her down the marble stairs. They hit the ground floor in the Galleria degli Arazzi, a long hallway with elaborate tapestries hanging on both sides.

"This way," Kate said, taking a right and running south down the hallway.

The radio squawked again. "Target is in the Map Gallery."

Kate burst through the door, into another long hallway called the Galleria delle Carte Geografiche. It had brightly colored maps along the walls and a high arched ceiling with frescoes almost as amazing as the Sistine Chapel's, but she didn't pause for even a second to admire her surroundings. Halfway down the gallery, a side door was just closing.

"Side room in the gallery," Kate said into the radio. "I'm on him."

"Agent O'Hare!" the voice came back. "You are an observer and you are not to engage! Do you hear me? *Do not engage!*"

She ignored the voice and kept running, with Nick on her heels. When she got to the door, she turned the knob but it was locked tight. She tried putting a shoulder into it, bounced backward a few feet, and said some words that shouldn't be said anywhere in the Holy City.

By this time, two members of the Rapid Intervention Group had entered the gallery. They were in Kevlar, helmets, and face shields, and carrying Beretta ARX160 assault rifles. One of the officers put a passkey into the electronic lock and the door opened.

The room was dark. The officers gestured for Nick and Kate to stay back as they turned on the flashlights attached to their assault rifles. They stepped into the doorway, shouting "*Sul pavimento, non muoverti!*" just in case the thief spoke Italian and also felt like cooperating and lying down on the floor so they could cuff him.

When there was no response, the officers moved into the room. Kate and Nick followed. There were several tables, high file cabinets, bookshelves, and display cases. The smell of strong chemicals hung in the air.

"This is a restoration room," Kate said. "Why would he—"

She was interrupted by the officers shouting again. They had found the rear entrance to the room. The door was open. The thief was gone, moving toward another part of the museum.

"Let's go," Kate said.

Without saying a word, Nick put up one hand to stop her.

"What is it?" she asked.

He pointed upward. High on the wall, between the bookshelves, was a window. It was open, and one of the ladders used to access the top rows of the shelves had been moved just under it.

"He's got them chasing their own tail right now," Nick said, again with an undisguised note of appreciation.

Kate climbed up the ladder, saw the rope hanging on the outside wall. She worked her way through the window, painfully scraping her shin against the stone sill, finally grabbed the rope, and was able to slowly work her way down. When she was on the ground, she turned around to see Nick standing next to her. There wasn't a single wrinkle in his jacket, not a hair out of place.

"I used the door," he said.

Before she could hit him, she spotted movement in the distance.

"There," she said, and started running again. She keyed her radio and reported that the target was outside the museum, heading toward the Sistine Chapel.

"Agent O'Hare!" It was the same voice who had told her not to engage the suspect. She was pumping her arms as she ran, making it hard to hear what the voice on the radio was trying to tell her.

Not that she was in any mood to listen, anyway. Her heart was beating fast now, that familiar rush she always felt when she was chasing down a suspect on foot.

Kate saw movement again, near the door leading into the cathedral. She ran through the same door, this time with her Glock pulled out from her belt.

She was breathing hard and paused one moment to orient herself. Leading with her weapon, she advanced into the Sistine Chapel. This time, she couldn't help but sneak a glance up at the ceiling, at the five-hundred-year-old frescoes and especially at Adam and the Big Guy himself, who seemed to be looking down at her, wondering what this crazy woman was doing waving a Glock 9mm semiautomatic in God's most holy of all holy houses. I'll do a hundred Hail Marys later, she thought, as she waited to spot another movement, hear some small sound, anything to let her know where the suspect was.

Footsteps behind her. She swung around, pointing her barrel at Nick. He wasn't breathing hard, and wasn't sweating. In fact, he looked like he'd just stopped at the Vatican barbershop for a shave and a haircut.

"Do I even have to say how wrong this looks?" he asked. "Although if you're going to shoot somebody, I suppose this isn't the worst place to spend your last moments."

"Quiet," she said. "He's in here somewhere."

She turned to scan the room again, as Nick looked up at the ceiling. There was a long silence, until it was broken by a door closing at the far end of the cathedral. Kate was off and running again, through the same door, until she picked up the intruder in the great expanse of St. Peter's Square, a hundred yards ahead of her. She grabbed her radio and tried to speak. "He's heading into the basilica."

"Moving in," the radio voice said. "Close off every exit."

She ran up the steps to the front doors of St. Peter's Basilica. One of the doors was ajar. She pushed it open. It was dark in the great lobby, the entire building closed down for the night.

Nick slipped in through the same door and stood beside her.

"My bat-sense is tingling," Kate said.

"Spidey-sense," Nick corrected. "But don't worry about it. I'm not here to judge."

They slowly made their way down the hallway, pausing every now and then to listen. The sound of footsteps came from above. Kate led with her Glock as she climbed the staircase. Every floor of the great basilica was dark and empty. Nick stayed close behind her.

They worked their way up each flight of stairs. A sign pointed them to the final staircase, leading to Michelangelo's Dome. Kate heard the last echo of footsteps. There was nowhere else for him to go.

"He's in the dome," she said into the radio. She was determined to ignore anything that was said next, any order to stand down, because she had tracked this man all the way to the very top of the city and she wasn't about to step back now.

Nick stayed behind Kate as she bounded up the staircase, which opened to the highest viewing platform in the city. In fact, it was the highest dome in the world. Under any other circumstances, it would have been a perfect night, with a million lights spread out below them, not just from the Vatican but from the city of Rome, which surrounded it.

"It's over!" she announced to the night air. "If you're armed, put your weapon down!"

She listened for a response.

Nothing. She picked one direction, went right, circling counterclockwise around the dome.

Nick appeared on the platform a moment later. He stood alone, looking down over the same view, until he heard a noise to his left. He edged around the dome, moving slowly, and saw nothing but the statues of the apostles that lined the platform's stone rail.

One of the apostles moved.

"It's time to give up," Nick said.

"I don't think so."

Nick wondered where he had heard that voice before.

The intruder had climbed up onto the edge of the stone wall, and now he was facing out over the square.

"Don't do it!" Nick said. He came forward, determined to grab the man by the waist.

The man turned to look at him. Both men were immediately frozen to the spot. They stared at each other, neither saying a word.

When Kate came around from the other direction, the spell was broken. The man spread out his arms and fell into the night.

Kate arrived at the wall just in time to see the man dropping to the square below.

There was a flash of white. A parachute! It unfurled within a fraction of a second. The air caught it and the man's fall turned into flight.

He made one great sweep across St. Peter's Square, then turned. The chute nearly brought him to a stop in midair before it regathered itself and took him toward the southern wall of the city. Kate watched, mesmerized, as the man disappeared over the wall, landing somewhere in the streets of Rome.

Kate stood motionless, trying to convince herself that she had really just seen the thief fly away.

"Why didn't you stop him?" she asked.

Nick slowly shook his head, looking numb. "That was my father."

CHAPTER TWO

There were two dozen people sitting in the Public Security Department's conference room on the upper floor of an office building in Rome's administrative subdivision, a few kilometers east of the Vatican walls. Present were members of the Gendarmerie's Rapid Intervention Group, Interpol agents with their intelligence analysts, plus Kate O'Hare and Nick Fox, the on-loan consultants from the FBI.

"This is the suspect we are now looking for," Inspector General Vitali said. For a man with such a romantic name, Lorenzo Vitali didn't appear to be in love with anyone. Today he looked like he wanted to kill most of the people in the room with his bare hands.

The other major player in the room was Special Agent in Charge Carl Jessup. He had arrived at the Rome airport just thirty minutes before, after flying all night from the FBI field office in Los Angeles. He was fifty-seven years old, a lean, sinewy man originally from Kentucky who still carried a trace of Old Appalachia in his speech. On his best day, Jessup's face looked like it needed a good ironing to smooth out all of the wrinkles and lines. After thirteen hours on an airplane, this did not come close to being his best day.

"The suspect's name is Quentin Fox," Vitali said.

The face of Nick's father was projected onto the screen that dominated one wall of the conference room. It was a simple passport photograph on a white background, the farthest thing from a glamour shot, yet it was impossible not to see the glamour, the charm, the confidence, the raw charisma, radiating from this face.

It was a face that had a few years on it, but clearly every one of those years had been good to him. A face that could open doors, close deals, remove clothes, get the best table at a crowded restaurant, and make everyone in the room hang on his every word.

Kate saw the resemblance immediately, especially in the eyes. Eyes that looked right through you. She looked over at Nick, who was now staring up at the face of his father without any expression on his own. She was dying to know what he was thinking, but now was not the time to interrupt with questions.

"Quentin Fox is sixty-two years old," Vitali said. "He was born in Paris, the son of an American diplomat and a French artist. He was educated first in Paris, then at Harvard when his father brought him to America. He majored in economics and art history."

Vitali clicked his handheld remote control. The photo on the screen was replaced by an old black-and-white shot of a much younger man leaning against a stone wall, his hands in his pockets, a long scarf draped around his neck, looking like he owned the entire campus.

"He ran a gallery in Boston for seven years before moving to New York City and opening his own business. As a dealer specializing in European and Middle Eastern art, young Quentin found himself operating in a very competitive world, but by all accounts he thrived in it."

The photo was replaced by another, and then another, Quentin Fox posing with artists and well-dressed buyers. Kate glanced over at Nick again, watched as the light from each new photo was cast on his face.

"This is Quentin Fox with a woman who was then named Olivia Price," Vitali said, projecting a photograph taken at a fancy party. Quentin was in a tux and Olivia was in a stunning, shimmering cocktail dress with her hair pinned up to show off her diamond earrings. "She was a painter whose work Quentin was showing, the daughter of very wealthy parents. Quentin and Olivia were married in Cuba."

Kate glanced over one more time. Nick allowed a faint smile as he looked at the image of his mother.

"Quentin and Olivia Fox returned to Miami," Vitali said, "where Quentin opened up a new gallery. She gave birth to a son six months later. Nicholas. Here's where it gets interesting." Vitali clicked his remote and a new image filled the screen. It was a man wearing a traditional keffiyeh, a red and white checked headdress favored by men in Arabic countries. "This is Quentin Fox in Cairo, about to meet with an international arms dealer who would be found dead two weeks later."

Everything about Nick's body language changed. He leaned forward in his chair, staring at the screen intently.

"Here he is two years later," Vitali went on, "in Barcelona, meeting with two members of a Basque separatist group."

Another image on the screen, the same man who'd been wearing the keffiyeh, now wearing a suit and sitting at a table with two other men.

"Three years later, in Cyprus. With a key figure in a human trafficking ring."

Another image, two men in another café.

"We don't have many other photographs," Vitali went on. "We did find three confirmed identities so far. I'm sure there are more."

One more image came up, with three more passports, Quentin's face in each, but each with a different name and country of origin.

Vitali stopped talking and stood in front of everyone, with the different faces of Quentin Fox still projected onto the screen behind him. He stared at Nick, clearly waiting for something to be said.

Nick stayed silent.

"Mr. Fox," Vitali said, "were you aware of your father's career as a foreign operative?"

"My father was an art dealer," Nick said. "He bought paintings, pottery, and rugs. He traveled a lot, brought items home, and sold them in his gallery. When he came home, he'd play with his model trains. I thought he had the most boring life in the world. I had no idea there was this whole other side to it."

"But you did find out?"

Nick hesitated. "I did. Later."

"Later as in when?"

"Later as in later."

Vitali stared him down.

"If you must know," Nick said, "I found out the day before my mother died. She made him promise to tell me. My father and I haven't spoken much since then."

Vitali nodded. "And were you aware that your father was capable of an operation like this?"

Nick almost smiled at that. "I didn't know he was this good, no."

"So you had no idea that he would be—"

"No," Nick said, cutting him off. "Of course not."

"We have just been informed that Quentin Fox worked as an off-the-books resource for the CIA," Vitali said, glancing over at Jessup. "Apparently, this was as big a surprise to the FBI as it was to myself."

Jessup shifted uncomfortably in his chair. "The CIA does not generally share such information with my bureau," he said. "Not unless there's a specific need to know."

"I believe we have that today," Vitali said, barely disguising his disgust at American bureaucracy, "but now that they've seen fit to share the information, it's clear that Quentin Fox worked for the CIA in *some* capacity for at least twenty years."

"It's a good cover," Nick said. "An art dealer has a plausible reason for traveling anywhere in the world."

"We've been told that his assignments ended twelve years ago," Vitali said, looking at Jessup again. "We've also been assured that Quentin Fox was *not* acting on behalf of the American government in any way. Whatever he was doing here, it was on his own initiative."

Nick shook his head. This didn't make any sense.

"I'm going to ask you one more time," Vitali said to Nick. "I'd like you to really think about your answer this time. Did you have any idea that your father would break into the Vatican last night?"

"Yes, that was our plan," Nick said. " 'Meet you at the top of the dome. Bring a parachute.' "

Vitali didn't look amused by this, but he pressed on. "The parachute, now that you bring it up, was found in an alley near the city wall. It's a specific type of chute that the SAS forces in the UK use. Again, I think I know what your answer is going to be, but do you have any idea how he might have gotten his hands on such a thing?"

"No."

"And you're not at all surprised that your father could make a jump like this? At his age?"

"He's sixty-two, not ninety-two," Nick said. "I think he just proved he can do it. And no, to answer your next question before you ask it, I have no idea where he is right now."

"Mr. Fox, if we find out you're not being honest with us—"

"You're the guys who asked me to come out here to help you," Nick said, keeping his voice level. "Are you going to accuse me, or not? Go ahead, Inspector Vitali, don't be shy. Just come out and say it. You'll feel so much better."

Agent Jessup recognized this as the moment he should shake off his jet lag. "Nick, that's enough. Just answer the questions."

"There's nothing to answer," Nick said. "I don't know anything about any of this. But I do have one question for the inspector, if he doesn't mind."

"Go ahead," Vitali said.

"What was stolen last night?"

"You mean what did your father steal from the Vatican?"

"If you want to put it that way," Nick said. "What did my sixty-two-year-old father steal after he single-handedly defeated your entire team?"

Vitali hit the button to advance to the next projected image. "*This* is what your father took from the Galleria delle Carte Geografiche, Mr. Fox."

It was a map, the paper yellowed and the ink faded. There were contour lines as if marking topography, and scattered across the map in a seemingly random sequence were a dozen crude symbols. Like something you'd scratch into the ground, a rough X, then an S, then something like an arrow. On the right side of the map, set apart in a separate banner, ran a string of words. *Auf dem Turm, Deutschland Siegt Auf Allen Fronten.*

Everyone squinted at the map, tilted their heads, trying to make sense of it.

"This map is seventy-five years old," Vitali said. "The inscription on the side translates to 'On the tower, Germany is victorious on all fronts.'"

"What is the purpose of this map?" Nick asked.

"We don't know for sure, but some of our experts believe this is, essentially—"

"A treasure map?"

"Pirates use *treasure maps*," Vitali said, his voice dripping with disdain. "With a dotted line to lead them around the quicksand and the alligators, and then the big X to mark where they should start digging." He turned to the map, pointed to some of the symbols. "This is a complex series of coded symbols, using Germanic runes from the eighth century as a lexicon."

"That leads to a treasure," Nick said.

Vitali let out a breath. "Ultimately, yes."

"So it's a treasure map," Nick said. "But for smart people."

There was a ripple of suppressed laughter in the room.

"This is a delicate subject we're about to discuss now," Vitali said. "In the last days of World War Two, when it was clear that the Allies were advancing on both fronts, there were a number of Nazi party members who thought they should gather together all of the gold they had plundered throughout Europe. The so-called *Raubgold*. Some of it had been hidden in Switzerland, some in Portugal." He paused. "According to *some* records, which are still in dispute, there may have also been a large reserve of gold stored in the Vatican. As much as one hundred tons. The gold was moved by a group of Nazi officials and sympathizers who called themselves *Die Bruderschaft*. 'The Brotherhood.' They may have moved as much as four hundred tons in all, from any number of locations and countries, if you count all of the rumors and stories. That would amount to around thirty billion in today's dollars. Four tons of it were recovered soon after the war, in the Merkers Salt Mine. That leaves ninety-nine percent of it still hidden somewhere."

"So follow the map," Nick said. "Go find the gold."

Vitali stepped aside to give Nick a clear view of the screen. "Be my guest, Mr. Fox. Decode these symbols for us and tell us where it is."

"It's not exactly my area of expertise, but if you print me a copy, I'll take it home and study it for a while."

Kate looked over at him. The moment this map had been projected on the screen, Nick's whole demeanor had changed again. No matter what else was going on here, there was a real-life treasure map involved, and that was something Nick Fox could not resist.

"You wouldn't be the only one trying," Vitali said. He brought up one more photograph. A man with a wide face, thin blond hair, and intense blue eyes magnified through rimless glasses, burning with sharp intelligence. If the Aryan Nations had a library, this man would be the head librarian, Kate thought.

"This is Klaus Egger. He was born in Austria, the grandson of a priest who joined the Nazi party, and who was one of the founding members of the original *Bruderschaft*. Egger attended Catholic seminary himself, but was expelled in his first year. He spent the next twenty years involved with various causes, some of them neo-Nazi, some of them extremists like the Society of St. Pius X, until he ultimately appeared at the top of an organization that has reclaimed the name of his grandfather's old organization. A new *Bruderschaft*. A new Brotherhood. We don't know exactly what their philosophy is, or what they're trying to achieve. We've intercepted communications about forming a 'Fourth Reich,' but we have no idea what that would look like."

There was another murmur in the room as everyone processed this idea.

"We have been collecting more dark web chatter all morning, and we now know that the Brotherhood is convinced that the *Raubgold* exists, and they are obsessed with finding it. We also know that they've put out open contracts, with an incredibly large bounty for any individual or group who helps them achieve that goal."

Vitali clicked one more time, to bring up the last image. It was a bright red star, emblazoned with the letters "RSK." Another murmur passed through the room.

"This is the insignia for the *Roter Stern Korps*, the Red Star Corps, a terrorist organization responsible for a string of bombings throughout West Germany before unification. The targets were mostly American military bases then, as well as the American embassy. They have been largely off the radar since then, but they reemerged three years ago. The current climate is ripe for any group that's nationalistic in nature, and the RSK is as extreme as it gets. And now they have recruited heavily from every country in Europe, not just Germany. Our current intel suggests that they're attempting to acquire sophisticated biological and chemical weapons."

Vitali paused to let all of this sink in. The room was deadly quiet.

"You may also remember that the top three leaders of the RSK were arrested in Belgium last year. The Brotherhood has capitalized on this leadership vacuum, and now it's safe to say that nearly every former RSK member, every *Red Star* as they often call themselves individually, is now working for the Brotherhood. It's a marriage of convenience for both organizations. If the RSK obtains these advanced weapons, they could create mass chaos across the continent. If this fortune really exists, we *must* prevent the Brotherhood and their hired guns from finding it. Which means we *must* recover the map that was stolen last night."

"I don't know why my father would take this map," Nick said. "But I can promise you one thing. If he has it, it's safe. He's not going to give it to any of these wack jobs."

"We know a lot more this morning than we did last night," Vitali said, "beginning with the fact that the *map* was the target, not the papal ring. We also know that the Brotherhood reached out to your father."

"That's impossible," Nick said. "He wouldn't have anything to do with these people."

"The father who hid a secret life from you for years? The former spy who you barely speak to anymore? That father?"

"He may have kept some secrets from me," Nick said, "but I know what kind of man he is."

"We have the intel, Mr. Fox. Encrypted communications, directly between Egger and your father. The specifics of the job. Negotiation on the price. If you want to see it for yourself, I'll arrange it."

Nick shook his head. "Don't bother."

"We've opened a Red Notice," Vitali said. "It will be broadcast to every Interpol office in the world."

Nick knew exactly what a Red Notice was, because he'd been the subject of one or two himself. Interpol couldn't actually create a global arrest warrant, but a Red Notice was the next best thing. Any country that chose to cooperate, and that was most of them, would keep an eye out for you, arrest you if they found you within their borders, and then turn you over to the country that originated the Red Notice.

The meeting adjourned and Nick was first out of the door. Kate followed, and then Jessup. As soon as all three were in the hallway, Jessup grabbed the young gendarme who was on loan from the Vatican to accompany Inspector General Vitali and to guard the door of the conference room. "Watch this man," he said, indicating Nick. "If he tries to leave, shoot him."

The gendarme was wearing the traditional navy blue uniform with the kepi hat, but he had checked his weapon before entering the building and he probably didn't speak much English anyway.

"Just watch him," Jessup said, doing the two fingers at his own eyes and then pointing at Nick. He walked fifty feet down the hallway and made a left turn. Kate knew to stay on his heels.

"As a warm-up," Jessup said, taking a moment to rub his bloodshot eyes, "did I hear correctly that you brought your *firearm* into the *Vatican*? Into the *Sistine Chapel* and *St. Peter's Basilica*?"

Kate was ready to tell him about Vitali seeing her put her Glock in her belt and not saying anything about it, but Jessup didn't look like a man who'd buy that story. "Do you think that's our biggest problem right now?" she asked instead, realizing as the words came out of her mouth that this was an even worse choice.

"You're right," Jessup said, after taking a moment to compose his thoughts. "We do have a bigger problem. And when I say *we*, I mean you and your partner."

"He's not my partner, sir."

"Are you really going to keep correcting me, Agent O'Hare? Do you really think that's the best strategy right now?"

"No, sir, I'm just saying—"

"Two days," he said, using a dead calm tone of voice Kate had never heard before, so drained of color that she couldn't detect even a hint of Kentucky in it. "You and your partner have two days to get that map back. And when you personally hand that map back over to the Vatican, I expect you and your partner to also personally hand over Quentin Fox. In cuffs."

Kate didn't bother to correct him on the "partner" business again. "With all due respect," she said, "the FBI sent us here to observe and advise, and that's exactly what we did. And if Nick wasn't here, they wouldn't even have any idea who to start looking for. I don't know if it's fair to ask Nick to go after his father, much less arrest him."

Jessup stared at her. He really does look like hell, Kate thought. This is a man who does not travel well.

"Two days," he said. "I'm going to the hotel to clean up."

He walked away, passing Nick with nothing more than one quick glare and a shake of his head.

"I'm getting a table at La Pergola," Nick said as Kate came by. "Will the boss be joining us?"

Kate rolled her eyes and took off down the stairs, two at a time. She caught up to Jessup in the parking lot.

"Why don't we send Nick home?" Kate asked.

He stopped dead, turned, and looked at her. "Excuse me, Agent O'Hare?"

"I'll stay and hunt down Quentin Fox on my own. Let Nick go back to the States and try to forget this one."

"He's not going to forget this one. And he's not going to walk away. You know that, Agent O'Hare. So you're going to watch him and you're going to make sure the right decisions are made."

"We don't always see eye to eye on 'right decisions.' But I'll do my best."

Jessup stared at Kate for a few beats. Kate suspected he was having a minor stroke.

Several cars were standing by, ready to transport on-loan personnel. Jessup waved his hand and one of the cars pulled up. He opened the back door and got in. "Two days," he said, and shut the door.

CHAPTER THREE

"I think I might remember something," Nick said to Kate as they ate Sardinian ravioli at La Pergola. "About the man who might have given my father that SAS parachute."

"I'm all ears," Kate said.

"When I was ten years old, this friend of my father's came to Miami to visit him. I remember, they went into the study and locked the door. Stayed in there for an hour, talking."

"And?"

"He had a very British accent. It was the coolest-sounding thing in the world to me back then. And he brought me a present from England. It was this gold pin, a sword with wings, and a banner that said, 'Who Dares Wins.'"

"That's the SAS motto," Kate said.

"Exactly."

"Do you remember his name?"

"No, I don't. It was a long time ago. But I remember the name was unusual. Something I might recognize if I saw it again."

A long moment of silence passed between them, until Nick finally spoke again. "Kate, no matter what my father has done, I don't know if I can help you bring him in."

Kate nodded. "I understand, but if you and I bring him in, he'll be in cuffs. If Vitali does, it might be a body bag."

———

Kate and Nick caught the next available flight from Rome to London. A driver was waiting outside Heathrow Airport to take them to the Ministry of Defence Strategic Command Center, a nondescript building down the street from the more famous Thames House, the headquarters of MI5.

Kate checked her Glock at the desk and they went up to the UK Special Forces office, home base for the 22nd Special Air Service Regiment. SAS for short.

It was a strangely familiar feeling for Kate, walking among the squad members. This was a different country, different insignias on the sand-colored berets, a different-sounding version of the English language. Yet the energy in the air was exactly the same. So was the self-assured way everyone carried themselves and the steely look in everyone's eyes. It took her back to the time she'd spent as a Navy SEAL.

Her chestnut-brown hair was several inches longer than when she was a SEAL. It was pulled back into a quick ponytail after her plane ride from Rome. Her jacket was wrinkled and she was wearing an FBI badge, but she felt totally at home.

"I bet anyone in this building could kill us in three seconds with a paper clip," Nick said.

"No doubt," Kate said, "and if you don't behave yourself, I'll kill you myself."

A man appeared in the hallway and headed straight for them. A little older than everyone else but no less imposing. Dress camo, hair cut high and tight.

"I'm Major Hannon," he said, with a West Country version of a British accent. "You must be from the FBI."

"Yes, Major," Kate said, shaking his hand. "I'm Agent O'Hare and this is Nick Fox."

The major looked Nick up and down like he couldn't quite understand the FBI connection. Kate didn't blame him. She felt the same way herself several times a day.

"I understand you already have the parachute used in the escape last night," Kate said.

"It just arrived." Hannon led them down a hallway, to an equipment room with enough armament to outfit a small army, which is exactly what they were. Assault rifles, pistols, a wide array of knives on the far wall. Kate couldn't help staring. This was her kind of room.

"It's here," Hannon said, showing them an unfolded parachute draped over a table. "It was already dusted for prints before it was sent here. None were found."

He gathered the featherweight material of the chute and started folding it as he kept talking. "It's definitely one of ours, but we do mostly HALO jumping."

"High altitude, low opening," Kate said to Nick.

"That's right," Hannon said, impressed. "You've jumped before?"

"Once or twice."

"Then I'm sure you used a backup chute. And a slider reefing device."

"Yes," Kate said. "Of course."

"This one's been modified." Hannon nodded to the fabric in his hands. "Quicker release, single chute with no backup. It's not the kind of thing we usually do here, jumping off buildings."

"Do you know where this chute came from?" Kate asked.

"We've got thousands of these all over the country. This one looks a little older than most. It might have been saved by someone who retired from the regiment. But I'll tell you one thing, whoever modified this knew exactly what he was doing."

"So how do we find out who did this, Major?" Kate asked.

"We've had a lot of smart men come through this building," Hannon said, "and most of them know their way around a parachute. I'm not sure how we're going to narrow this down."

"I might have an idea," Nick said.

———

Nick, Kate, and Hannon sat in a conference room, high above the streets of London.

"I was ten years old," Nick said. "The man who came to visit us, he gave me an SAS pin."

Hannon listened to every word, and the look on his face made it crystal clear he wasn't buying any of it. "If this man was in the regiment, he never would have said so. That's the first rule."

"First rule of Fight Club, never talk about Fight Club?" Nick said.

Hannon looked at him like he had no idea what Nick was talking about.

"He didn't say a word about being in the SAS," Nick said. "But who else would have a pin like that?"

"Nobody."

"That's what I thought. And you just told us five minutes ago that this chute definitely came from the SAS. So why not follow up on it?"

"What was this man's name?" Hannon asked.

"It was a long time ago. But it was an unusual name. Something that sounded funny to me at the time. I think there's a chance I'd recognize it if I saw it."

"There's anywhere from four hundred to six hundred active members at any one time."

"If we know the year, can you show me the active roster?"

It was obvious Hannon didn't love the idea. He thought it over for a moment and finally gave in. Using the year that Nick was ten years old, he went off to another room to find the roster.

"This sounds like a long shot," Kate said. "There must be some other way you can contact your father."

"I tried calling him. His phone is dead. I called his neighbor, too, and he said the house has been empty for weeks."

Hannon came back into the room with a roster sheet. "You'll see we're divided into four squadrons," he said. "Each squadron has four troops, led by a captain. The troops have specialties.

Mobility, Mountain, Boat, and Air. The Air lads use most of the parachutes, no surprise, so that's where I'd start."

Nick went through the names in each squadron list, focusing on the air troops. There were sixteen names in each Air Troop, sixty-four in all. He stopped and closed his eyes like he was transporting himself back to a ten-year-old version of himself, hearing his father's friend being introduced to him. A friend with a cool British accent and an unusual name.

"I'm sorry," he finally said. "It's just not jumping out at me."

Hannon took back the list and looked at the names. "I know most of these men. I'll be honest, Mr. Fox. I find it hard to believe that any one of them would help train your father, much less modify a chute so he could make a clean getaway from a robbery at the Vatican. I'm not surprised you didn't find a name here, because I still don't believe a single word of this."

"I understand why you'd say that," Nick said. "I'm just going by what I remember."

"Memory's a funny thing. I won't hold it against you, sir."

"We appreciate your help," Kate said. "I'll report to Interpol that you did everything you could for us."

Hannon made an effort not to laugh at that. To him, Interpol was nothing but a bunch of computer geeks and pencil pushers, with tin badges and popguns.

"I'll see you out," he said. "And good luck finding your man."

They had booked two rooms at a hotel in the West End, near Covent Garden. It was still early in the evening, but they were both exhausted and jet-lagged. Nick passed on a nightcap and Kate was grateful, but suspicious.

As soon as Nick was alone in his room, he opened up his laptop and started searching. Thirty minutes later, he opened the door quietly, looked up and down the hallway, and stepped very softly past Kate's room, toward the elevator.

In another few minutes, he was down on Monmouth Street, hailing a taxi. Thirty seconds later, Kate hailed her own, and told the driver to follow the taxi in front of them.

"I'm going to kill him," she said. She kept saying it over and over, until the driver gave her a funny look and she made herself stop.

They stayed on Nick's tail, through the city, onto Whitechapel Road. There were a few anxious moments, making their way through the evening traffic and trying to keep in contact with a single taxi that looked like any other. Finally, Nick's taxi turned down a narrow residential street and came to a stop. Kate watched Nick get out. She threw some pound notes at the driver and did the same. She was a block away, partially hidden in the shadows between streetlamps.

Now she had a choice to make. Go strangle the man, or wait and watch. She decided to wait and watch.

After five minutes of standing in the shadows, she started to get that old feeling, which had never failed her, that she was being watched herself.

———

Nick stood down the street from the address he'd given to the driver. The owner of this little row house was a retired SAS captain named Richard Duckworth. It had been half a lie that he didn't know the name. He remembered the man calling himself "Duckie," and then that half lie was followed by a full lie when he scanned the list of names and acted like a man coming up empty. In truth, the name had jumped right out at him, and the fact that he had been the Air Troop captain for B Squadron clinched it. The man he had met when he was ten years old, and who might have given his father the parachute, lived in this row house.

Nick's first order of business was to come up with a plan, a script, and possibly a character. Or maybe this was the one time when he should play it straight? Just tell the man he was the son of Quentin Fox and needed to talk to him?

Because that's really all he was doing here. He felt bad leaving Kate behind, but he was certain that if he could just get five minutes with his father, alone, he could find out the truth. Without the truth, there was no way to know what to do next. Return the map. Give his dad to the authorities. Or go hunt for treasure.

Nick was halfway to the door when it opened. Two men came out. One was the same model of man he'd seen in the SAS headquarters, brick-wall solid, with a high and tight haircut. He may have been a little older, retired from service, but he couldn't help but carry himself like a soldier. The second man was his father, and he was holding a hard metal tube about a foot long.

Nick knew this had to be the map.

Nick followed them several blocks, back to Whitechapel Road. He watched them enter a narrow two-story building that was tucked into the middle of the block. He gave them a minute, then carefully peeked into the little window set high on the front door.

It was a pub, the kind of place meant only for the locals who'd been drinking there for most of their lives. There wasn't even a sign on the front announcing the Bell & Crown or the Stag & Spit Bucket.

Nick stepped inside. There was a single rail of a bar running down one side of the room, with a rough-looking bartender on the other side. There was a game of "footie" on the "telly," but nobody else but the bartender was watching it. There was no sign of Nick's father or Duckworth.

The bartender stopped wiping a glass, looked at Nick as if he must have gotten himself seriously lost and walked through the wrong door. "Help ya, mate?"

"You got a bathroom?" Nick asked.

The bartender hesitated, then said, "Loo's back there."

Nick went down the narrow hallway, found the empty men's room and an empty women's room that was probably never used. He pushed open the third door and scanned the small kitchen. Nobody was here.

He pushed open the back door and glanced up and down the filthy alley. Nick was about to go back inside, then stopped himself and looked up at the second-story windows. How do you get up there?

Nick came back down the hallway, into the bar.

"All set, mate?" the bartender said.

"How about one quick pint," Nick said, sitting on one of the stools.

"We'll be closing soon."

"Just one. Then I'll be on my way."

The bartender tilted a glass and filled it, put it in front of Nick, then walked to the other end of the bar to watch the match. So much for Nick stalling, making conversation, or anything else that might help him figure out where his father had gone.

A minute later, another man walked in. He was wearing an old tweed jacket and a bow tie, but otherwise he looked just as uncomfortable and just as out of place as Nick. "I'm Professor Lewis," he said to the bartender. "I believe they're expecting me?"

The bartender put his rag down. "Right this way, Professor."

He led Professor Lewis to the hallway. Nick leaned back to watch what was happening, but lost sight of them as they turned the corner. The bartender returned a few seconds later, alone.

"Thank you, sir," Nick said. "You have a great evening." He threw a few pound notes on the bar and walked out.

When he was at the end of the block, he made a right turn, worked his way back to the alley, and found the back door of the pub. He opened it quietly. This time, as he made his way up the hallway, he felt along the surface of the ancient wooden wall.

His fingers hit a vertical seam. He kept going until he hit another seam. This could be a hidden door, he thought. He tapped lightly. It sounded hollow. He pressed against one side of the panel, then the other side.

From the bar, he heard footsteps approaching the hallway. The bartender's coming back here, Nick thought.

Nick pushed on the wall again, higher, then lower. The footsteps were getting closer. He pushed one more time and felt it give, then the panel slid all the way open and he stepped inside, closing the panel behind him.

Kate tailed Nick to Whitechapel Road and watched him go into the little pub with no name. She still couldn't shake the feeling that she was being watched herself.

She was about to approach the pub when Nick came back out. She ducked into a doorway, holding her breath as he walked by. A few seconds passed. She poked her head back out, looked down the street. He was gone. Damn, I can't lose him, she thought. Kate hurried down to the end of the block, but still didn't see him.

She guessed to the right, went in that direction, came to the alley, and spotted Nick. She darted back just in time to avoid being made. When she peeked around the corner, he had disappeared again. Kate went down the alley and found the back door to the pub. He must have gone in here, she thought. But why? He just walked out the front door a minute ago.

She cracked open the door, in time to see the bartender leaving the men's room. Moving down the hallway, she stopped for one moment, pushed the men's door open. The bathroom was empty.

Kate continued into the bar. The bartender was wiping down some glasses and looked over at her like, *what the hell?*

"Where is he?" she asked him.

"Where's who, luv?"

"The man who came in here."

"He wasn't here more than a minute," the bartender said. "Then he was on his way."

Kate came closer to the bar, took out her FBI badge. With no official jurisdiction, no official reason for this guy to give her the time of day, she knew she'd have to really sell this next part. "I'm going to ask you again," she said, flashing the shield. "Where is he?"

The bartender looked at the badge, his world clearly not rocked one tiny bit. "I think we've already covered it, luv. Your man came in and left."

"He snuck around to the alley and came in the back door. He's not in the bathroom. So where is he?"

The bartender stopped smiling. "Bloody hell," he said, throwing down his bar rag and moving quickly to the hallway.

Nick stood motionless inside the doorway. He waited for the sound of footsteps to end, let out his breath, and turned toward the stairs behind him. A dim glow of light was coming from somewhere above. He heard voices. Nick couldn't quite make out what they were saying. He took a step on the old boards, winced at the squeak, then kept going.

"*Auf dem Turm, Deutschland Siegt Auf Allen Fronten*," he heard one voice say. It sounded like the professor who had just come in.

"On the tower, Germany is victorious on all fronts," the man said. "Which makes sense, because those were the exact words hanging on the tower. They cut the cables, you know, so that nobody could use the lift. They didn't want someone to sneak up and cut the banner down."

"Are you saying that's where the treasure is?" It was Nick's father's voice. "That's impossible."

"I'm just telling you what I see here," Lewis said. "These runes in the center section, they call them the *Elder Futhark*. They go back to the eighth century. It's a code, very common for the Nazis. Hitler was obsessed with the occult, with astrology, ancient symbols, omens."

Nick stayed frozen where he was, listening intently.

"Can you decipher the code?" his father asked.

"I need to see more of it. Are there other documents?"

Before Nick could hear another word, the hidden door opened behind him. He turned to see the bartender, with Kate standing beside him. Nick didn't have more than one second to react when he heard a riot of heavy footsteps coming through the front door of the pub. Kate pushed the bartender toward the back door, pulled the Glock from her belt, and aimed it down the hallway. A bullet passed over her head and dug into the doorway. She returned fire.

"Move!" she said, coming up toward Nick.

As Nick hit the top of the stairs, the three men in the room were already in motion. Duckworth had his own semiautomatic drawn and Quentin Fox was rolling up the map, while the professor just looked like he was deciding which window to jump out of. Quentin pushed open another secret door on the far wall, grabbed the professor by his tweed coat, and pulled him through.

Duckworth aimed his barrel at Nick. "Don't move," he said. "I'll put one right through your eye hole!"

"Captain, it's me," Nick said, raising his hands. "I'm Quentin's son."

Duckworth froze, trying to understand what he was hearing.

Kate flew into the room, firing back down the staircase. "Get down!" she said.

Nick took cover behind the upended table, but Duckworth was an old SAS man and there was only one thing he knew how to do. He joined Kate at the stop of the stairs and fired down at the intruders.

"Who are they?" he asked Kate between rounds.

"I was hoping you could tell me."

One of the men tried to come up the stairs. Duckworth kept the "eye hole" promise he'd made to Nick and put one through the man's left eye. When the man went down, another appeared from behind him. He sprayed bullets wildly, one of them hitting Duckworth under his arm.

Kate took aim and fired, killing the second intruder.

"Get out of here!" Duckworth said. "Through that door! I'll hold them!"

Kate pushed Nick ahead through the other secret door. It led to another staircase, this one caked with dust and cobwebs, obviously not used for years. They followed the two sets of footprints down to a door that had already been pushed open. They emerged in the alley behind the pub. Another man fired on them immediately. Kate took dead aim and put one into his chest.

"Which way did they go?" Kate asked Nick.

Nick saw one set of dusty footprints leading in one direction, another set in the opposite direction. "Both ways!"

Kate grabbed the gun that the man in the alley had just dropped. She got her first good look at the man, saw nothing more remarkable than his raw, stubbled face, his thick sweater and heavy boots, like a dockworker would wear. There was a tattoo on his neck, a hint of something red barely peeking out from under his collar, but Kate had no time to examine it. "Here," she said to Nick, handing him the gun. "You go that way."

It was one of Nick's oldest rules to never touch a gun if he didn't have to, but today was a great day to make an exception. He gripped it in firing position, finger off the trigger, and headed left down the alley as Kate went in the opposite direction.

As Kate drew nearer to the alley's opening to the street, she saw one of the men who'd been in the upper room, now splashing through the filthy puddles just ahead of her. It wasn't Quentin Fox, but rather the third man, the one with the tweed jacket and the bow tie. He ran out onto the street, but before Kate could reach the same opening, it was blocked by the largest man she had ever seen in her life. And he had a gun.

She dove behind a garbage bin as the huge man fired on her. She fired back and caught him high in the right shoulder. The man barely flinched. He kept firing, until he finally ran out of bullets.

The big man came toward her, as if Kate being armed meant nothing to him, but then someone called to him from the street. He turned and left the alley. When Kate caught up, she saw him getting into a black van. He had left a thin trail of blood from where she'd hit him in the shoulder.

She turned and looked back down the alley, but saw no sign of either Fox, father or son.

———

Nick emerged from the alley and spotted his father running across Whitechapel Road. He gave chase, dodging oncoming cars, catching sight of him again as he entered a park. He lost him, almost gave up, until he finally saw him running toward a pedestrian bridge.

Nick's lungs were burning as he reached the bridge. He stood at the apex, which gave him a good view of the rest of the park. He saw nothing but trees, the darkness broken only by a few more streetlamps and a dozen people walking calmly. Nobody running.

"Where did you go, Dad?" he asked out loud.

Nick leaned over the edge of the pedestrian bridge, taking long breaths of the cold evening air. On the street directly below him, opening the door to a taxi, was his father. He was holding the metal cylinder containing the map.

Quentin Fox sensed the presence above him, looked up, and saw Nick staring down at him. The two men were frozen like this for several seconds. Nick still had the gun in his hand. He could have pointed it at his father, ordered him to stop. He could have shot the gun into the air. He could have put a bullet into the taxi's hood, scaring the driver out of his vehicle and drawing the attention of everyone around him, including the police.

He didn't do any of those things.

He kept staring into his father's eyes until the driver honked his horn. Quentin nodded to Nick, got into the back with his treasure map, and then the taxi drove away.

CHAPTER FOUR

Nick answered the call on his cell phone. He didn't recognize the number, but he immediately knew his father's voice.

"We have to stop meeting this way, Nick."

"Where are you?" Nick asked.

"I'm on the run," his father said, "apparently being hunted by my own son."

Nick was standing on the sidewalk outside the pub, watching the stretchers roll by, each one carrying a black body bag.

"Interpol says you're working for some seriously bad people," Nick said.

"I don't care what *they* think," Quentin said. "What do *you* think?"

"I think you're in a lot of trouble. I can help you."

A moment of silence passed.

"What happened to Duckie?" Quentin asked. "And the professor?"

"The captain is in surgery. He'll be fine. The professor got away. So are you going to tell me where you are, or not? And who were those people shooting at us? A hit squad from some government? Or just another group of competing psychos?"

"I don't have time to explain," Quentin said. "But don't listen to what Interpol is telling you. You know me too well to believe any of that."

"Tell me where you are," Nick said.

"Good-bye, son."

The call ended. Nick stood there under the streetlamp, staring at his phone, until an idea came to him and suddenly he wasn't so tired anymore.

———

On the other side of the building, Kate was on her own call.

"I told you to watch your partner," Special Agent in Charge Carl Jessup said. "I told you to make good decisions. Your career is dangling by a thread, Agent O'Hare."

Kate nodded in silent acknowledgment. She wondered how she had ended up in this London back alley, in the middle of the night. A dozen of the Crown's finest officers were combing through both floors of the pub. The three dead intruders were not yet identified. Former SAS captain Richard Duckworth was in surgery to repair a partially collapsed lung. The professor was probably still out there, running.

"I thought returning fire was a good decision, sir," Kate said.

"What were you doing there, anyway?"

"Following Nick. Just like you instructed."

From there, Kate knew it would only get worse. Like an immediate one-way ticket home worse. Nick tricked me, she thought. He lied to me and the SAS major. And then, in the moment of truth, he went off to find his own father. He didn't trust me to help him.

"This supposed pub, what is it really?" Kate asked, a game effort to change the subject. Two hidden staircases and a secret second-story room? Quentin Fox, a professor, and an ex-military man who just happens to have a loaded gun?

"I haven't heard anything yet," Jessup said, "but it's obviously *something* because everybody at the CIA is doing a great job of playing dumb. I'll keep digging, but right now I need both of you back here in Rome. After I debrief you, I'm going to personally put you on a plane to Los Angeles, and sit right between you. Kiss your two days good-bye."

Kate looked up to see Nick coming down the alley, waving to her. "Sorry, call you back," she said, and ended the call.

"We need to go," Nick said.

"They're not done asking us questions here."

"Since when do you care about obeying the authorities?"

"I'm dead serious," Kate said. "Do you realize what I had to do here? How close I got to being killed myself?"

"I'm sorry, Kate. I really am. But I think I know where we can find my father."

———

Kate stared straight ahead, not looking at Nick. They were riding on a late-night train from London to Paris.

"I'm going to spend the rest of my career in a cubicle because of you," she said, breaking the silence. "I mean, I *really* put myself out there this time."

"I'm sorry," Nick said. "I'm not sure my father knows how much trouble he's in. Before you arrived, I overheard them talking about a German banner that got put on a tower during the war, and cutting the cables to the lift so nobody could tamper with it. If I remember my history, that has to be the Eiffel Tower."

"You think that's where he's going next?"

"It's a guess, but I think it's a good one."

They had just entered the "Chunnel," the thirty-one-mile underwater tunnel that ran beneath the English Channel. The train would go 400 feet below the channel surface and another 250 feet below the seabed. It was the kind of thing that would make both of them claustrophobic if they thought about it for too long.

"Never mind your father's trouble," she said. "You're one inch away from having your deal revoked, which means going to prison."

"It's my father, Kate. You wouldn't think twice about going to prison for your father."

Kate leaned her head back on the seat and groaned. It was true.

"Fine," she said. "We'll go to Paris and find your dad. But if you ditch me one more time, I swear I will hunt you and your father down like a badger after a couple of squirrels."

CHAPTER FIVE

"I don't understand," Kate said, squinting as she looked up into the morning sunlight. "This can't be where the treasure map leads."

Above them loomed the wrought-iron latticework of one of the most recognizable landmarks in the world. Over a thousand feet tall, for a time the tallest building in the world, still considered by many native Parisians as a colossal eyesore. The Eiffel Tower.

Nick was squinting into the same sunlight. "It's worth a shot," he said.

They had checked into a hotel on Avenue de Suffren and gotten what felt like one hour of sleep. Now they were out on the street, a half block away from the entrance to the tower. It would officially open in five more minutes.

"Do you think he'll be here today?" Kate asked.

"Every day he waits, it increases the risk that someone catches up to him."

"We should tell the Interpol office here in Paris that Quentin might show up. They can help us watch."

"It's one tower," Nick said. "We can handle it. I don't want my dad to run again. I need to talk to him, find out what's really going on."

"Okay," Kate said. "You're on lead."

Nick and Kate stationed themselves at opposite sides of the Champs de Mars. Nick had to be careful about hiding his face, but Quentin Fox had never seen Kate before.

The tourists lined up to take the first lift rides. The traffic increased throughout the morning. It was a perfect day, sunny, not too hot. What a great day to be in Paris, Kate thought, if only I wasn't about to get chewed out by my boss for disobeying a direct order.

They took turns spelling each other for food and bathroom breaks. The noon hour hit. More lunch vendors came out to sell food from their carts. There was no sign of Quentin Fox. Another hour passed, then another.

Nick was beginning to have doubts, until he finally saw his father.

Nick called Kate on her cell phone and they watched Quentin board one of the lower lifts. Nick followed on another of the lower lifts, which rose at an increasingly steep angle on the tower's pedestals to the intermediate level. Nick spotted his father boarding one of the two upper lifts, which would take him all the way up to the top. Nick caught the next car. When Nick arrived at the top platform, he scanned the crowd and located his father, the only one not looking out at the city. Instead, Quentin was studying the structure immediately above him like he was trying to work out some kind of engineering problem in his head.

Nick approached him, stopping when he was next to him. He looked out over the city below. It was an impressive view.

"You didn't bring your parachute this time," Nick said.

Quentin Fox didn't move. "You need to turn around," he said in a dead calm voice. "Get in that lift and go back down."

"Is anyone else here with you?" Nick felt his phone buzzing in his pocket. He ignored it.

"I'm alone. Nick, you have to listen to me. You have no idea what's going on here." Quentin was still facing ahead, and hadn't yet looked Nick in the eye.

"You're after the *Raubgold*. I don't know why, but I do know there are other parties after it. Dangerous people. They'll kill you over this treasure. Or worse." His phone continued to vibrate.

Quentin turned to face Nick. "I know. You have to trust me. I spent the better part of my life protecting you. I know you're a grown man now, capable of leading your own life, but I can't stop being your dad. You don't want to get involved in this."

The next lift opened. Two armed members of the *Préfecture de police de Paris* came out, followed by Kate. Kate went to stand by Nick, and together they watched as the cuffs were snapped onto Quentin's wrists.

The look on his father's face burned in Nick's mind as he was taken away.

51

They took Quentin Fox to the nearest police station on Place Louis Lépine. He sat alone on a hard wooden bench in the holding cell. It wasn't his first time behind bars. There had been that one night in Kiev, another night in Athens. On both occasions, all he had to do was wait for his CIA contact to find out about his arrest, then make whatever quiet arrangements were necessary for him to be sprung. Today there was nobody to call.

The sound of a door opening jarred him from his reverie. He looked up to see his son standing on the other side of the bars. Next to him was the woman who had been at the tower.

"This is Kate O'Hare," Nick said. "She's an FBI agent."

Quentin stood up. "It's nice to see you again. If you don't mind me saying so, you're a lot more attractive than most of the FBI agents I've come across."

"I'm afraid there isn't anything I can do to help you, Mr. Fox," Kate said. "You'll be going back to Rome tomorrow."

"I understand. How do you know Nick, anyway?"

Nick and Kate looked at each other. "It's a long story," Nick said.

"I'm sorry I won't have time for it," Quentin said.

"Could you give us a minute?" Nick asked Kate.

"Sure," Kate said. She turned to Quentin. "I'm glad nobody was hurt today, Mr. Fox. Good luck with whatever happens next."

Quentin smiled as he watched her leave.

"I may not get to see you again," Nick said. "You need to trust me and tell me what's going on. What were you doing in London?"

"Captain Duckworth was helping me. He's the one who trained me to jump, and modified that chute for me."

"I remember when he came to visit us," Nick said. "That's how I found you."

Quentin smiled. "He's hard to forget."

"Do you work for the SAS, too?"

"Let's just say I helped some people coordinate things with them. That pub you tailed me to was the old safe house we all used to exchange back-channel information."

"If you aren't moonlighting for the CIA anymore, and you aren't SAS, why are you looking for the *Raubgold*? According to Interpol's intel, there's dark web chatter about the Brotherhood hiring you. Tell me that's not right."

Quentin came closer to the bars, looked his son in the eye. "It's half-right. They contacted an identity I used to maintain, a certain kind of art dealer with a lot of contacts in the museum world. As soon as I found out who they really were, what they stand for, I realized I had to go in a different direction."

"Did you try calling your old buddies at the CIA?"

"Yes, but I was never officially on the books at the Agency, and everyone I knew there is gone. A bunch of kids there now, and as soon as I started talking about *Raubgold*, I could practically hear them laughing."

"So you decided to steal the map yourself?"

"I didn't see another choice," Quentin said. "This gold needs to go back to the people who rightly own it. Or at least *something* good has to be done with it. If I didn't try to make that happen, I would have regretted it for the rest of my life."

Nick shook his head. "Can you imagine what Mom would say if she could see us now?"

"I think she'd tell you to help me."

"Are you serious?"

"The two Foxes, working together," Quentin said. "Why not?"

Nick gestured to the bars Quentin was standing behind. "Not going to happen now."

"Maybe not," Quentin said. "But then I'm not on a plane to Rome yet."

The two men looked at each other for one more long moment. Neither man knew what else to say.

The officer opened the door and poked his head in. "It is time, sir."

Nick went up to the bars. Quentin stretched out a hand, and Nick took it. "Good-bye, Dad," Nick said.

"No touch, please," the officer said.

Nick put up both hands. "Sorry."

"Thanks for coming to see me," Quentin said.

Nick nodded. "Good luck," he said, following the officer through the door.

———

Just after two in the morning, Nick Fox walked back and forth on Place Louis Lépine. The vehicle traffic was light and the foot traffic practically nonexistent. The bars and the nightlife were several blocks away.

Finally, at 2:15 a.m., a single figure emerged from the alley that ran alongside the building.

"Took you long enough," Nick said.

Quentin gave him back the tools Nick had slipped into Quentin's hand when he had reached through the bars to say goodbye. "Do you always carry lock picks with you?"

"Like I said, it's a long story."

"Well, next time bring me a good old-fashioned hook pick instead. And a tension bar with actual tension on it."

"Noted," Nick said. "Now let's get off the street."

———

On the top floor of the hotel on Avenue de Suffren, Kate O'Hare was sleeping soundly. On the empty pillow next to her was a box with chocolates from Pierre Marcolini, plus a handwritten note from Nick Fox, apologizing for ditching her again.

CHAPTER SIX

The first time Kate O'Hare caught up to Nick Fox, after five years of hunting him down, she had him cornered on the roof of a sky-scraper. As a helicopter swooped down to pick him up, he told her that she wasn't going to shoot him. He was right.

The second time she caught him, she ran into his car with a bus as he was escaping from a jewel heist. This time he didn't get away, and she could still remember the feeling that ran through her body when she finally put cuffs around his wrists.

Just a few days after she handed over his case files to the federal prosecutor, Nick Fox "escaped" from custody. Kate tracked him down *again*, this time halfway around the world, only to find out that he had been offered a deal to work unofficially for the FBI. In the years since, he and Kate had broken a dozen major cases to-gether. They'd also broken every rule in the FBI handbook about fraternization between an agent and a "confidential source."

She never thought she'd have to hunt him down again. Never thought she'd have to relive the moment when she slipped those handcuffs on Nick Fox's wrists. Now she would have to apprehend Nick *and* his father.

———

Kate had already eaten three of the Marcolini chocolates when the phone rang. She knew exactly who it was and was only surprised that the call had taken so long.

"You let Nick Fox break his father out of prison!" The voice belonged to Agent Jessup, but it sounded a full octave too high.

"You let Nick Fox break his father out of prison!" he said again.

"Agent Jessup, sir!"

"You let Nick Fox break his father out of prison!"

"If you could just calm down a moment, sir. Try to breathe. Drink some water."

He tried to say the same thing a fourth time, but now it sounded like he was hyperventilating.

"Can you sit down and put your head between your knees?" Kate asked. "Maybe breathe into a paper bag?"

There was a momentary silence as Agent Jessup pulled himself together, found his breath, and then read off a quick list of orders for Kate.

"Number one, you are officially suspended. Number two, you are on the next plane to Los Angeles. Number three, the second I see you, I am going to *unsuspend* you just long enough to suspend you again, only this time in person."

"I understand you're upset, sir."

"No, you don't. My boss is upset, and her boss, and his boss, all the way to the director himself. Those people are all upset. Me, I'm something else. I don't even think there's a word for it."

"I'm sorry, sir. I'll pack right now." She hung up the phone and looked in the hotel mirror, asking herself if she was ready to find a new career. She stopped to read Nick's note one more time.

Kate,

I know how much you love chocolate, and these are the very best Paris has to offer.

I'm taking my father to a country where there is no extradition to any country in the European Union, nor the US or UK.

I can't drag you into this any further. This quest is a personal matter and it might end your career, if not your life. You'll have to let your inner badger loose to see me, which I hope will be soon.

Love,

Nick, your favorite squirrel

There were about fifty countries that met the extradition criteria, but only a couple where Kate could see Quentin Fox hiding out for the rest of his life. The Maldives, maybe Indonesia. Yeah, that felt right, she thought, a nice little place on the beach, on the island of Bali.

She wondered if Nick would dare to come back to Los Angeles after helping his father to hide away forever. His assignment with the FBI would obviously be over, which meant he would probably be looking at a prison cell again, but with no last-minute deal to save him this time. Unless of course she killed him first, then *she'd* be the one going to prison. At that moment, it felt like a toss-up. She threw the rest of her things into her travel bag and went downstairs to get a taxi to the airport.

———

Nick stood on the other side of the street and watched Kate get into the taxi. He waited half a minute, then turned toward the Champs de Mars. His father was waiting for him there.

A thin leather messenger bag was slung over Quentin's shoulder. He ended a call on his cell phone, put the phone in his bag, and watched Nick approach.

"How's Professor Lewis?" Nick asked.

"Finally calmed down," Quentin said.

"He's never been chased by a bunch of assassins before?"

"Professor of Germanic literature, you'd think he'd get that all the time."

Nick looked up at the Eiffel Tower. It had just opened for tourists again. The first lifts had gone up and people were already getting in line for the next.

"Does your professor have any more ideas on where we're going?" Nick asked.

"He's had a chance to do a little more research since we talked at the safe house. Apparently, there's this other Nazi map, called the 'Lue Map,' brought to America just before the war by a Nazi or at least a Nazi sympathizer. The history is kind of hazy, but Professor Lewis thinks we're working with something based on the same idea as the Lue Map. It's actually different pieces of one master map that need to be collected and put together. Even when you do that, you end up with a complex code that has to be deciphered before you can follow the directions."

"So what does this mean for us?"

"It means that the banner on the right side was probably a pointer to the next section of the map. The key 'locator' symbol, he said, was over that Nazi slogan. I had to describe it to him to help him remember what it looked like. I forgot the name he had for it, but it represents the sun."

Nick looked back up at the tower, shielding his eyes from the bright morning sunlight. "Still not getting it."

"It means *up*, Nick. The highest point on the tower. That's where we have to go."

Nick blinked away the glare, looked at his father.

"At least, that's where *I'm* going to go," Quentin said.

"Not going to happen, Dad. This time, it's my turn."

———

Kate placed her unloaded Glock, a box of 9mm shells, and her Ontario MK 3 knife into her hard travel case and locked it. As she waited in the baggage check line at Charles de Gaulle Airport, she knew she would have twelve uninterrupted hours in the air. Twelve hours to consider the end of her career and just how badly Nick had betrayed her.

It had always been a complex relationship between the two of them. As much as she tried to keep it professional, there was always something more. There had been moments when she had let him get close to her, in spite of her best judgment. There was that one time when she had come home to find that he had broken into her apartment and had left a trail of Toblerones lead-ing to him. He definitely knew the quickest way to her heart.

To add insult to injury, she would be flying on the FBI dime, which meant "Economy Comfort" instead of the automatic first-class upgrade whenever she traveled with Nick. So maybe six inches of extra leg room. No fully reclinable seat that felt like a La-Z-Boy chair, no gourmet food, no free cocktails. Even though it was morning here in Paris, it was whatever-the-hell time it was back in Los Angeles and she really wanted something to drink.

When she reached the front of the line, she put the travel case on the scale and told the ticket agent about the weapons that were inside it, as required by law. As the agent printed her luggage tag, Kate found herself picturing two squirrels sitting on another air-plane, surely already off the ground by now, flying toward the South Pacific. In first class, of course, toasting Quentin Squirrel's new life. Next, she pictured herself as a badger, sitting in Econ-omy, eating a bag of broken, stale pretzels. A badger, she thought, who should be out chasing squirrels. And one of those squirrels just told her he hopes to see her soon.

"You lousy son of a bitch!" she said out loud. *Way* too loud. The agent looked at her like he'd been slapped across the face.

"I'm so sorry," Kate said. "I was talking about someone else. Can I get that bag back?"

The agent had just put the tag on it and was about to drop it onto the belt.

"I need it back," Kate said. "Please."

He hesitated again, then gave it back to her. "Is there a prob-lem, ma'am?"

"Yes, I'm a total idiot! Badgers don't get on airplanes, they chase squirrels!"

She turned and pushed her way through the people in line behind her. The agent called after her, but she didn't break stride.

"Idiot, idiot, idiot!" she said, all the way out the door. A few minutes later, she was in a taxi, heading back to the Eiffel Tower.

———

Quentin Fox opened up his messenger bag. The security guard took a quick look through it and pulled out the largest medical inhaler he'd ever seen.

"That's for my asthma," Quentin said. "Just in case. It's very high up there."

The guard put the inhaler back into the bag and let him through. Quentin and Nick took one of the first lifts to the intermediate level.

"Do you know what I'm going to be looking for?" Nick asked.

"I told you, you're not doing this."

"I'm not letting you climb the Eiffel Tower, Dad. Watching you jump off that dome was bad enough."

Quentin thought about it. "Have to admit, that was pretty terrifying."

"So it's settled, my turn today. Just tell me what I'm looking for."

"I was hoping to figure that out when I got up there. Something that could hold an old piece of paper inside it. For seventy-five years."

"No problem," Nick said. "Piece of *gâteau*."

When they got to the first deck, they went directly to the next set of lifts.

"That was quite a highlight reel they showed us in the Interpol briefing," Nick said. "Cairo, Barcelona, Cyprus."

"Cairo was my first. They had just recruited me. I sold a rug to an arms dealer. God, was I nervous."

"So how do you go from selling a rug to a bad guy to a part-time secret career as a spy?"

"They told me they wanted me to be an 'independent operative,'" Quentin said. "An 'off-the-books resource.' Whenever they needed someone who could infiltrate the art world, or a museum, or anything to do with ancient artifacts, they kept coming back to me, and I kept getting the job done. And I started to really like it."

"But I personally watched you circumvent the Vatican's entire security system. Where did *that* come from?"

"That was another one of my specialties. Remember, I had to deal with security systems every day as a high-end art dealer. I even helped other galleries set up their systems. A few museums, too. Alarms, video surveillance. Who better to break a system than the man who knows every way to build one?"

Nick shook his head in amazement. He could have used his dad on a few jobs over the years.

"Enough about me," Quentin said. "I want to hear about you and Kate."

They were interrupted by the lift door opening. They rode all the way to the top, stepped out, and surveyed the upper platform. There were four sides, each identical. Approximately twenty other people were up here on the platform with Nick and Quentin. Nick counted at least five languages being spoken.

There was yet another level above them, but this one was inaccessible to the public. It held only satellite dishes and other electronic equipment.

"Last chance to let me do this," Quentin said.

Nick took the "inhaler" from his father and removed the fake shell to reveal the spindle of thin steel cable underneath, with a hook on the end. Quentin pulled a pair of black rubber gloves from his pocket and gave those to Nick, too.

"I'll create a distraction," Quentin said.

"Fake a heart attack?"

"Come on, that's amateur stuff."

Quentin took out a deck of cards from his other pocket. He grabbed Nick by the arm, looked him in the eye, and said, "Be careful, son."

Nick nodded. A couple walked by, speaking English. "Hey, folks," Quentin said to them, "can I show you a quick magic trick?"

As Nick moved to the other side of the platform, Quentin had the woman pick a card, sign it, then put it back in the deck. He shuffled, took out the wrong card, then passed his hand over the card to turn it into her card, complete with signature. It was basic magician's sleight of hand, a pinkie break, a force, a color change. The key is to put some charm into it and really lean on the reveal, get a big reaction from your mark. That's all it takes.

A few other people wandered over to see what the attraction was. The whole city of Paris was laid out below them, yet they'd rather watch a stranger do a silly card trick. Nick had to admit, it was the perfect one-minute diversion.

Nick checked one more time to make sure he was not being watched by anyone on the platform, then he tossed the metal hook onto the railing of the electronic deck above him, grabbed on to the cable, and used it to help pull himself up. He climbed over the railing, got his bearings on the platform full of electronic equipment, and took a moment to gaze out over the city. He looked up at the next part of the tower that led most of the way to the top.

It was a warm, still, sunny day down on the ground. A thousand feet above, it was a different world. A stiff breeze hit Nick broadside. He kept climbing, resetting the metal hook, wondering if this thin metal cord would be enough to stop him if he lost his grip. There was yet one more structure that led even higher, and then the worst part of all, a thin column of smooth metal, at least another thirty feet tall. There were a series of horizontal indentations on the column, one every two feet, barely enough to give him a handhold and foothold.

He didn't think about how he would find the map link when he reached the top. That was another problem to solve, once he got up there. Right now, all he wanted was to not fall off and die. He didn't look down. He just kept going.

It was late morning. The Paris traffic was already heavy. Kate swore to herself in the backseat as the taxi made its way into the heart of the city. Far ahead of her, she saw the Eiffel Tower rising above the other buildings. It was still at least two miles away. She opened her hard case, took out the Glock and her shells, slid out the magazine, and loaded it.

The taxi driver caught sight of what she was doing and watched her in the rearview mirror.

Kate took out her FBI shield and showed it to him. "It's all good," she said. "Keep going."

She lifted her right pant leg, strapping her knife sheath to her calf. This time the driver smiled in appreciation. It was the sexiest thing he'd seen all week. The taxi ground to a halt again. The driver honked his horn, the universal language of taxis everywhere.

"This is a really nice case," Kate said, putting it down beside her on the backseat. "Take care of it." She slipped the gun into her belt, threw some money into the front seat, got out of the car, and started running.

———

Nick finally reached the top of the column. At the very top of the tower was one final structure, a round base holding a single rod with a light on top. He clipped his hook onto the base, caught his breath, and looked carefully at the rod. A gust of wind caught him. He closed his eyes and held on tight. When he opened them, he saw a metal cuff circling the rod. He looked closer. It was a slightly different metal, a slightly different color, and very faintly embossed on the surface was a tiny swastika.

He wondered if the French knew that there was such a symbol, no matter how small, on the very top of their national monument. How many people had even been up here? Maybe the one guy unlucky enough to have to change the lightbulb every few months. He was probably too busy holding on for his life to notice a tiny symbol on a piece of metal.

Nick reached up and grabbed the metal cuff, tried to move it. It wouldn't budge. He took the spindle holding his metal cord, hit it against the bottom of the cuff like a hammer. He hit it again. And again. It moved. He kept hitting the bottom of the cuff, driving it upward a quarter inch at a time. Finally he saw the edge of a piece of folded paper, and he had to work around it as he kept striking at the cuff. This is going to be tricky, Nick thought. As soon as it's free, it's going to fly away.

He hit, grabbed at the paper, hit, grabbed at the paper. He hit one more time and then it was free, soaring into the air like a runaway bird. He lunged for it, feeling his fingers touch it at the same instant his other hand lost its grip on the base. For one eternal moment, he was in free fall, a thousand feet above the ground, looking down for the first time and seeing the whole city about to rush up toward him. Nick grabbed with his free hand, refound the spindle, felt the cord tighten, and hoped to God that it would hold him.

It did. It held. He was practically horizontal to the ground, his legs wrapped around the column and the thin cord holding the rest of him suspended in the air.

In his other hand was the old piece of paper.

———

Quentin Fox looked at his watch. He paced back and forth nervously. He had no more card tricks to perform. The diversion was less of a priority now that his son was up there. If he was seen dropping back onto the platform, that wouldn't be such an issue, because at that point they would be in motion, heading back to the ground.

"Beautiful day," a man standing next to him said.

Quentin couldn't place the accent. German, or something farther east. Maybe Czech. Maybe Polish. Maybe Ukrainian.

Quentin turned to see the man. He had dark eyes, dark stubble on his chin, jet-black hair tied into a ponytail. The sleeves of a black T-shirt were stretched over his carefully toned biceps.

"I'd like to know where he is." The man spoke his English carefully, as if weighing each word to make sure it was correct.

"Sorry, I don't know what you're talking about," Quentin said.

The man lifted his chin, indicating the rest of the tower above them. "Up there? Right now?"

Quentin shook his head. "Can't help you."

The man stepped a few inches closer, lowered his voice a notch. "If he finds something up there, he will give it to me. Along with the other item that was taken. I will take both of them, and then you will be free to leave."

"Okay, you got me," Quentin said. "I did take those towels from the hotel. They were so soft, I couldn't help myself."

"Do you see those people behind us?"

Quentin glanced over his shoulder. A family of four were looking out over the city. Mom, dad, one boy about twelve, a girl maybe eight or nine.

"The girl will go over the railing first," the man said. "Then the father, who will try to fight me. I will break his nose first, which will blind him and make it easier to throw him over. Then the boy. Then the mother, after watching the rest of her family die."

Quentin looked into the man's eyes. Then he noticed the red star tattoo on the left side of his neck. Quentin hadn't received the same briefing that Nick and Kate had, but he didn't need it. He already knew all of the major players in this game. The Brother-hood had hired the *Roter Stern Korps* to help find the *Raubgold* for them, and this man standing in front of him was one of them. If he got his hands on this map, they'd all be one big step closer.

The man reached into his jacket pocket and pulled out a black carbon fiber knife with a six-inch blade. "When is he coming down?"

"How about now?" Nick said, as he swung down from the rail-ing and kicked the man in the face.

The knife fell to the ground. Behind them, the mother screamed and grabbed one child. The father grabbed the other.

"This way," Nick said to Quentin. He went to the stairway that led down to the lower levels. The gate was closed and locked, with a sign indicating it was for emergencies only. Nick kicked the gate and it flew open.

The two men pounded down the metal stairs two and three at a time, each flight cutting back and forth in a crisscross pattern. From below them, Nick and Quentin heard the pounding of foot-steps, coming up to cut them off. The footsteps were getting closer.

Nick looked above them, saw the man from the top platform coming down. "You sure you didn't bring your parachute?" he asked. "And maybe an extra one?"

He looked through the interior of the structure. The opposite side was about twenty feet away, up here where the tower was at its thinnest, but there were no stairs on the other side. Nick took the spindle of metal rope, weighed the hook with one hand for a half second, and tried to hurl it across to the other side. It clanked against the metal and fell. Nick pulled up the hook, tried again. It clanked and fell again.

"We're about to have a real party here," Quentin said, looking up at the one man coming down, then down at however many men were coming up. It sounded like at least three or four of them.

Nick took a breath, gave the hook a kiss for good luck, and tossed it across the gap again. This time it caught and held.

"Go," Nick said. "You first."

Quentin looked down the interior of the tower, at what had to be a five-hundred-foot drop to the level below them, then he looked at the metal cord stretched across the twenty-foot gap.

"Go!" Nick said.

The man above them was just a few flights away. Quentin climbed over the railing, grabbed on to the cord, and tested it to see if it held his weight. It sagged, but it didn't break. He let go of the railing, trying not to look down. He passed one hand over another, like a monkey traversing a vine. Although a monkey would have done it without thinking, without expecting to die every second.

The man from the top had reached Nick and stood a few feet away from him on the same platform. It was Nick's turn to notice the gym-toned arms and the red star on his neck. Nick put both hands up.

"Give it to me," the man said.

"Sorry," Nick said. "Can't do that. Do you have any idea what I went through to get it?"

The man charged, and Nick sidestepped at the last possible moment, deftly wrapping both hands around the man's wrist and guiding his blundering momentum over the railing. The man had half a second to look back into Nick's eyes, not so much terrified but totally dumbfounded, before he fell five hundred feet and crashed onto the roof of one of the lifts.

There was a brief silence as the men below them paused to watch their fellow soldier sailing by at terminal velocity, then they started pounding their way up the stairs again. Below them, the intermediary deck was in pandemonium, with everyone screaming and trying to get away from whatever had just caused such a stunning impact.

Quentin had worked his way across the cable and reached the other side of the tower. He turned and saw his son following behind him, moving much easier and faster.

"Sure, you got the gloves," Quentin said, freeing one hand at a time to shake them out and blow on the cable burns.

"We have to keep moving," Nick said. "Be careful."

"Too late for that," Quentin said, as he started to follow his son down the interior of the latticework, working from one horizontal to the next like a giant ladder. From below, they heard police officers shouting instructions and blowing their whistles. By the time Nick and Quentin hit the ground, the whole tower would be on full terrorist-event alert.

"If we get separated," Nick said, "I'll meet you at La Terrasse. It's on the Seine. We'll have a nice lobster bisque with champagne."

"Can we get out of this alive first before we make lunch plans?"

Nick kept climbing down the latticework, warning Quentin whenever he found a handhold with too much oil or pigeon shit on it. When they reached the bottom of this interior section, they were still only halfway to the ground.

"How do we get out of here?" Quentin said, looking around him. With all of the lifts in the tower shut down, at least four hundred people were jostling in every direction at once, trying to reach the stairs.

"Just act natural," Nick said, brushing off his jacket. They both joined in the throng, going with the flow to the nearest set of stairs. They got halfway down when they saw another group of three men fighting their way against the tide, elbowing their way up the stairs.

"There he is!" one of the men shouted, as soon as he spotted Quentin.

The Foxes both turned around and went back up, pushing their way through the crowd. When Nick finally reached the top of the stairs, he turned to locate his father.

Quentin was gone.

———

Kate heard the police whistles as she got closer. A dozen tourists rushed by her, running away from the tower, then another group and another until she was pushing her way through a wave of humanity.

As she got closer to the stairs leading up to the first level, she saw Quentin Fox flipping a much younger man over his shoulder.

The man landed hard on the pavement. When the man came to his feet, he was holding a gun. The tourists all around him started screaming and clawing at each other to get away. Kate fought her way through, just as the man leveled his barrel at Quentin. She slid out her Glock and put it against the back of his neck. The man froze, not sure what to do next.

"Drop the gun," Kate said.

The man complied, but a fresh wave of panicked tourists engulfed them. Kate was swept away, nearly falling over. When she regained her bearings, the man was gone. So was Quentin.

Nick searched frantically for his father, until he spotted two more men coming after him. One of them might have been the biggest man Nick had ever seen in his life. Nick hurried across the deck level, trying to find another staircase.

With all of the lower lifts closed, a guard was now standing at the gate to shoo people away. Nick glanced behind him and saw the two men closing in on him. He tried to push his way past the guard, but the man put up a hand to stop him.

"Do me a favor and stop *them*," Nick said, slipping by the guard just as the two men were about to grab him. The guard and the men tangled with each other, until the big man literally lifted the guard with one hand and threw him aside. It was just enough of a delay to let Nick climb his way around to the tracks on which the lower lifts rode up and down the tower's pedestal. There was a service ladder next to the tracks. Nick started climbing down the ladder, but when he looked up, he saw one of the men coming after him. When the man was close enough, he tried kicking Nick in the head. Nick ducked, grabbed on to the man's leather boot, and pulled. The man lost his grip and fell, half sliding, half bouncing his way to the bottom.

Nick kept going, but when he looked up again he saw the big man coming down next. With such long legs, the giant was able to take five and six rungs at a time. Nick grabbed on to the handrail next to the ladder and stepped off, sliding down the railing like a fireman going down a pole. Thank God for the gloves, he thought.

When he looked up, the big man was right on top of him, holding on to the same railing and moving fast. Nick squeezed the railing with his gloves, slowing himself down as much as he could. He knew he'd have to time this just right.

When the big man was just a few feet away, Nick put one foot back onto the ladder. He slipped off a few of the rungs, finally caught one, and came to a bone-rattling stop. He stepped away from the railing just as the big man's fingers brushed against his arm.

Nick watched as the big man, now a prisoner to the basic physics of *way* more mass-times-acceleration, kept sliding past him on the railing. The big man's speed was too much to handle, and as he tried to slow himself down, he caught one foot and launched himself right off the pedestal, falling a hundred feet to the pavement below.

Nick continued down the ladder until he reached the ground. He turned to look back up at the tower.

"I hope you got out, Dad."

———————

Thirty minutes later, Nick arrived at La Terrasse. He sat down at a table, his back to the wall so he could see anyone coming in. His father came through the door a few minutes later.

"I didn't even get to ask you," Quentin said, joining him at the table. "Did you find what we were looking for?"

Nick nodded. "You don't have the first piece anymore, do you?"

Quentin reached under his shirt, opened the money belt around his waist, and brought out the original map section he had stolen from the Vatican. "They did a lousy search on me last night," he said. "They were just holding me until the Interpol agent could get there."

Nick reached under his own shirt and brought out the second map section from the tower. They glanced around to make sure they had a little privacy, then they put the two pieces together and leaned over to examine them.

The second piece was just as cryptic as the first, with squiggly lines that seemed to suggest topography, dotted with a random assortment of ancient runes. As on the first piece, this second piece had a separate line of text inside a banner, running down the right side. *Der verrückte König würdigt den Schwanenritter.*

Nick took out his phone and entered the words into the Google translate app. "The insane king? Something about paying tribute, and a swan and a knight? Any idea what that means?"

"You got me," Quentin said. "But something tells me we're not done yet."

They had a couple of drinks, and then Nick wandered outside

while Quentin paid the bill. Nick walked down through the patio area, to the dock, and stood there for a while watching the boats cruising by on the Seine. He wondered where Kate was. Surely she had gotten his note. She was missing out on all the fun.

The barrel of a gun pressed into his lower back. "Where is he?" a man's voice asked.

"What are you going to do?" Nick asked. "Shoot me right here?"

"That's up to you. And your father."

Then another voice. "Put it down."

Kate!

Nick turned, saw Kate standing behind the man. She had her gun on him, while he still had his gun on Nick. It would have been a Mexican standoff if they weren't doing it in France.

"Put it down *now*," Kate said.

"Go ahead," the man said. "Mr. Fox and I will both die together."

Nick flashed Kate his charming smile. "Took you long enough," he said to her.

"Seriously? It looks like I'm right on time. Saving your ass once again."

"I've been told it's one of my best features," Nick said. "I see you got my note?"

"It was a bit cryptic."

"I'm glad you figured it out. I wanted to give you something you could show Jessup. Something that would hopefully keep you from wasting away in a cubicle."

"Hey!" the man said, jabbing Nick with the gun. "Both of you, shut up!"

Nick turned, as if to answer the man, and saw his father come into view. The man with the gun sensed the same movement, diverting his attention for a quarter of a second. Nick pushed the gun barrel away with his left hand, chopped down on the man's wrist with his right. He kept twisting the gun counterclockwise, away from the man's trigger finger, away from his grip strength. As the gun came free, he put one hand in the center of the man's chest, gave him a good shove, and watched him fall into the river, five feet below the dock.

When he looked up, his father had Kate in a wrist lock, her gun pointed harmlessly toward the sky.

"I'm glad I got this chance to thank you," Quentin said to her. "Kate, is it?"

"Yes," Kate said. "Let's all go somewhere where we can talk about this."

A sharp whistle cut through the air, as several Paris *officiers de police* came charging down from the street.

"I'm sorry, Kate," Quentin said, "but we can't do that right now."

Then he pushed her into the river, too.

CHAPTER SEVEN

Kate dragged herself out of the Seine River to see a throng of onlookers staring at her. Nick and his father were long gone. She stood dripping on the dock, in a country where she had no dry clothes to change into and she didn't speak the language. She had no hotel room, nobody to help her, just the wet clothes wrapped around her body, wet shoes and socks on her feet, wet hair, wet face, wet bills in her pocket, wet passport, wet cell phone, wet knife strapped to her leg, and a wet gun.

She went into the bathroom of La Terrasse, past a hundred lunchtime diners staring at her, and used up all of the paper towels drying herself off as much as she could. After googling the nearest clothing store on her phone, which thank God was still working, Kate walked to the store, shivering. She found some decent enough clothes, jeans, T-shirt, and some athletic shoes a size too big. After throwing her wet clothes away, she went out and found a taxi, then found another store where she could buy a new hard travel case for her weapons, because she sure as hell wasn't about to leave those behind. She made her way back to the airport with her hair still wet.

Kate looked at her phone. Her ringer was off, but now that she was checking she could see that Jessup had already called her three times. She also saw a text from a number she didn't recognize. The message read "Sorry, that was an accident and the police were coming so we had to leave! I'll buy you new dry panties that I'm sure you will find just ducky, I promise. Love, Mr. Peanuts." Mr. Peanuts, she thought. Peanuts as in squirrel, as in Nick, as in I'm going to kill you when I catch up to you.

Kate went to the British Airways counter and caught a flight to London.

––––––––

Kate was on the ground in Heathrow ninety minutes later. She took a taxi to the police station that had handled the shooting at the safe house, flashed her soggy FBI badge, and managed to catch the right person on the right day. He gave her the hospital and room number of Captain Duckworth, the man who'd stood next to her and helped her fire on the assassins coming up the stairs. If that doesn't bond you, she thought, what else will?

She took another taxi to the hospital. When she walked into the room, Captain Duckworth was sitting up in his bed.

"Private room," Kate said, looking out the window at the garden below. "With a view."

Duckworth smiled at her and tried to lean forward but that was obviously a bad idea. "I'd normally stand when a lady enters the room," he said, with an East End Cockney accent, sixty-plus years thick.

"I'm glad to see you're on the mend, Captain."

"And I'm glad to see a pleasant face."

"I need to know where Quentin Fox is," she said. "There are some very bad people on his trail right now. I'm sure you don't want to see him killed any more than I do."

"I know about the bad people," Ducky said, patting his ribs. "But I'm afraid I can't help you. He's just an old friend I was helping out. Put him up for the night, introduced him to another friend of mine. Then he was off running, and I promise you, I haven't heard from him since."

"You have no idea where he could be right now? His son is with him."

He raised an eyebrow at that. "Well, that's a kick in the head. The Fox boys together?"

"Yes, they were just in Paris."

"Lovely day for it," he said.

"They were almost killed, Captain. I'm trying to help them."

"Maybe they don't need any help."

"This other friend you introduced him to," Kate said. "The professor. Tell me about him."

"Hadrian Lewis. He's a professor at Oriel College, Oxford. Germanic literature, I think. Sounds like a pretty dry topic to me."

"He was helping with the map?"

"It was something mysterious, is all I know."

"But you heard what they were talking about," Kate said. "At the safe house."

"Safe house? You mean the pub?"

"The pub that was used by the SAS and the CIA as a safe house, yes. I know all about it."

Duckworth made like he was racking his brain on that one. "Now what would the British SAS and the CIA be doing using the same safe house?"

"Come on, Captain," Kate said. "I know Quentin Fox came to see you for a reason. Did you two used to work together?"

"Working with an off-the-books American operative on SAS business? No, that doesn't sound right, either."

Kate was about to press him, but then she backed off. She knew what kind of man Duckworth was, a retired Special Forces captain who would never truly leave the job behind him. Just like her own father, the man who still wouldn't talk about many of his missions.

"I'm going to give you my card," Kate said, taking one out of her pocket. "If you see him, or if you hear from him, please make sure somebody calls me, okay? Will you do that much, at least?"

Duckworth took the card from her, looked at it. "Why is it all wet?"

"Long story." As she was about to leave, she paused in the doorway. "Hadrian Lewis, you said? At Oxford University?"

"Germanic literature," he said. They both smiled, because they both knew where Kate was going next.

Kate rented a car, took a few minutes to get accustomed to being on the other side of the road, and drove the eighty miles to Oxford University. Now she was doing the last thing she ever thought she'd be doing that day, listening to a lecture on the *Nibelungenlied*, a Middle High German epic poem written in the thirteenth century. Kate listened to Professor Lewis compare the three different surviving versions of the poem, then express his own opinion about which was the most reliable. He made it clear that he didn't agree with most other Germanic literature scholars on this topic, so right away Kate could see she was dealing with a real gunslinger.

She caught up to him as he was leaving the lecture hall. He was wearing a Harris tweed jacket, with a white dress shirt and a red bow tie.

"I was at the safe house the other night," she said, showing him her FBI shield. "I'm glad you got away unharmed."

"I thought it was just a pub," he said as he continued to walk down the hallway, increasing his speed by a notch. "I don't know anything about a safe house."

Kate wanted to grab him by the tweed jacket and tell him that everybody needed to stop pretending it wasn't a safe house. Instead, she took a moment to compose herself. "Look, I know you were there, and I know you saw the map."

Lewis stopped dead. He looked up and down the hallway, then at Kate. "I'm sorry, Miss, what was your name?"

"FBI Agent Kate O'Hare," she said, leaning on the first half. It occurred to her that with the way Professor Lewis had run away from that safe house, he had probably never even talked to the police that night.

"I was just doing a favor for an old friend," Lewis said as he straightened his bow tie.

"That's the second time I've heard that line today."

"I wasn't there for more than five minutes before everything went to pot," he said, describing a gunfight as only a British professor could. "If I'd had any idea that such a thing were going to happen—"

"Quentin Fox's son climbed the Eiffel Tower today," Kate said. "The map sent them there, didn't it?"

Lewis swallowed hard. "They really did that?"

Kate nodded. "Not something you try every day. He must have had a good reason."

Lewis just looked at her. He was the very definition of a man trying to act natural. At least Captain Duckworth had been charming about stonewalling her.

"What was he looking for?" Kate asked.

Lewis straightened his bow tie again and looked her in the eye. "I'm sure I have no idea, Agent O'Hare."

Kate smiled. This was a sophisticated and highly educated man, but he also a man who had no idea how to lie. Saying her name to punctuate the statement, even the way he was standing, one foot turned out as if to get a head start on escaping. All classic tells.

She took out one of her cards and gave it to him. "Will you let me know if either of the Foxes contacts you?"

"Of course," Lewis said, putting the card into his jacket pocket. "Now, if you'll excuse me."

"Friday afternoon," Kate said. "You have any big weekend plans?"

He straightened his bow tie one last time. There might as well have been a neon sign glowing over his head, exclaiming that he had a plan.

"Nothing exciting for me. Just grading papers."

"Thank you for your time."

When they were both out of the building, he took a left and she took a right. She doubled back after fifty yards and picked him up walking across campus toward the parking lot. The ancient buildings loomed all around her as she tried to blend in with the students. Everyone seemed to be in a good mood after another week of classes had ended.

Kate noted the car that Professor Lewis was driving, hustled back to her rental, and took off after him. She fielded a few honks that reminded her which side of the road to drive on, and caught up to him. She tailed him to a little cottage on the edge of town and watched him go inside.

Five minutes later, Professor Lewis came back out the door. He'd taken off his bow tie and he was carrying a leather travel bag. Now we're getting somewhere, she thought.

As she pulled out behind him, she didn't think he would be in the habit of checking for tails, but she tried to be careful, anyway. He went to the A420, took that southwest to Swindon, then cut directly south and headed for the coast.

It was getting close to dinnertime when she saw him pulling

into the ferry dock at Poole. Kate hadn't eaten anything except a few pieces of chocolate that morning, had run two miles through Paris, had been dumped in the Seine, then sat on a plane where all they had given her was one lousy bag of stale pretzels.

She watched Professor Lewis get out of the car and go into the ferry dock office. He's buying a ticket to go across the English Channel, she thought. I need to be on that ferry.

She was about to get out, then stopped herself. Wait, he didn't take his bag, she thought. He's not going anywhere.

Twenty minutes later, she saw the ferry from Cherbourg, France, coming around Brownsea Island. It moored at the dock. Forty or fifty people got off. Two of those people were Quentin Fox and Nick Fox.

Kate watched Professor Lewis and the two Foxes squeeze into the car. She stayed behind them as they left the dock. There was only one road leading around the inlet, so it was easy to follow them. The professor drove them all the way around and into a little Channel-side town called Swanage.

Kate watched the car park, then watched all three men go into a seaside house just across from the beach. She had driven past a little fish-and-chips stand on her way through town, and now her stomach was growling. She would have killed for a nice greasy bagful of bad food, but right now she had two squirrels to catch.

———

Nick and his father were sitting at a small kitchen table while Professor Lewis put the teapot on the stove. "Nice little place you got here," Nick said. "Right on the channel."

"I'm sorry, gentlemen," Lewis said. "I can't wait any longer. May I please see what you recovered today?"

Quentin took out both map pieces and put them on the table. The professor leaned over without touching them, instead pressing both hands together as if praying.

"Extraordinary," he whispered. "Absolutely extraordinary."

"What can you tell us?" Quentin asked.

The professor gently moved both map pieces together. "I mentioned the famous 'Lue Map' when I saw this first piece, but this is different." He tried moving the pieces around, reversing their position. "The Lue Map was more of a pure mathematical puzzle. Like something the Freemasons would create. *This* is more symbolic. More occult in nature. Which is exactly what you'd expect in a Nazi artifact. I believe it's actually a form of *Angeketteter Schatzkarte*. A map designed to lead you to a certain destination. But *Angeketteter* means that the pieces of the map are like the links of a chain."

Quentin let out a breath, looked over at his son. "Meaning there are more links we have to find?"

"I believe so," Lewis said. "Look at the banner on the right side of this new piece." He turned the piece so he could read it. "*Der verrückte König würdigt den Schwanenritter.* The mad king pays tribute to the—"

The professor paused and tilted his head in confusion.

"The Swan Knight," he said. "That might be referring to the *Lohengrin*, an opera by Wagner."

"Who's the mad king?" Quentin asked. "And how is him being an opera lover going to take us to the next link?"

The professor kept staring at the map pieces, utterly transported, until something else came to him. "Oh, an FBI agent came to see me today," he said. "She was looking for you. I did a crackerjack job of playing dumb, if I do say so myself."

"Wait," Quentin said, "she came to see you *today*?"

"Yes."

"She's in England?" Quentin said. "Right now?"

He looked over at his son, but Nick was busy texting on his burner phone.

In the car outside, Kate's phone beeped. She picked it up and read the message. "The fries are getting cold. Are you getting warm?"

Twenty seconds later, the door burst open.

"Hand over that food!" Kate said. She took the bag of fish and chips from Nick and sat down while Quentin and Professor Lewis looked at her in amazement.

"*You*," Kate said, glancing up at Quentin as she took a big bite. "You threw me in the river!"

"I'm sorry?" Quentin said, tentatively.

"No, you actually threw me into the Seine River!"

"It's my fault," Nick said. "He didn't know you were coming to help us. And then we had to scram when the police showed up."

"Oh, there's plenty of blame to go around," Kate said. "And by the way, you're buying me a pair of shoes that actually fit."

"Fair enough."

"And thanks for all of *your* help" she said to Professor Lewis.

"You're welcome," Lewis said, still looking completely bewildered by everything that was happening in his kitchen.

"I think she's speaking ironically," Nick said.

"How were you so sure I'd follow you so I could *help* you?" Kate asked Nick, slowing down to take a breath. "I could arrest you right now."

"You're in England. You can't do that."

"I could call Interpol and have them send the local police," Kate said.

"You're not going to do that," Nick said. "Number one, you *know* we're doing the right thing here and you want to help us. And number two, I got you some really good junk food."

"You're right about one thing," she said. "These fries are fantastic." She put three more in her mouth.

"Actually, we call them *chips* here," Lewis said.

Before Kate could answer that, they all heard a vehicle pull up on the street. Kate got up, went to the small window in the door, and looked out at the street. She saw a black van, unmarked. The front and back doors opened in perfect choreography. Four men got out. One of them was the giant Kate had shot in the alley. As the foursome approached the house, each man took a quick glance up and down the street.

"We gotta get out of here," Kate said, turning to see the three men still sitting at the table. Nick was stealing some of her chips. "*Move!*"

"Where's your back door?" Quentin asked Professor Lewis. "Come on, sir. Let's go."

"But, but," Lewis stammered, "whatever's happening, I'm not a part of this!"

"You are now," Nick said, pulling him to his feet. "Back door."

Kate saw the intruders just a few feet from the house now. She hurried after Nick, Quentin, and Lewis, running into Lewis as he paused to turn off the burner under the teapot. She gave him a wide-eyed look, like *seriously?*, and pushed him forward.

The front door was kicked open just as Kate made it out the back. She closed it quietly, hoping they'd spend a few seconds clearing the house before coming out the back. Ahead of her, Nick and Quentin were helping Professor Lewis over the fence of his garden. Lewis went up to the back door of the house behind his and politely knocked on it. Nick pushed past him, put his shoulder into the door, and then pulled him inside. Quentin followed, and then Kate. The house was empty.

"Which way?" Nick asked as he pushed open the front door. As Kate looked back, she could see all the way to the rear window of the house. The other men were already climbing the same fence.

"That way," Kate said, pointing south, toward the Swanage Pier. It was a quarter mile away, but she saw some of the locals out for their after-dinner strolls.

"How fast can you run?" Nick asked Professor Lewis.

"I was a speedy lad in my day."

"Well, your day just came again," Nick said. "Let's go."

Nick and Quentin ran on either side of him. Kate brought up the rear, turning to look behind her. Three of the four men were on the street, moving toward them. They didn't seem to be hurrying. It was like they knew there was nowhere to escape.

Kate had a good idea where the fourth man had gone, back out to the front of Professor Lewis's house, just in case she tried to double back for her rental car. These guys are pros, she thought.

As they got closer to the pier, Kate surveyed their options. There were no police officers in sight, just a few dozen innocent people walking around, worst case collateral damage, best case a stampede running away once the shooting started. Neither scenario would help them.

"I'm going to hang back," Kate said. "Tie them up. You guys take the professor and find some help."

"You're not doing that," Nick said. "There's got to be a way out."

They were about to reach the pier. A left would take them back to the house, where the fourth man was waiting. A right would take them away from town and make them isolated on the empty road. They'd be easy targets if the men got back in their van and followed them. Straight ahead was a short walk to the end of the pier and then the English Channel.

Kate spotted a boat on the water, a twenty-five-foot cruiser, cutting in from the channel toward the pier. It was moving slowly, maybe too slowly to reach the pier in time, but it was their only hope. She ran ahead and waved at the driver of the boat. She didn't see anyone else on board.

"I'm done for the night," the owner called to her. "Just bringing her in for fuel."

"We need your help!" Kate called back, taking out her FBI badge. The man was fifty yards away, but she hoped the flash of gleaming metal would look official.

She glanced back up the pier. The men behind them were moving faster.

"Please hurry!" she said.

The boat angled in toward the pier's edge. Kate leaned over, trying to grab the bow. She misjudged the distance, lost her balance, and went into the channel. Son of a bitch! she thought. Twice in one day!

The boat owner helped pull her up out of the channel, just as Quentin and Nick arrived with Professor Lewis, who was breathing so hard it looked like he was about to have a heart attack. As soon as they made it into the boat, Nick pushed the driver away from the controls and took over. The men on the pier were twenty yards away, their weapons already drawn.

"Get down!" Nick yelled.

Quentin pulled the driver onto the floor of the boat and Kate covered the professor as Nick gunned the engine. The propeller churned at the water, the bow lifted, and the boat lurched away from the pier just as the first shots rang out.

Nick ducked his head but had to stay high enough to see where the boat was going. One shot shattered the boat's windshield. Another pinged off the top of the engine. Several others dug into the gunwales. The good people of Swanage out for their after-dinner stroll on the pier were screaming and running away. The gunmen ignored them and kept firing shots at the boat as it sped away.

Finally, the shooting stopped. Kate peeked over the gunwale and saw the men running back up the pier.

"They'll get in their van and follow in this direction," she said to Nick.

Nick nodded. "I'll keep going for a while, then double back."

"What's going on here?" the boat owner asked. "Who were those men shooting at us? At *my boat*?"

He surveyed the pebbles of glass that had once been his

windshield, the dent on the engine casing, and the divots dug into his gunwales.

"We're sorry," Kate said. "But we would have been dead if you hadn't showed up."

———

An hour later, Kate was wrapped up in a bathrobe and sitting by the window on the third floor of a little inn, in another channel-side town called Bournemouth. Her cell phone, just one month old, was sitting in a public garbage can a half block down the street.

The boat had brought them to this town, several miles down the coast. They had checked into this inn for the night. To recover, to catch their breath, to figure out what to do next.

She took a sip of hot tea and kept watching the street. A few minutes later, the black van came rolling by, moving slowly. It stopped directly next to the garbage can. The men got out, looked up and down the sidewalk, and peeked into the windows of the storefront. The big man dumped out the garbage and kicked through it. He picked up Kate's phone and showed it to the other men. He put it in his pocket, the men got back in the van, and it drove away.

Kate looked up when the door opened. Nick came into the room, with Quentin and Professor Lewis behind him. Quentin took a laptop out of his bag and set it up on the desk. Lewis took a seat and started typing.

Nick came over and sat in the chair across from Kate. "Need any help warming up?" he asked.

"What I need is a clean phone, if you have one."

He pulled out a burner phone from his pocket. "Did they show up for yours?"

"Tracked it down to the exact can," she said.

"You know what that means."

"They were already close behind me," Kate said. "Somebody was feeding them the GPS from my phone."

"That's got to be Interpol," Nick said. "Who else could even do that?"

"Meaning Interpol is compromised," Kate said. "I need to make a phone call."

She got up, padded across the room in her bare feet, went into the bathroom, and closed the door.

Jessup answered on the first ring. "Who is this?"

"It's me," Kate said. "I'm on a burner phone."

"Where are you? No, let me guess, you're in a little town in England called Swanage?"

"I'm not there anymore, but how did you know?"

"I saw the report," Jessup said. "I'm still at Interpol. They say everyone on the pier was running around talking about men shooting at a boat."

"Nobody was hurt?"

"Nobody was hurt, thank God. But you were supposed to be on your way home. What were you doing in Swanage?"

"Please listen to me," Kate said. "This is very important. Interpol has a leak. We can't trust them."

There was a long silence. When Jessup's voice came back, it had changed. He sounded more worried than perturbed now. "You know I can't help you as long as you're in another country."

"I know that, sir. But these people have to be stopped."

"Think about what you're saying, Kate. If Nick and his father keep going down this road, it could turn into a suicide mission. I'm surprised they've lasted this long."

"I hear you, boss. But I think I need to stay and help them."

Another silence. "What can I do?" he asked. In one second, he had gone from the hard-ass boss to the boss who really did care about the safety of his agents, especially Kate.

"Try to track down the leak at Interpol. They're compromised and it's going to make this a lot harder for all of us."

"I'll do everything I can, Kate. But you have to promise me you'll be careful."

"I'll do my best, sir."

"You've got to promise me one more thing, too."

"What's that?" she asked.

"If you find the *Raubgold*, make sure none of it ends up in Nick's pocket."

She ended the call and went back out into the room, where Professor Lewis was done tapping on the laptop.

"*Der verrückte König würdigt den Schwanenritter*," Lewis said. "The mad king pays tribute to the Swan Knight." He turned the laptop around so that Quentin, Nick, and Kate could see the image. "The mad king was Leopold the Second of Bavaria, and he paid tribute to the *Lohengrin* by building the *Schloss Neuschwanstein*. It's probably the most famous castle in all of Europe. Definitely the most photographed."

Kate bent down to look. She'd seen pictures of this castle before. Its gleaming white sandstone walls rose from the forested hill on which it had been built, the Bavarian Alps rising in the background. The castle was Romanesque in design, incredibly ornate, with towers, turrets, gables, balconies, statues, and more windows than she could count. Almost too beautiful to be real. It had supposedly been the inspiration for Cinderella's Castle in Disney World, but right now, no one in Kate's group was appreciating the beauty.

"Look at those sheer walls," Quentin said. "The road up the hill is the only way in, and it's going to be heavily guarded after hours."

"We'll need climbing gear," Nick said. "Communications. Maybe more weapons. I'm sure we'll be running into the Brotherhood's men again."

Kate started hitting numbers on the burner phone again.

"Who are you calling?" Nick asked.

"Climbing gear, communications, weapons," she said. "There's only one man I know who can help us with that. My dad."

CHAPTER EIGHT

Nick, Kate, Quentin, and the professor were on the Euro Star train, speeding through France, destination Metz. From there they would catch another train into Germany, where they'd meet Kate's father at the Munich airport.

"I have to admit," Nick said, sitting next to Kate, "I wasn't one hundred percent sure you'd come help us."

"What else am I supposed to do?" she asked. "Go home and sit in my cubicle while you have all this fun?"

"Well, I think you deserve a little more thanks. Maybe I can make you breakfast in bed sometime?"

"Only if it's waffles and real maple syrup," she said. "Not the fake stuff."

"It's a deal."

"Just promise me one thing," she said.

"Anything."

"You don't go off the reservation again. That goes for your father, too. If I'm on the team, I'm on the team all the way."

Nick put his head back against the seat, closed his eyes, and smiled.

"I'm going to need a verbal promise from you, Nick."

"Yes. I promise."

In the row ahead of them sat Quentin Fox and Professor Lewis. Lewis was practically vibrating with nervous energy. Instead of having tea at his little house on the channel, he was speeding into the heart of Europe, following a cryptic set of clues to an unimaginable treasure. This was slightly more exciting than grading papers.

"Nick always did love trains," Nick overheard his father saying. "He used to play with them for hours when he was growing up."

Nick leaned over the seat. "No, that was you, Dad. You were the train nerd."

"I was the one buying them, sure. But that was all for you."

Nick nodded and smiled, then closed his eyes again. Some things aren't worth arguing.

When Jake O'Hare walked through the customs gate, Kate was waiting for him. She gave him a hug and then she stood waiting for more. Jake pulled out a big jar and gave it to her.

"Thank God," Kate said. "Can you even imagine an entire continent of people who never eat peanut butter?"

Jake O'Hare was an ex-Marine, currently retired and living in a garage casita behind Kate's sister Megan's house in Calabasas,

California. He was square-jawed, square-shouldered, barrel-chested, and big-boned. His gray hair was still buzzed to military specifications. He walked with a slight limp, the result of an injury he'd sustained on a mission that he still insisted was classified.

"Never thought we'd both get back to Germany at the same time," Jake said. "How long has it been?"

"I was just a kid," Kate said. When she was sixteen, she and her sister had lived on the USAG Stuttgart base with their father. It was there that Jake had taught her how to drive, but with his own unique twist. From the beginning, he had challenged her on the driving course with obstacles and oil slicks, and had even shot out her tires one time, just to make sure she'd be ready for anything.

"Nick Fox," Jake said, shaking the younger man's hand and nearly crushing most of Nick's metacarpal bones. "What have you gotten my daughter into now?"

"The usual amount of trouble," Nick said. "Jake, this is my father, Quentin."

The two men shook hands, sized each other up.

"Heard a lot about you," Quentin said.

"And this is Professor Lewis," Nick said. "From Oxford University."

The professor gave him a slight bow, perhaps sensing that he'd never write again if he shook hands with the man.

"Gentlemen," Jake said, "I flew over here because Kate asked me to. She said I'd get the full story when I was on the ground. So here I am."

"It's Munich and it's lunchtime," Nick said. "Let's go have some brats and a few beers."

They found a little *Brauhaus* where they could grab an isolated table in the back garden. Once the food and beer were delivered, Quentin launched into the story, starting with the Brotherhood contacting him about infiltrating the Vatican museum and stealing a seventy-five-year-old map, his own investigation into the group, what they stood for, and how they had contracted with the *Roter Stern Korps* to help recover the four hundred tons of *Raubgold*. And how Quentin had decided to find the gold himself, before they could get near it.

Jake listened carefully. When Quentin finished the story by recounting the theft at the Vatican, the gunfight at the London safe house, and then the trip to the top of the Eiffel Tower, any normal father would have pulled his daughter aside and made immediate arrangements to fly them both home on the next plane. Instead, Jake ran one hand through the stubble on his head, looked over at his daughter, and asked her one question. "What can I do to help?"

"We need climbing gear," Kate said, "communications equipment, and weapons."

"I have a contact here who can get us anything we need," Jake said. "Where's the next mission, anyway?"

"You know how I never wanted to be a princess when I was a little kid?"

"That was your sister," Jake said. "You wanted to be a ninja."

"Well, it's too bad Megan's not here," Kate said, "because we're going to Cinderella's castle."

It was another two-hour train ride from Munich to the Bavarian town of Hohenschwangau. As soon as they stepped out onto the station's outdoor platform, they saw the spires of Neuschwanstein Castle rising a thousand feet above the tree line.

"Piece of *Kuchen*," Nick said, looking up and blinking in the glare of sunlight.

They checked into a small inn and then gathered outside in a private courtyard to plan out their next steps.

"I've been studying the symbols on the second map," Lewis said, tapping on his laptop. "They are like links in a chain. In the first link, there was a rune meaning *up* just above the banner, indicating that the next link would be found at the highest point of the tower. But here in the second link, the rune is next to the *swan* in *Schwanenritter.* Which helps answer another question: Why did the creator of this link use the general *Schwanenritter* when he could have used the specific name *Lohengrin*?"

"Cut to the chase," Nick said. "What does this all mean?"

"The rune next to the swan indicates *food*, or *mouth*. So you're looking for a swan in the castle, and inside the swan's mouth—"

"Is the next link," Nick said.

"Correct."

"So we should start by taking a scouting mission to the castle," Nick said.

An hour later, they were all on the public shuttle to the castle. It ran for miles, up the steep access road. Jake and Kate looked out one side of the shuttle, watching the road and the forest that lay beyond it. Nick and Quentin looked out the other side. The professor read the little guidebook he had picked up at the ticket stand.

"Much of the castle's interiors are still unfinished," Lewis said. "That's good news."

Nick looked over at him, then at the twenty other people who were on the shuttle. He had heard four or five languages being spoken, but he was sure half the bus probably spoke some English. He put one finger to his lips.

Lewis got the message, nodded, and made like a man locking his mouth up tight and throwing away the key.

When the shuttle van reached the top, it drove through a great stone archway. They all noted the massive iron gate that would slide shut after hours. When the vehicle stopped and everyone got off, they also spotted the two German police officers standing by the entrance. A hard-looking man and a woman who, Nick thought, looked like she could kick the man's ass *and* their asses at the same time. They had eagles on their badges, meaning *Bundespolizei*, the federal police. What were they doing here? You don't deploy your top police resources guarding a tourist site. Unless that was exactly the point. The Vatican and the Eiffel Tower both get hit, within days of each other. Maybe Interpol was advising its member countries to keep a close eye on all major cultural sites. If that's true, Nick thought, our lives just got a lot more complicated.

The group was led past a kiosk where everyone received an audio device with the tour information recorded in several different languages. A sign reminded them that any form of photography was strictly forbidden on these grounds. That was Nick's cue to glance over at the police officers, then start the micro 4K video recorder he had peeking out of his shirt pocket.

Jake, Kate, Nick, and Quentin let Professor Lewis go ahead of them so they could lag behind the rest of the group. The entrance led directly to a spiral staircase that went up a hundred feet to the main level of the castle. The first window appeared, blocked with three iron bars. Nick tried to look downward to judge the distance, but all he could see was the tops of the trees below. He turned to Kate and shook his head.

Kate put the audio device in her ear to hear the recorded tour. Nick didn't bother with the audio. His job was to look for creative ways to get in and out.

When they reached the main level, they saw the first painting decorating the great foyer. It was a swan. Nick turned his head and saw another swan, then another. Kate came over to stand next to him, took the audio device from her ear.

"You remember that opera the professor was telling us about?" Kate asked. "The Swan Knight?"

Nick nodded.

"The guy who built this castle, he wasn't just a fan of Wagner's. He was the official president of the fan club. And this castle we're standing in right now was basically his love letter to swans."

Nick smiled. "This is getting more fun by the minute."

He stayed close to Kate as she trailed behind the rest of the tour, moving from one elaborately decorated room to another. Jake and Quentin stayed just ahead of them, ready to distract any tour guides who came looking for the stragglers.

There were two separate throne rooms, a great hall, and several royal bedrooms. Professor Lewis might have been right about much of the castle being unfinished, but there was still plenty of castle that *was* finished, and it was all finished with swans. Nick stopped counting at seventy.

They caught up to Professor Lewis at the end of the tour. He was staring intently at a fresco on the ceiling. "It's one of the most remarkable things I've ever seen," he said. "I don't know why I ever put off coming here."

He turned to them and said, "I don't know if you noticed, but there are quite a few swans here."

When they were back at the inn, Nick called the team together in the courtyard. "The federal police are on-site," he said. "Is there any reason to believe they know we're going to hit this place?"

"I can't imagine how they'd know that," Quentin said.

"The Brotherhood might," Nick said. "If Interpol is leaking to them, maybe the leak goes both ways."

"I told you, there's no way they'd know the castle is next," Quentin said. "They don't have the map."

"But they must know that the map is going to lead you to *some* place that's important," Nick said.

"How many major tourist sites are there?" Quentin asked. "If we're talking all of Europe?"

"We're not," Nick said. "From what we know of the map's history, the sites would only be found in countries that were once controlled by the Axis powers. Like Italy and France."

"And obviously Germany," Quentin said, thinking it over.

The professor was sitting by himself at another table nearby, going through Nick's video footage. "I don't see how the next link can be hidden in a swan's mouth if the swan is just part of a painting," he said. "Although I suppose you could construct a little trapdoor. Or maybe in one of these tapestries. You could cut a flap in the fabric. The map could be behind it."

The video tilted upward, pausing at a great swan carved into the wooden pilaster against the wall.

"King Leopold had carpenters working on this room for four years," Lewis said. "There could be a hidden compartment in one of these carvings."

The video tilted all the way up to the ceiling, which featured a swan gracefully posed in a pond.

"If it's *that* swan," Lewis said, "then we're in quite a pickle."

"Yeah, it's a pickle, all right," Jake said. "We used to call missions like this one-percenters."

"Meaning one percent chance of success?" Quentin asked. "I've been on a few of those myself."

Jake smiled. "I'm not being trying to be pessimistic. As a matter of fact, one-percenters are usually the most fun. There's no pressure when you're trying to do the impossible."

"So when do we move?" Kate asked.

"There's a new moon tonight," Jake said. "I say we go get ready."

CHAPTER NINE

Jake O'Hare had spent most of his life in the military, and still thought like a soldier. Nick Fox had spent most of his life in the world of international crime, and still thought like a thief. Where a soldier sees strength, a thief sees overconfidence. Where a soldier sees a glaring light, a thief sees the shadow next to it.

That's how the two men, with two different minds formed by two different lives, created the best possible plan to infiltrate the castle.

"There's a reason why they build castles on hilltops," Jake said. "You control the highest ground, you control *everything*."

"But this castle was built in the nineteenth century," Nick said, "not the Middle Ages. It was never intended to be a defensible position. The whole thing was built for show."

"The elevation is real," Jake said. "Those exteriors walls are real. Those iron bars on the windows are real. If King What's-his-face

JANET EVANOVICH AND STEVE HAMILTON

was trying to *fake* an impenetrable castle, he did a pretty damned good job of it."

"We can't go through the front gate," Nick said. "We'll be playing right into their strength."

"*Whatever the other team does best, that's what you have to do better.* It's an old Knute Rockne saying we used to have taped above the door to our barracks."

"If Knute Rockne had been a thief, he would have spent most of his life in prison," Nick said. "But let me ask you this. When we were up there, did anyone happen to see a state-of-the-art security system? Surveillance monitors? Motion sensors?"

"No, we didn't," Jake said.

"Because they assume that the walls and the gate are enough to stop *anybody*," Nick said. "They don't think they need anything else. That's the arrogance that comes with having an advantage you *think* is unbeatable."

"Okay, so how do we take advantage of that?"

"We start by finding a way up that wall," Nick said, spreading out a detailed map of the castle and the surrounding terrain. "Between the two of us, I know we can do that."

———

A few hours later, just after the night went full dark, a black van was dropped off in the largest public parking lot in Hohenschwangau. Jake put on thin latex gloves, got behind the wheel, and moved the van to within walking distance of the hotel. He took stock of the equipment in the rear of the van, all carefully packed in boxes.

"We're even, buddy," he said. A long-ago favor had been repaid.

The team dressed in dark clothing, then left the inn through a side door. From his window on the second floor, Professor Lewis watched them walking down the road. He wished them well, switching from his beloved German literature to Shakespeare. "To do a great right, do a little wrong."

Nick, Kate, Quentin, and Jake climbed into the van and Jake drove, heading for a secluded spot near the *Poellatschlucht*, the gorge that ran along the base of the hill on which Neuschwanstein Castle had been built. The access road leading up to the castle ran on the northern side, turning at the top toward the entrance. The team would stay south to remain out of sight of the great front gates. They would use the foreboding height of the castle's sheer walls, rising straight up as if part of the rocky hill itself, as their own counter-advantage. The new moon would be an additional ally.

Jake was driving. Quentin sat up front in the passenger's seat. Nick and Kate were in the back. Everyone was quiet. Getting into their own heads and into the zone.

Jake backed the van as deep into the woods as he could go, not so far that he couldn't drive out when it was time to leave. He opened the back of the van, leaving the interior lights off. In the dim glow of a penlight, he gave each team member their equipment. Lightweight grappling hooks, for use in the interior of the castle only. The exterior climbing would take something a lot sturdier. He also gave them Bluetooth earpieces, already live and connected to each other, so that they would remain in constant contact.

Finally, Jake handed Quentin and Nick Walther PP semiautomatics, each loaded with rubber plugs. If they needed them, the weapons would look realistic, and if fired, the rubber plugs would deliver "nonlethal but incapacitative trauma" upon impact, which was a fancy way of saying it would put you down and only make you *wish* you were dead.

Jake gave Kate a Beretta 92X semiautomatic, loaded with her preferred 9mm ammunition. The contact had also left a SIG Sauer P226 for Jake, along with a 10,000-volt stun gun.

"Remember our rules of engagement," Nick said. "We take down the Brotherhood's hired soldiers only. We do not expect to see them in the castle, but you never know how close they may be." He paused to survey the darkness around them, as if someone could be creeping up on them at any moment. "No unnecessary force against police, security, or any other innocent parties. And when we're done storming the castle, I'll pick up the check for strudel."

"Sounds good to me," Jake said. He took out the camo tarp, and they quickly covered the van with it. Even in the dark, it was one extra measure of protection. He threw a heavy rucksack over his shoulder, with the equipment they'd need to scale the exterior wall.

As they headed into the forest, the ground quickly descended toward the stream that cut through the bottom of the gorge. They worked their way carefully down the hill, avoiding the steepest drops, until they reached the bottom. There was a rough wooden bridge crossing the stream.

"This is fun," Nick said to Kate. "It's like we're married and on a family vacation to see the castles of Europe."

She looked at him and shook her head. "If we were married, I wouldn't be sharing a room with my father."

"Want me to talk to him? See if he's willing to switch?"

"Only if you have chocolate."

"Sorry," he said. "That was Paris. Best I can do here is bratwurst."

The woods grew thicker, which gave them more handholds, but the thicker canopy also made it darker, and they all kept scraping their faces against the rough branches. As they got closer to the base of the castle, Jake started looking for one specific tree. He and Kate had stood on the road, in the last of the daylight, using his Zeiss binoculars to scan the cliff and identify the best candidate. It had to be tall enough, easy enough to climb, and sturdy enough in its upper branches to support his weight.

The trees were almost exclusively pine. There was one particular tree, about halfway along the southern wall, that Jake and Kate had chosen.

"This is it," Jake said as he reached the base of the tree. "How's everybody doing?"

They all took a moment to catch their breath, and to mentally prepare themselves for the next step. Nick looked up at the castle wall, which from down here looked as high as the Empire State Building.

"Are you sure there's not an elevator we can take?" Nick asked.

Jake squared the load on his pack and started climbing the

tree. The climb was as easy as he had hoped. Lots of horizontal branches, regularly spaced. It was their first good break. As he neared the top of the tree, he could feel it holding steady for him. It wasn't swaying or bending. Second good break.

He worked himself into a solid semi-seated position, unslung the rucksack, and took out the one piece of equipment he was glad he wouldn't have to carry anymore. It was a military grappling hook launcher, seriously old school, but air powered and therefore nearly silent, and it could easily shoot that hook over a hundred feet.

He would only have one shot, so he had to make it count. That's why he had already picked out his target. Not a window, because that would be an almost impossible shot, even if the upper windows didn't have iron bars like the lowers. Not a balcony, because although the castle had plenty overlooking the interior courtyard, the exterior had none. Jake's one and only best shot was to fire over the courtyard wall, here in this part of the castle where the courtyard met the much higher main building. If he cleared the wall and then pulled back on the hook, there was a good chance it would meet resistance where the two levels joined.

If it didn't, they would have to retrieve the hook and reload, which Jake knew from experience to be a colossal pain in the ass, even under ideal circumstances.

Jake took a breath, took dead aim with the launcher, then fired. The hook came out with a *whoosh*. It sailed over the top of the wall, clearing it by maybe two feet. He pulled on the rope, slowly, waiting to feel the hook grab on something. It did. He gave it a good yank. It was solid. Good break number three. Now the fun part, he thought.

Jake hung the launcher on a branch so it wouldn't fall on anyone below him. He held on tight to the rope with both hands and pushed himself away from the tree. He was maybe twenty-five feet away from the wall, and braced himself as he slammed against it. The rope held.

He caught his breath again, then began climbing, but not like a man climbing a rope in gym class. Instead he used what the Marines call an "S wrap," looping the rope around and under one foot, holding it secure with the other, using this temporary base to launch himself up a few feet, gaining a new hold with his hands, and then rewrapping the rope through his feet again. The same process, again and again, saving his stamina.

Kate watched her father from below, marveling at what he was doing, so many years past his official date of "retirement." Jake had packed a lightweight "caving ladder" rope in his pack, and this was what he was securing to the top of the courtyard wall. He dropped the rope and it unrolled as it came all the way to the ground.

Kate grabbed hold. It was still a long way up, but the rope had a loop placed every two feet, on alternating sides. The world's trickiest rope ladder, but better than a pure free climb and easier than using the S wrap. She pulled herself up, hooked a foot, then another and kept repeating the process, concentrating on the rope, on her next action, and not looking down. When she reached the top, her father put out a hand to help her over the wall. She dropped to the stone floor of the courtyard. The spires of the castle loomed above her, silent and dark. Way better than Disney World, she told herself.

She heard Nick's voice in her earpiece. "On my way up!"

He came up quickly, got over the wall, and was followed soon after by Quentin. The team went through the archway to an alcove where one stairway led up, another down.

"Orient yourself to this exact point," Nick said. "This is where we rendezvous. Have your escape route clearly laid out in your mind at all times. Always ask yourself, how do I get back here as fast as possible?"

Everybody nodded.

"Stay on your comms," Nick said. "Keep talking. Now let's go find it."

They broke the huddle, splitting off in four different directions. Kate went up the stairs, heading for the top floor. She would start in the royal bedroom and work her way down. She turned on her penlight, moved quickly and quietly. The door was open. They didn't have much reason to close doors around here, not if tour groups were coming through every day and you wanted them to see all of the fancy stuff.

"God, this is the worst room of all," Kate said as she stepped into the bedroom. "They might as well call it the Royal Swan Room."

Each wall was covered by a mural, floor to ceiling. Swans were swimming, drinking, eating, communing, and probably having sex in some corner of the artwork.

Kate started with the nearest wall, ran a gloved hand across the mouth of a swan. No secret compartment or trapdoor or whatever she was supposed to find.

"One down," she said. "A million more to go."

In one of the great throne rooms, Nick looked at the wooden carved swans placed high on a dozen pilasters running along each wall. They were at least fifteen feet off the ground.

He took out his grappling hook, a lightweight version of the great hook they had used to scale the outside wall. It was connected to a much shorter version of the same caving ladder rope, with the loops for quick climbing. He tossed it over the neck of the first swan and pulled himself up.

In the other throne room, there was a balcony high against the walls. This made life easy for Quentin because all he had to do was walk along the rail and inspect each of the carved swans. The fun part came when he shined his penlight to the ceiling and saw the great fresco above him, the idyllic pond with the great swan in the middle of it. A huge chandelier hung from the center. That was his only hope to get up to the ceiling.

He came back down from the balcony, looked up at the chandelier. "You wouldn't hide it in the ceiling, would you? Nobody could be that cruel."

But of course, all's fair in love and treasure hunting, so he swung his hook at the chandelier and hoped that it would hold when he started climbing.

———

On a level far below Kate, her father was moving through the room they called the Hall of Singers. There were dozens of paintings on the walls, but here they were mostly human characters from Wagner's operas, a sea of faces that all seemed to look down at Jake with great disapproval for his invasion of their sanctuary. Jake pressed a gloved hand against each of the swans he saw in the backgrounds of the painting, working his way clockwise through the room.

Then he went down a story, into the great kitchen. No swans. He moved to the dining room, where a large swan, elaborately carved from ivory, was featured on the mantel above the fireplace.

Jake moved closer and shined his light into the swan's mouth.

———

Minutes had passed, but it felt like hours to Kate. She had worked her way through the bedroom, interrogating every swan she could see. She even went down on her knees and felt the rug with the swan image braided into it, then moved some furniture so she could pull up the rug and inspect the floor underneath it. Nothing.

"How's everybody doing?" she asked.

"No luck yet," Nick said.

"I'm trying to get to the ceiling," Quentin said. "If you hear a fall, that's me breaking my neck."

Kate went to the window and looked out at the dark courtyard. For just one moment, she borrowed her sister's daydream about being a princess who lived in a place like this, who woke up every morning and looked out this very window at her kingdom.

Something in her kingdom moved. It was just a shadow, but it shifted unmistakably beyond the open gate. Had the gate been open this whole time? Or did this just happen?

The shadow stopped. She saw another shadow move beside it. Vans. Doors opening, no lights, but one quick burst of a flashlight and Kate saw a uniform.

"Police at the gate," Kate said. "Two vehicles."

———

Nick dropped to the floor in the throne room. "Where are you, Kate? I'm coming to get you."

"I'm on my way down," Kate answered. "Go to the meeting place."

As Nick was about to turn a corner, he sensed movement ahead of him. A door opening.

"They're inside," he whispered.

———

In the second throne room, Quentin listened to the voices as he was about to climb back down the great chandelier. He heard footsteps and stopped dead.

His ladder rope was still hanging from the chandelier, reaching all the way down to the floor. As he leaned over, he felt the chandelier start to sway. Quentin extended his fingertips, just enough to grasp the rope. He pulled up slowly as he heard the footsteps getting closer and saw the faint glow of a light near the far door.

He pulled harder, cursing under his breath as the chandelier started to sway again. A hundred fragile old-fashioned lightbulbs rattled in their little cages.

The light grew brighter. He pulled the rope all the way up, feeling the chandelier rocking back and forth.

Two shadows appeared at the doorway. One pointed a flashlight into the room, scanning from one wall to the next. The two men came into the room and crossed it, stopping just beneath him. Quentin held his breath as he stared down at the top of their official *Bundespolizei* hats. The Walther semiautomatic was in his belt, loaded with the rubber plugs. As soon as one of them looked up, he would pull it out and fire. He rehearsed every part of it in his mind. Shoot one with a rubber plug, then the other. Apologize on your way out the door.

The two men moved on. When they were gone, he lowered the rope and slid down almost as fast as a fireman coming down a pole. He whispered into his comm, "Where is everybody?"

———

Jake came up the stairs, reaching the alcove that was their designated meeting spot. Nobody else was there. "Locations," he whispered. "Everybody say something."

"I'm making my way over," Quentin said.

Jake waited to hear from Kate and Nick. The silence was not good.

"I'm trapped," Nick finally said. "There's no way out."

Jake closed his eyes. "Kate," he said. "Where are you?"

Nothing.

"Get ready for World War Three," Jake said. "Don't worry, it'll just be lights and noise. Start moving as soon as you hear it."

Jake pulled out the last supplies from his bag, stepped out into the courtyard, and threw the first of the flashbang grenades. The explosion shattered the silence of the night. He threw another, then another.

Footsteps approached. He took out the flare gun, ready to fire. But then he saw Quentin and pulled back.

"Where are the kids?" Quentin asked him. "Those are armed *Bundespolizei*. They do not mess around."

They were interrupted by more footsteps, then by voices speaking German. Jake pointed the flare gun into the archway and fired, following that with another flashbang. Nick emerged from the smoke, holding his ears.

"Where's Kate?" Nick asked.

More silence, all three men looking at each other, until finally, they heard her voice. "I'm coming down! I need cover on the stairs!"

Jake stepped back into the alcove and looked up the winding staircase. He heard several sets of footsteps coming down. Kate reached the bottom first. As soon as she was clear, he fired a flare up the stairway and threw another flashbang.

"Get out to the rope!" Jake said, firing another flare.

Kate and Quentin both climbed up to the top of the wall, where Nick was already waiting.

"I'll go first," Nick said. "Come right behind me."

As she nodded, she heard the distant sound of a helicopter's rotors. She glanced up into the sky and saw the lights from the chopper, maybe a mile way, moving fast toward them. While she was still looking skyward, she spotted a statue on the very top of the main building. The statue represented a man looking out over the great valley below.

He was holding a swan.

It all came to Kate in an instant. This was the one swan in the entire castle that wasn't easily accessible, the one swan that would have the best chance of remaining untouched for seventy-five years. Because who would be crazy enough to go up there?

"Let's go!" Nick yelled.

"What's wrong?" Jake said, appearing below her. "Why aren't you going down?"

"Because I'm going up!" Kate said. "Cover me!"

The roof of the main building was three stories above her, but the surface of the stone was rough and there were ledges across the bottom of each floor. Kate jumped up onto the corner edge of the building before Nick could stop her. She scaled up the wall, one floor, then the second, then the third. Below her, her father was firing more flares and throwing more flashbang grenades. The helicopter was getting closer, sweeping its searchlight over the forest.

She kept moving, grabbing on to the edge of the roof and pulling herself up onto the tiles. As she got to her feet, she struggled to keep her balance on the sloped roof, making her way over to the statue. The life-size swan was tucked politely under one arm, its wings folded. She grabbed the swan's neck to hold herself steady.

A sudden flash of white light blinded her. It was the searchlight from the helicopter. She held tight to the swan's neck and felt it move. Scrambling with her feet, feeling herself losing her balance, she regripped lower on the swan's neck and felt herself going off the edge of the roof, swinging herself all the way around and catching the statue on the other side.

The swan's head and neck had come off in her hand. She looked down into the hollow space inside and thought she saw something, but then the searchlight swept over her again. The helicopter was even closer now, the wash from the rotors making her hair whip around her face. Harsh words roared at her from the chopper's loudspeakers, but they were German and meant nothing to her.

Kate put the swan's head into her pocket and made her way back down to the roof's corner. There was a terrifying moment as she eased herself over the edge, feeling herself hanging in space, finally finding the wall with her feet, feeling the rough surface, trusting in the leverage, in the laws of physics, letting go and half-climbing, half-sliding down until she was back on the wall.

"Get down the rope!" her father yelled at her. "Go!"

Nick had already slid down the rope a few feet, waiting for her to follow. She grabbed on tight and swung her body over the wall, into the open air again, feeling herself slam against the stone and almost lose her grip.

"Are you okay?" Nick asked.

"Don't worry about me!" Kate said. "Just keep moving!"

She found the rope with her foot again. She went down to the next loop and then the next, moving faster, and as the searchlight stayed on them and the booming voice continued to bark at them.

She looked back up and saw Quentin on his way down, her

father still on top of the wall, firing another flare and throwing another flashbang. As they got closer to the ground, Nick slid down the rest of the rope and caught Kate as she fell the last few feet.

"Keep moving!" Jake said from above them. "I'll find you!"

They threw themselves through the forest, sliding back down the side of the great hill, barely catching themselves on one branch after another. The helicopter blades roared high above them and the searchlight tried to find them, but here the forest was too thick. Nick and Kate both fell, scraped up their legs and their arms and their faces, got back up, kept moving, then fell again. Finally they reached the bottom, both landing in the stream. The shock of the cold water braced Kate like a slap across her cheek. She looked back up the slope, but she didn't see Quentin, or her father. In the distance she heard a police siren, then the faint sounds of dogs barking.

Nick and Kate did the one thing anyone should do with dogs on their trail. They stayed in the stream, following it a hundred yards to hide their scent, then broke back out and made their way up the other side of the gorge. Kate's feet were so numb from the cold water, she couldn't feel them anymore.

"Where's the van?" Nick asked. "I don't recognize where we are."

Neither did Kate. They were climbing back up now, but she had no idea where they would end up. When they reached level ground, they kept moving forward, vaguely in the right direction, back toward the town, but they had lost the road. Finally Kate spotted a clearing in the moonless night, and when they got closer they saw the pavement.

"The van's back there somewhere," she said. "But how far?"

They heard the sound of a vehicle approaching. They ducked behind trees, watching to see what was coming their way. The vehicle was running with only its parking lights, two wavering red dots weaving back and forth on the dark road.

It was the van! Kate stepped out, waving her hand, then threw herself back into the woods as the van locked its breaks and slid, almost turning sideways. Nick and Kate piled in and the tires spun on the gravel as Jake gunned it.

"Thank God," Quentin said. "I can't believe we found you."

Jake didn't join the celebration. He was too busy keeping the van on the road, driving as fast as he could with almost no light. The road turned suddenly and two wheels spun out in the dirt. Jake fought to bring the van back onto the pavement, slowing down as they came to the crest of a hill. Far ahead of them, they saw the flashing lights of police cars coming toward them.

"Hold on," he said, and threw the wheel hard to the right. They rumbled through a rough field, ran over a fence, then another fence, sprayed water through a pond, but kept moving. There was a barn ahead of them. Jake aimed for it, sailing through the open door and coming to rest when the front bumper hit a stack of hay and knocked it over.

He turned the van off. Everything went silent, except for the ticking of the van's hot engine and the sound of four people breathing.

"Is everybody okay?" Nick finally asked.

"I can't feel half my body," Kate said. "But I think so."

"What about you?" Quentin said to Jake. "That was a nasty fall off the rope."

"Sprained ankle," Jake said. "I've had worse."

There was another long silence as they all processed what they had been through. They had gotten out.

"What were you doing up on the roof?" Jake asked Kate.

"I was getting this," Kate said, pulling the swan's head from her pocket. She took out her penlight to examine it. While the rest of the statue had been stone, this one section appeared to be something like carved ivory. The exact same color, but removable. With a small swastika carved onto the neck.

"Whoever hid that clue at the Eiffel Tower," she said, "it was at the very top, right? This guy, whoever he was, he liked his heights."

"You have got to be kidding me," Jake said.

"No way," Nick said.

Quentin didn't say anything at all. He was too transfixed on the swan's head in Kate's hand, and then on the old piece of paper that she pulled from inside it.

It was the next piece of the map.

CHAPTER TEN

They all boarded on the Euro Train leaving from Munich just before dawn. They were speeding east, toward Austria, even if they didn't yet know exactly where they needed to go next. Right now, it was all about *motion*, all about getting out of Germany.

They had a private compartment this time, two long bench seats with a table in the middle. Quentin leaned back in his seat with a large bag of ice over his head. His ears were still ringing from the flashbang grenades. Next to him, Kate slept with her head on Nick's shoulder. On the other side of the table sat Jake, his right ankle wrapped up tight and still visibly swollen. Professor Lewis sat next to him, poring over the next link in the map.

"I don't have this one quite figured out yet," Lewis said, "but I believe we're moving in the right direction. There's a clear reference to Austria here."

Quentin made a point of not showing any of the map pieces in public, but here in the private compartment Lewis was free to lay all three pieces out on the table. The latest piece was similar to the others, with the strange ancient runes arranged along the topographical lines in the center, and the separate banner on the right side. This one read *Der Eisbär dient dem Erzherzog von Österreich und dem Heiligen Römischen Kaiser.*

"We've got an 'ice bear,'" Lewis said, "the Archduke of Austria, and the Holy Roman Emperor. It's quite a puzzle, isn't it?"

"If there's anyone who can figure it out," Nick said, "it's you."

Lewis smiled at him. "Thank you, I'll give it my best go."

Quentin struggled to stand up, his head pounding with every slight movement. "I need more ice," he said.

"I've got it," Nick said. He opened the compartment door and stepped out into the hallway. He made his way slowly down the side hallway of the car, passing through one more car, then into the dining car. The tables were half-full of normal people leading normal lives, having breakfast on their merry way to Austria.

Nick asked the server behind the bar for a bag of ice for his father. He was ready to try the request in French, then Italian if he needed to, but the server spoke enough English to get the idea. Nick grabbed the bag of ice and thanked the server. He was about to turn and leave when he felt the presence of the man next to him.

"You threw Nils from the tower," the man said.

Nick turned slowly to look at him. He had the bent nose and scar tissue of a man who'd lost at least half of his street fights. He was wearing jeans and a black leather jacket. More important to Nick, one point of a red star tattoo was visible over his collar.

Nick looked over to see another man in one of the dining booths. This one had a shaved head and the same red star tattoo on his neck.

"I think Nils threw *himself* off the tower," Nick said. "But where's the big guy?"

"You'll meet Franz in time," the man said. "I promise."

"Franz? Really? Like Hans and Franz from *Saturday Night Live*? 'We're going to pump you up'?"

"I don't know what you're talking about," the man said.

"You're missing out," Nick said. "I'll email you a YouTube link."

"Where are you and the others going?"

"What do you mean?" Nick asked. "I'm alone."

"Let's try this again. You are all in one compartment, two cars ahead of us. Where are you going?"

"Oh, *them*," Nick said. "We're just going to Salzburg for some of their famous sausage."

The man dropped his voice down a notch. "We could shoot you right here. You think we care about anything else?"

Nick looked at him again, then at the man in the booth. Clearly they don't, he thought.

"Let's go," the man said. "Walk."

The second man stood up and led the way through the dining car. Nick was nudged into the middle of the parade, with the first man following him. They opened the door and went into the space between cars, a sudden rush of wind blowing across Nick's face. When they were in the next car, they squeezed over to the side to let a very old woman totter by them.

Another door opened, another blast of wind, then they walked into the car containing everyone in the world who was important to Nick Fox. He still had no idea what to do.

The two men walked directly to the compartment and threw open the door. Kate looked up in surprise. The professor looked up like he was about to wet his pants again. Quentin was asleep, his head leaning against the wall of the compartment.

Jake was gone.

The lead man looked up and down the hallway, took out his gun, and pointed it at Kate. "Where is he?"

"Bathroom," she said, nodding her head toward the other end of the car, away from the direction in which they'd come.

The first man said something to the other in German, pushed Nick into the berth, and kept his gun pointed at Kate. The second man went forward to the other end of the car to find Jake.

When the second man reached the end of the car, he saw that he had to go on to the next to find the bathroom. He opened the door and went out into the rushing wind one more time. Jake was waiting for him.

He put his stun gun against the man's neck and hit the button. Ten thousand volts raced through the man's body in a fraction of a second and shut down his entire neuromuscular system. As the man slumped to the floor, Jake took away his gun and stuffed it into his own belt. When the man started to recover, Jake lifted him back to his feet.

"*Auf Wiedersehen*," Jake said as he pushed him through the gap. Because it was a Euro Train, the man probably hit the ground at 150 miles per hour, maybe more, but he had a theoretical chance of surviving.

———

Back in the compartment, the first man's attention was momentarily drawn away from what was going on in the car ahead. He had spotted the map lying on the table and knew exactly what it was.

Kate slid one hand down below the table, into Nick's leather travel bag.

"I'll take that," he said. "Slide it over here."

Kate carefully riffled through the contents of the bag, feeling for something metal.

"I said, *slide it over*."

This time he gestured with the gun, pointing it at the map. Kate pulled out the Walther semiautomatic that Nick had carried the night before in the castle. She aimed at the man's abdomen and fired. In the same instant, Quentin opened his eyes and took the man's gun.

As all of the air went out of the man, he made a low half-yell, half-gasp, sounding exactly like a man who's just been hit in the gut with a rubber plug traveling 350 feet per second. Nick caught him as he fell, and pushed him back out into the hallway. The old woman was making her way back through the train.

"He's having a seizure," Nick said, holding the man out of the way, long enough for the woman to pass. "I'm getting him some help, don't worry."

Either she didn't understand English, or she didn't care, because she just kept walking.

Jake opened the door just as Nick reached the end of the car, half-pushing, half-carrying the man. Jake took him from Nick, looked down the hallway to make sure the woman was out of sight, and threw the man through the gap.

"Say hello to your friend for me," Jake said.

Before Nick could thank Jake, he glanced through the window leading to the cab ahead of them. The man named Franz, the largest man on the train, possibly the largest man in the combined nations of Germany and Austria, was pushing his way down the center aisle. In this cab, there were open double seats on either side, and a passenger was currently blocking the aisle, struggling to put a big suitcase in the overhead rack.

"I don't think we're quite done," Nick said. He watched the big man push the suitcase into the rack with one hand, as easily as a normal man would stick a letter in a mailbox. He deposited the passenger into his seat just as easily.

"Help me up," Jake said, nodding to the top of the car. "When he comes through, I'll hit him like a ton of bricks."

Nick put his hands together to make a step. Jake winced as he went up on his sprained ankle, but with one quick lift he was able to grab on to the top of the car and pull himself up. He got his stun gun ready again, hoping it had enough time to recharge.

Nick watched as the big man fought his way to the end of the car, leaving looks of outrage and pure terror in his wake. Nick waved to him as he stepped back through the door into the car behind him.

Kate poked her head out of the berth. "Is everything okay?"

"Give me that gun with the plugs," Nick said. When Kate handed it to him, Nick told her to close the door to the compartment, to lock it tight, and to shoot anything bigger than a Coke machine if the door was pulled open. "Use real bullets this time," Nick said. "Keep shooting until the gun goes *click*."

As the door closed, Nick turned just in time to see big Franz entering the gap between the two cars. Jake dropped down from his vantage point, driving his elbow onto the big man's skull. Franz didn't flinch.

Jake took the stun gun, stuck it against Franz's neck, and hit the button. There was a loud crackle of electricity. Franz looked down at Jake like a man vaguely annoyed by a buzzing mosquito.

Franz picked Jake up by the neck with one hand and carried Jake toward the edge of the gap. The ground was rushing below Jake's feet.

Nick opened the door and fired with the gun, hitting Franz with every plug in the cartridge. Abdomen, chest, neck, forehead. Each blow was enough to put a normal man on the floor for a very long time. As Franz let go, Jake was barely able to grab on to the ladder that ran up the side of the car. The wind rushed past him at 150 miles per hour, trying to blow him off the train.

Inside, Nick was backing away from the door as Franz tore it open and stepped inside the car. "Let's talk about this," Nick said. "*Sprechen Sie Englisch? Français? Italiano?*"

Franz took three more steps forward. The compartment door

opened and Quentin's foot came out to trip him. Franz landed so hard, it was a wonder the train didn't derail. As he was shaking his head clear and starting to push himself back up, Kate came out and wrapped her father's thin metal cable around the man's ankles, tying it into a quick knot.

"Hey, didn't I shoot you in London?" she asked.

Franz looked up at her like, *Do you really expect this to do anything other than slow me down for maybe three seconds?*

Kate showed him the grappling hook on the other end of the cable.

Franz's eyes grew wide. He scrambled to untie the cable, but Kate had already led it through the door and into the gap between the cars. Jake was just managing to climb back off the side ladder.

"You might want to step aside, Dad," Kate said.

As soon as Jake was behind her, Kate spun the grappling hook three times and out through the gap.

They happened to be going over a bridge, spanning high above a river. The hook hit one of the bridge's tension wires and caught immediately. One half second later, Franz was pulled through the door to slam violently against the other car, and .000001 seconds after that he was yanked by his feet through the gap.

Jake and Kate both heard the sound of a great weight hitting a hard metal beam at very high speed. As they poked their heads through the gap, they saw Franz's body dangling from the cable over the river. Franz's ankles finally worked free of the cable and he fell at least two hundred feet to the rocky riverbed below.

When they went back to the compartment, Nick, Quentin, and Professor Lewis were catching their breath. Especially the professor. "This is not what I signed up for, guys," Lewis said. "I've never had a gun pointed at me before."

"You did great," Nick said. "Everybody did."

"No, I really think it might be time for me to go home," Lewis said.

Everyone else looked at each other.

"It might not be that easy," Nick finally said. "They found us at your house, remember? They know you're with us."

The professor thought about that one, closed his eyes, and nodded. "Looks like my unplanned vacation is going to last a while longer."

"Which brings up an even more important question," Nick said. "How did they know we'd be on this train? We didn't even know we'd be on it ourselves until we decided this morning."

"They can't be tracking us anymore," Kate said. "I dumped my phone in England."

"My phone's always clean," Nick said.

"And mine," Quentin said.

"Same here," Jake said.

A moment passed, and then everyone turned to Professor Lewis. Another moment passed as he noticed everyone staring at him. "What?"

"Professor Lewis," Quentin said, measuring each word. "Do you still have your own personal cell phone in your possession?"

He took out his phone from his tweed jacket. "This one?"

Jake, Nick, and Kate all let out breaths, rolling their eyes. Quentin stayed focused on Lewis. "You brought that with you from England."

"Yes. Is that a problem?"

"Not for long," Jake said, grabbing the phone from Lewis's hand.

"Wait," Nick said. "Don't just throw it out the window. We can use it to our advantage."

"A false flag?"

"Exactly," Nick said. "When this train arrives in Salzburg, the phone will still be on board, but we won't be."

"The next stop is Rosenheim," Kate said. "We get off there, but then what?"

"Then we go to Vienna," Lewis said.

Everyone looked at him again.

"When that gun was pointed at me, I think I had an inspiration and figured it out. *Dem Erzherzog von Österreich und dem Heiligen Römischen Kaiser*. The Archduke of Austria and the Holy Roman Emperor. For a short period of time that was one and the same person, beginning with Francis the First. When Francis was crowned as both, he lived at the Schönbrunn Palace in Vienna."

"So we go to the palace and we look for what?" Kate asked.

"*Der Eisbär*," Lewis said. "The literal translation is 'ice bear,' but what that really means is 'polar bear.'"

"So another crazy king," Kate said. "Or archduke or emperor or whatever. And another animal clue for us to find. Is that what you're telling us?"

The professor winced. "Not exactly. This time, it's a different kind of animal clue."

"What do you mean?" Kate asked.

"The Tiergarten Schönbrunn," Lewis said. "It's part of the palace, and it happens to be the oldest zoo in the world. The polar bear exhibit, in fact, is quite famous."

"Wait a minute," Kate said. "Are you saying what I think you're saying?"

"Yes," Lewis said. "The next link is guarded by real-life polar bears."

CHAPTER ELEVEN

It was another beautiful day in another beautiful European city. Kate sat on the balcony outside her hotel room, looking out over the baroque architecture of Vienna. Her father came out, stood at the rail, and looked down at the same view. "How you doing, kid?"

"I just talked to Jessup," she said, holding up a burner phone. "He's been working on the Interpol leak."

"Getting anywhere?"

"Not yet," Kate said. "As long as Interpol is compromised, it's going to keep feeling like the whole world is trying to stop us, even the guys with badges."

They both looked out at the city for a while.

"You really think we're going to find it?" Kate finally asked.

"Is your gut telling you to keep looking?"

"Yes," she said, surprising even herself at how quickly the answer came to her.

"Then I know we're going to find it. Because your gut is *always* right."

She nodded. "Okay, so what now?"

"I say we go check out the zoo."

As the taxi took Jake, Kate, Nick, and Quentin past the front gates of the palace, they all spotted the *Bundespolizei* cars parked conspicuously on both sides of the street, along with the uniformed officers watching all of the tourists as they entered the grounds. They had to wonder, once again, if every single major European cultural landmark was being provided a higher level of security now that three of them had been hit in succession. But then, this is the palace, Kate thought. Would they actually think it was necessary to guard a zoo?

There was a separate entrance to the Tiergarten Schönbrunn, a few blocks down the street from the palace's front gates. When the taxi let them out, they didn't see any extra *Bundespolizei* standing around to guard the peacocks and penguins. So the answer is no, Kate thought. We are officially crazier than even the most careful security analyst could ever account for.

They bought their tickets and made like any other tourists enjoying a nice trip to the zoo, strolling through the grounds, a true mixture of the new and the old. As Professor Lewis had told them, many of the original buildings had been built in the nineteenth century, and it was the oldest continuously run zoo in the world.

They made their way past the rhinoceroses, past the bison,

past the insect house and the bat house and the snake house, finally arriving at the polar bear habitat, which took up an entire curve on the main path. It was an open-air complex terrain of jutting stone that had been built for the bears, with roughly half the surfaces covered in green moss. There was also a waterfall and a slide leading down into a deep pool of water, and a beach made from thousands of smooth stones.

It was a popular exhibit, with at least a hundred people standing in front of it. A huge adult female polar bear was calmly sitting on the rocks, seemingly watching the people who were watching her. At one point, she seemed to look directly at Kate, holding her gaze as if saying, *Don't even think about it.*

The biggest attraction was the cub, whose birth had made news around the world earlier that year. Now he was a healthy six-month-old, splashing around at the edge of the water.

Jake and Kate stepped up to the rail together, while Nick and Quentin stood together on the far end. The rail formed a large arc, a hundred feet long, and the entire habitat must have covered well over fifteen hundred square feet. Kate noticed the fenced-off walkway along the upper rim, from which the handlers probably threw the bears their raw fish or whatever else they got to eat.

"It's big," Kate said.

Jake nodded. He was studying the terrain carefully, taking in every detail.

Kate felt a cold wave of air against her face. "Bet it's a lot colder when you get in there, too."

Jake nodded again.

Somewhere behind her, Kate overheard one of the zoo guides

talking to a young couple. She was speaking English. Kate wandered over to pick up on what she was saying.

"An adult female will usually weigh about five hundred pounds," the guide said. She was plucky and blond, with perfect English pronunciation, and she probably spoke at least four other languages. Austria at its finest. "They can eat twenty percent of their body weight in one sitting, so that's one hundred pounds of meat!"

The young couple were appropriately impressed by this, thanked the guide, and moved on. Kate put on her best smile to draw the guide's attention. "Is this still the original exhibit?" she asked.

"We're going to be shutting down this exhibit for a major renovation," the guide said. "The new 'Franz Josef Land' will have three times as much space, with a much more natural habitat for the bears. But yes, the habitat you see here now has been around for almost a century. It was one of the few that didn't get damaged by the bombings in World War Two."

"Isn't that interesting," Kate said. "And those doors I see in the rocks, does that mean the polar bears go inside to sleep at night?"

"Actually, fun fact! Most of the other animals in the zoo do go inside to sleep at night, but polar bears are one of the few animals that don't ever do that. They can't sleep in enclosed spaces, so they have the run of the place all night long!"

"That is a fun fact!" Kate said, suddenly feeling a little sick to her stomach.

"I'll tell you something else," the guide said, stepping closer like she was about to share a secret. "Did you know that polar bears are one of the only mammals in the world who don't have a natural fear of humans?"

"You don't say."

"If you're ever in the Arctic Circle and you see a polar bear," the guide said, "you'd better start running. Because they will seriously hunt you down."

"Another fun fact!" Kate said. "Thank you so much."

The guide squeezed Kate's arm and wished her a great day. As Kate went back to her father, her fake smile disappeared.

We are so screwed.

Back in Professor Lewis's hotel room, Kate and Nick sat next to each other on the bed. Jake was leaning against the edge of the desk, watching the professor tap away on his laptop. Quentin was at the window, looking out at the city.

"This zoo has a tragic history," Lewis said. "During the war, they had to choose which large animals to save, and then they killed all of the smaller animals and used them as food. Then, when the Russians were advancing through Austria, the two head zookeepers committed suicide."

Nick and Kate looked at each other. "Does this have anything to do with where we're looking?" Kate asked.

"In 2002, three jaguars attacked a handler," Lewis said. "Killed her in front of everybody. A few years later, another handler got crushed to death by an elephant. Do you get the feeling this place is cursed?"

"Professor," Kate said, "you're not exactly helping the mood here."

"You're right, I'm sorry," Lewis said. "I should focus on where this next clue is pointing." He held out the map so that everybody could see it. "Look at the rune next to this next banner. This is *Gebo*. It means *gift*."

"It just looks like an X," Kate said.

"Correct. That's *Gebo*."

"So what's the gift that's inside the polar bear exhibit?"

"That's what I'm trying to figure out," Lewis said. "It had to be before or during the war, but I can't find anything in any of the records. Of course, they didn't have Facebook or Instagram back then to show off a new toy for the polar bears. You may have to do a hard search when you're inside the exhibit."

"I'll go," Quentin said. "The one thing we know is that whatever I'm looking for, it'll be marked with a small swastika, like the others."

"We should start high," Nick said. "Like at the Eiffel Tower and the castle."

"Maybe," Quentin said. "Or maybe whoever hid it didn't have to worry about keeping it out of reach like at those other places."

"Right," Kate said. "Because the polar bears would eat anyone looking for it. I did mention the part about them being outside all night, right?"

"I found this one old postcard of the exhibit," Lewis said. He brought up a rough black-and-white drawing on his laptop, then switched back and forth between the drawing and a modern photograph. "The drawing is from the 1890s, and I don't see a waterfall here. It was definitely added later, so it's possible that this was the gift added to the exhibit."

"It's a place to start," Nick said. "Let's see that map of the whole zoo."

Jake spread out a map of the zoo on the desk.

"There's a service entrance down here on the southern gate," Nick said. "It's the most wooded section of the zoo. Working our way north, there's a large tree about fifty yards west of the polar bears, next to the zebra pen. Someone can climb that tree and watch out for any security doing their overnight rounds."

"Jake's the best climber," Quentin said. "He should take that lookout."

"And I'll go into the exhibit with Quentin," Kate said.

"Let's make one thing clear," Jake said. "I am not going to be the man sitting in a tree, watching his daughter get mauled by a polar bear."

"I'll go," Nick said. "It'll be a good chance for some more quality father-and-son time."

"Being eaten together," Quentin said. "I think that qualifies."

"If Jake is in this tree to the west," Nick said, "Kate can be our eyes on the east side." He pointed to the reptile house. "There has to be a way onto the roof."

Jake nodded. "We'll have our comms on, like last time. As far as the rules of engagement go—"

"They'll be the same," Nick said. "No innocents hurt. Period. That includes people *and* polar bears."

"We're still close to a new moon tonight. No sense waiting."

Everyone in the room nodded. Nobody said another word,

because there was nothing else left to say. As soon as the sun went down and the zoo was empty, Nick Fox and his father had a date with the polar bears.

After dinner, Jake slipped away from the group and went outside to hail a taxi. Kate caught up with him and asked him where he was going.

"Nick and Quentin need to save their energy for tonight," Jake said. "I'm going out to get some more supplies."

"I'm coming with you," she said.

Jake asked the driver to take them to the nearest gun store. They ended up in a shop in Kagraner Platz, a modest little place by American gun shop standards. It carried mostly hunting equipment, some decent rifles but not many handguns.

"We can't buy guns here," Kate said. "We're not citizens."

"I know," Jake said as he picked up two canisters of pepper spray. "But if they need a few extra seconds, these might help."

He took the canisters to the counter. "Do you have anything bigger?"

The man at the register had his glasses hanging from his neck, halfway down his ugly sweater vest. He put on the glasses and looked Jake and Kate up and down like they'd just landed a spaceship and walked into his store.

"I do not speak English," the man said, in perfect English.

"Just these two, then," Jake said, sliding the canisters toward him. He counted out the right number of euro coins and plunked them on the glass.

The man shook his head. "I cannot sell to you."

"I'm pretty sure you can, friend." Jake dropped a few more euros on the glass.

"*Nein.*"

"*Ja.*" A few more euros.

"*Nein!*"

Jake emptied his pockets and put every euro he was carrying on the glass. "Do you want my daughter here to post a bad Yelp review?"

The man brushed the euros into his hand, opened up his till, and threw them inside. "Good day," he said.

"And good day to you," Jake said, taking the two canisters and walking out the door.

The man kept scowling as he came around the counter to help another customer. But the other customer was a young man with so many tattoos, you could barely make out the red star on his neck, and he had just taken a picture of Jake and Kate with his phone. He waved the shop owner away, went outside to watch the taxi pull out into traffic, and started texting on his phone.

CHAPTER TWELVE

Just after midnight, Nick, Kate, Quentin, and Jake approached the southern wall of the zoo. There was a large gate for service vehicles to pass through. Quentin quickly worked the padlock, snapped it open, quietly removed the chain, and pushed one side of the gate slightly open.

After they had all passed through the gate, Quentin replaced the chain and padlock, but left the shackle unlatched. They moved through the mini-farm, with all of the animals tucked away for the night, passed under a canopy of trees, and crossed over a bridge. Some of the zoo's pathway lights were on, most off. Just enough for the night security to do their rounds.

Kate veered to the east, toward the reptile house. Jake went west to find the tall tree near the penguins. Nick and Quentin stayed huddled behind the bat house for the moment. They would make their next move after receiving the all-clear from Kate and Jake.

Jake reached the tree and looked in all directions. There was nothing to hear but the faint white noise from the waterfall in the polar bear exhibit. No living things, animal or human, were moving. He put on his gloves and shimmied up the tree to the first large branch. The climbing was monkey-easy the rest of the way to the top. He settled in, checking every point on the compass.

"In position," he said into his comm. "All clear."

Kate was behind the reptile house, where she found a dumpster from which she could reach just high enough to grab hold of the gutter. She pulled herself all the way up and moved across the roof to the front.

"In position," she said. "All clear on this side."

Nick gave his father a quick nod, and then they were in motion.

"There they are," Nick whispered as they approached the polar bear exhibit. A mound of gray-white fur lay motionless on the lower level of rocks. "I'm sure Baby Bear is tucked in there with Mamma."

"Maybe they'll both stay asleep," Quentin said.

"Here's hoping. You know any polar bear lullabies?"

"Looks like we're going in from the top," Quentin said, nodding to the upper platform.

"We'll go down those steps," Jake said, indicating the rough stairway carved into the rocks. "Stay to the right, approach that waterfall from the opposite side."

The two men went around to find the rear access door to the exhibit. A set of metal stairs ran up the back of the rocks, protected by a cage with a roof. Nick worked the lock and had it open within a minute. They pushed the door open and climbed the stairs to the upper platform. They both rolled themselves over the railing, dropping the few feet to the upper rocks. They were now officially in polar bear territory.

As quietly and carefully as two men can descend a rough stone staircase, that was how Quentin and Nick Fox moved. Kate's voice entered the ears of both men. "Still clear."

"Do me a favor," Nick whispered. "Don't say anything unless there's a problem."

"Roger."

Nick took a moment to let his heart rate return to double digits, then kept moving. Another step, then another, until they could peek over the edge and see the sleeping bears. Baby Bear was indeed tucked under the arm of Mamma Bear.

They worked their way all the way down to the main level of the exhibit. It was a strange and terrible feeling for both of them, putting their boots on the same level on which the bears were sleeping. From this point on, if Mamma Bear woke up and decided to have a midnight snack, at least one Fox, whichever was the slower man, would be on the menu.

The waterfall was still flowing, long after the park had closed. Maybe the white noise helps them sleep, Nick thought. I sure as hell hope so. Either way, he was glad to have the sound to cover his footsteps.

Quentin moved a few steps ahead of him, took out his penlight, turned it on to the weakest setting, and held it in his mouth as he started to examine the gap in the wall through which the water flowed. Nick worked his way down one side of the torrent, peering at each rock. His back was to the bears. He tried to put that out of his mind and focus. Look for the swastika, he told himself. And then you can get out of here.

They examined every rock around the waterfall. Quentin looked at Nick and they both had the same thought at the same time. Maybe the rock is *behind* the waterfall. Nick plunged his hand into the icy torrent, trying to feel the rocks behind the falls. His hand went numb within a matter of seconds.

As he was shaking the feeling back into his hand, Nick saw his father remove his earpiece, take a deep breath, then put his head into the water with the penlight still in his mouth. Nick looked over at the bears. Had one of them rolled over in her sleep? Their position looked slightly different. He shook that off and got back to work, moving down to the bottom of the waterfall, shining his light on the rocks. All the while, he kept glancing first at the bears, then at the stairway, then at the sheer walls on the far side of the pond. It was an impossible climb unless you could levitate on the water and then jump ten feet straight in the air.

"We have a guard on the east side of the park, walking your way," Kate said. "One hundred yards, moving slowly."

Quentin brought his head back out of the waterfall and looked at Nick. They searched the terrain around them. There was a door leading inside, for the rare occasion when someone needed to access the lower level. Nick moved as quietly as he could to try the door. It didn't move, obviously latched from the inside. There was nowhere else to hide, because that was the way this exhibit had been built. You pay to see the polar bears, you don't want them tucked behind a big rock.

"Fifty yards," Kate said.

"I see him now," Jake said. "You need to find some cover, guys."

"Easy for you to say," Nick whispered.

Quentin pointed to a rough slab of stone that extended out over the water, like a raised dock for bears. You gotta be kidding me, Nick thought, but he knew it was their only choice.

Nick went into the water on one side of the peninsula, Quentin on the other. The water was an icy shock against his skin, but Quentin went in all the way up to his neck and moved under the slab, where there was maybe twelve inches of space for their heads. He was already trembling uncontrollably.

"Just breathe," Nick said.

"The guard is in front of the exhibit," Kate said in his ear.

"I have him now," Jake said. "He's walking past."

"Tell him to hurry up," Quentin said, his teeth chattering.

"Stay down," Jake said. "I'll let you know when it's clear."

A minute passed. A frigid, icy eternity, long enough for Nick to process everything he'd seen from inside the exhibit.

"Question," he said into his comm. "Why are we looking for a *gift* again?"

"Because that's what the rune means," Kate answered. "According to the professor."

"What did that symbol look like?"

A moment of silence, until Kate spoke again. "It was an X."

"So why can't the rune just be the rune this time? Not what it *represents*, but the symbol itself?"

Jake broke in. "What are you talking about?"

"Where the bears were sleeping, just a few feet above them, I noticed an X on one of the rocks. I didn't think anything of it then, but now—"

"It's worth checking out," Jake said. "The guard is gone now."

"I'm glad you guys are figuring this out," Quentin said, "but I have to get out of this water before I die."

He went to the edge of the slab to pull himself up. What he saw next was heart-stopping, both in its sheer beauty and in its absolute terror.

Quentin Fox was staring directly into the coal-black eyes of a curious polar bear cub.

———

From his vantage point in the tree, Jake watched the polar bear cub leave his mother and wander over to the stone slab that jutted out over the water. The cub moved with the playful innocence of a young and inquisitive animal, but Jake knew that the stakes had just changed, because nothing on this earth is more deadly than an animal like a polar bear, already bad news in *any* situation, who suddenly perceives that her cub may be in danger.

"Try not to move," Jake said. "I'm coming down."

"To do what exactly?" Quentin asked.

"To do whatever I have to do," Jake said, hitting the ground and reaching for his SIG Sauer. No matter what rules of engagement they had agreed to, Jake was not going to let Quentin get eaten without at least trying to stop it.

———

Quentin put a finger to his lips, like he could actually convince the bear cub to be quiet and not wake its mother, but from the corner of his eye, he saw the slow movement of something very large. Nick grabbed him and pulled him back under the slab.

"Listen to me," Nick said. "I'm going to distract the mother bear, and you're going to get out of here."

Jake's voice broke through on both of their comms. "I've got another idea. I'm going to toss a line directly across where you are. Then I'll make a pulley with the railing posts to create some leverage. You get out of there one at a time, grab the line, and I'll lift you. Then you can swing over to the railing."

"What about the map link?" Quentin said. "We didn't come here to leave it behind."

"We'll regroup," Jake said. "Do better recon tomorrow. Right now, I'd rather keep you both alive."

"Okay," Nick said. "My father's coming out first."

Quentin's body felt like it was starting to shut down from hypothermia. He was too cold and too exhausted to argue.

"Give me a minute to set up," Jake said. When Jake reached the railing, he checked up and down the walkway. Not like the guards are our biggest problem right now, he thought.

The mother bear was on her feet now, wandering over to her cub. Jake took out the team's last grappling hook, spun it a few times, and launched it toward the very upper level of the exhibit. He didn't care exactly where it hit. He just needed to be able to drop the line in the vicinity of the stone peninsula.

The hook hit something he couldn't see, but when he tested it, it held. He gave it enough play so that the line was just brushing the surface of the water. Then he looped the line around one post, led it to another, brought it back, looped it one more time for good measure. Basic physics: each loop in the pulley doubles your lifting power.

"The line's ready," Jake said, wrapping the free end around his waist. "But the mother bear is on the slab. You might want to wait a minute."

Mamma Bear nuzzled her cub, gently at first, then with more insistence. She wanted the cub away from the water, but if the cub could have spoken it clearly would have announced that there was something interesting under the slab.

The mother bear practically rolled the cub back toward their sleeping spot, but then she stopped and sniffed the air. In the back of Jake's mind, he remembered something about how a polar bear could smell a seal something like twenty miles away. He didn't know how well that sense of smell applied to prey that was underwater, and he didn't know if smelling humans all the time had changed this particular bear's behavior.

"I think you've got to move," Jake said. "Look for the line as soon as you come out of the water. And Nick, if that bear goes in the water, I think you need to get out."

The mother bear was already coming back to the edge of the water when Quentin's head broke the surface. Within the span of one second, he turned, saw the bear looking at him, and reached for the line. As soon as Jake saw Quentin grab it, he threw his weight away from the rail, using the pulley system to pull the line taut. Quentin felt the bear's claws brush against one foot as he was raised into the air.

The bear's momentum took her into the water. Nick heard the splash and felt the huge presence of the bear displacing the water all around him. It was his turn to move, because a polar bear underwater is in its natural element.

Nick pushed away from the slab, staying underwater like a backstroker pushing away from the wall. When he came up for air, he saw his father dangling from the wire, just a few feet away from the reach of the mother bear, who was churning away in the water. Nick had already watched his father hanging from a similar wire in the interior of the Eiffel Tower. Somehow this felt a hundred times more terrifying.

Quentin locked eyes with his son on the other side of the exhibit. He stopped trying to move sideways toward the rail and stayed where he was, suspended over the middle of the pool, hoping to keep the bear occupied so that Nick could get out of the water and make it up the rocky stairs.

Nick swam to the edge and stumbled up onto the rocks. He'd been denying the effects of the frigid water on his body, locking it out of his mind. But as he left the water his whole body felt numb, as if he could barely move at anything beyond slow motion.

The sleeping spot was in front of him. Nick went to the X. He was just tall enough to reach it. He willed the lifeblood back into his hands so he could feel the rough surface.

"Get out, Nick!" It was the voice of his father calling to him, sounding like it came from a place many miles away. Everything was going dim around him, but he kept moving his fingers across the rocks.

"Nick, move!"

Nick felt something, a slight difference in the resistance as he tapped one finger on one small, round rock. He had a knife strapped to his belt, and fumbled with his almost useless fingers until he had it in his hand. He opened the blade, put the tip in the tight seam around the rock, pushed with gentle pressure, then harder until it gave way.

The rock fell out of the hole. Behind it was a metal tube. He worked in the knife a little farther and pried out the tube. It was sealed at both ends with a gummy substance that might once have been wax.

"Nick!"

He looked up from his task. The mother bear had given up on reaching Quentin, and now had wandered over to this side of the exhibit for a much easier meal. She was four feet away from Nick, not moving, just watching him.

Nick took the canister of pepper spray from his pocket, nearly dropping it with his still-frigid fingers. He recovered, flipped the switch over to the ON position, pointed it at the bear's face, and fired. A dribble of liquid came out and ran down his hand. The damned thing wasn't waterproof.

———

Kate looked down at the two night guards as they passed by the entrance to the reptile house. They were both wearing black windbreakers with "Zoosicherheit" printed across their backs in large yellow letters.

"Two coming from the east," she whispered, even as she

realized that the men on the other end were already dealing with something a lot more serious than the approaching security guards. Still, it was her job to monitor the situation outside of the polar bear exhibit and to keep it from getting worse.

Kate scrambled over to the back edge of the roof, eased herself over and hung down low enough to land on the dumpster without making too much noise, then started running toward the polar bear exhibit.

———

Jake heard Kate's voice. "Two coming from the east." He wasn't worried. Kate would handle it. He had to focus on the polar bear currently staring down Nick. Jake pulled out his SIG Sauer and manually cocked the hammer for a faster shot.

He watched Nick take one careful step backward, then another. The bear advanced with him, but did not charge yet. Another rough set of steps was carved into the rock formation, directly behind Nick. It was much steeper than the steps they had used when they first entered.

"Nice bear," Nick said, taking another step backward, then another until he was at the bottom step.

Jake took dead aim at the animal's center mass. Do not make me do this, he thought. Let the man leave.

Quentin was still hanging above the water, watching his son backing away from the other bear. He couldn't move. He couldn't watch. He couldn't *not* watch.

"Nice bear," Nick said one more time, then it was time to *move*.

He took one step, drove his other leg up as high he could, caught another step, then another. The bear took a moment to realize that his prey was trying to escape before coming after him.

Jake moved the sight of his gun along with the bear's motion, leading slightly ahead. His brain was set on pure reaction mode. The instant he needed to fire, he would do so without hesitation.

Nick scrambled, briefly lost his footing, regained it, climbed another step, then another. The bear was closing the gap. Jake kept his aim, starting to apply pressure to the trigger. Nick took one more step and could practically feel the bear's breath now. Jake's trigger was halfway down.

Nick saw the lower rung of the upper railing, coiled his entire body like a spring, and jumped. His hand touched the rail. He kept pulling, drawing his body upward. A claw raked against his leg, cutting through the fabric like it was tissue paper. Four sharp nails cut into his skin.

He pulled once more, desperately drawing his body parallel to the concrete platform. He caught one foot, then the other, regripped with his second hand on a higher rung and kept pulling himself up like a pole vaulter arching his entire body to clear those last few inches over the bar. He hung on the top of the railing for one sick moment, feeling like he could go either way, then landed hard on the concrete. Nick was freezing, bleeding from his leg, sucking in oxygen as fast as he could, but he was alive.

Jake took his finger off the trigger, just in time to refocus on Quentin. Quentin had used pure survival reflex to keep moving himself. He was now close enough that Jake could reach out and grab Quentin's arm, pulling him up to safety.

Kate was about to draw the attention of the guards when they stopped, turned around, and walked back toward her. She ducked behind the corner of the bat house as the men passed. She could hear an animated conversation, in German, being conducted over their radios.

"They're leaving," Kate whispered. "I don't get it."

When they were gone, she came out and ran down the pathway to the polar bear exhibit. Quentin was lying on the ground, soaking wet and breathing like he'd just set a personal best in the marathon. Jake was unwinding his line from the rail posts.

"Where's Nick?" she asked.

"Top deck," Jake said. "He might have taken a swipe to the leg, but otherwise he's in one piece."

Kate ran around to the back of the exhibit, up the stairs to the top deck. Nick was still stretched out on the concrete platform. His right pant leg was torn and soaked with blood, just above the knee.

She kneeled down next to him. "How bad is it?"

"Hard to say," Nick said, pushing himself to a seated position. "I'm so cold, I don't think I have any blood flowing."

"Can you get up? We need to get out of here, fast. I saw two guards turn around and leave their beat. I have a bad feeling about what's coming next."

CHAPTER THIRTEEN

Jake and Quentin were waiting for Nick and Kate on the pathway.

"I'm guessing zoo security has been replaced by Red Star security," Jake said. "If that's true, they'll have all of the exits covered."

Kate nodded. "We'll need a counterattack. Something that will allow us to get Nick and Quentin out of here."

"Agreed," Jake said. "You and Nick go back toward the gate. Quentin and I will see who we can take out here."

Jake watched Kate and Nick as they headed for the bridge and the southern exit. Then he and Quentin ducked back behind the polar bear exhibit, opened the gate, eased it closed behind them, and climbed up the back stairs.

Two men arrived at the front of the exhibit, spotted Jake's line wrapped around the rail posts, and looked in at the polar bears. They were both wearing the zoo's official black windbreakers, but they were carrying semiautomatics with suppressors. The disguise isn't meant to fool us, Jake thought. It's a way to slip out undetected after we're dead and the police start showing up.

Jake could have come over the rail and taken a shot, probably hit one of them. With a lot of luck, maybe both of them, but his gun didn't have a suppressor, meaning his shots would let everyone else know he was there. That meant everyone else in the zoo, plus whoever was outside the zoo but close enough to hear the noise.

"Get ready," Jake said to Quentin. "We're going to have to improvise."

———

As Kate and Nick made their way through the forested area, moving carefully from one tree to the next, Kate's mind settled on the same problem that had just hit her father. If she fired her Beretta, she would alert the entire palace complex, and God knew who would show up five minutes later.

Nick was still shivering and bleeding from his leg. They spotted a pair of figures moving in the shadows ahead of them, two men coming through the southern gate. Kate steered Nick toward the nearest building.

"You got your lock picks?" she asked him. "Think you can open a door?"

Nick nodded. "In my sleep."

They went around to the back of the building and found the rear door. Nick shook his hands, blew on them, pulled his lock pick set out of his soggy pants, and got to work.

There were three entrances to the park. Two men came through each gate, with strict orders to kill anyone else on two feet. It had taken this pair an extra minute to get down to the southern entrance, but now they were on the zoo grounds, each carrying a Heckler & Koch USP Tactical Combat semiautomatic with a Brügger & Thomet suppressor.

The man named Moritz nudged his partner, Oskar, and pointed with his gun to the path that led over the bridge. Something hit their ears, a metallic scraping noise, from somewhere to their left. Oskar aimed his gun in the direction of the sound and was just about to fire when Moritz stopped him.

Oskar and Moritz moved carefully along the edge of the minifarm, toward the building on the other side of it. The metal gate protecting the front entrance was open. The sign above the entrance read *Insectarium*. Oskar went in first, turning on his flashlight as he stepped into the dark building. The light flashed off the glass surfaces all around them, reflecting back on both men.

Before Moritz could tell his partner to turn off the flashlight, he was covered with a blanket of *something* that had been dropped on him from above. The blanket turned into a hundred separate living things, crawling over his head, his face, his neck, into his ears, his nose, his eyes, his mouth. Beside him, Oskar was screaming and started shooting his gun indiscriminately. *FWOOMP FWOOMP FWOOMP*. Moritz was too busy with all of the insects covering him to do anything about it, until he heard two sets of feet dropping to the floor from somewhere above them.

He tried to aim his weapon, but he had to close his eyes as the horde of roaches continued to crawl over his face. When he cleared his vision, he saw that Oskar's weapon was now in the hands of a woman, and that the barrel was pointed directly at his chest.

Moritz had a decision to make now, whether to drop his weapon or fire. When a large roach crawled down his shirt, he forgot all about his decision for a moment, just long enough for his gun to be kicked out of his hand. He started tearing off his clothes and got as far as his windbreaker. A closet door was opened and Moritz was pushed inside, landing on top of Oskar.

On the other side of the door, Nick wedged a chair against the knob to keep it shut, at least for a while. When he was done, Kate handed him one of the official black windbreakers.

"Congratulations," she said. "You've just been promoted to Zoo Security."

———

The two men who entered through the northern gate had just reached the center of the zoo when they heard a muffled scream coming from somewhere to the south. They were armed with the same HK USP Tactical semiautomatics and the same suppressors. Neither of these two men was as trigger happy as Oskar, but they held their weapons in a ready-to-fire position as they ran down the pathway.

They slowed down as they came to the trees, recognizing the danger of being out in the open. That was when they saw the movement of two figures stepping into the faint glow of one of the light posts. Black windbreakers. It was Oskar and Moritz. The two men put down their weapons.

But then Oskar and Moritz were suddenly firing on them, *FWOOMP FWOOMP FWOOMP FWOOMP*, and the last thought running through the mind of each man was that maybe this wasn't Oskar and Moritz after all.

Both bodies slumped to the ground.

"Is there anything sexier than a woman with a semiautomatic and roaches in her hair?" Nick asked, stepping close to Kate. He picked a roach off her ponytail, threw it over his shoulder, and kissed her.

"You're a hopeless romantic," Kate said. "You know that, don't you?"

Nick smiled. "I can't help it. It's in the Fox genes."

"We can deal with your genes later," Kate said. "Let's go find our fathers and get out of here."

The two men who'd come in through the eastern gate, and who were now standing in front of the polar bear exhibit, had heard the same muffled scream. They moved quickly along the rail until they were interrupted by a voice. *"Guten Abend!"*

The two men looked all around them, spotted Quentin standing on the upper platform over the exhibit, and started firing. *FWOOMP FWOOMP FWOOMP FWOOMP.* Quentin dove for cover as the bullets chipped away at the concrete platform and bounced off the railing with a loud *ding*. Below Quentin, the mother bear and her cub were becoming agitated by the commotion.

Jake slipped out of the stairway door and was on top of the men before either could react. Jake's first move was to redirect the first man's gun toward the second. He got off two shots. The second man was already dead on the ground when the first man threw an elbow at Jake's face. It glanced off the side of his cheek, stunning him.

They both struggled for the gun. Quentin was about to join the fight when a shot was fired and barely sailed over his head. Quentin went looking on the ground for the second man's gun, but by the time he found it, Jake had already disarmed the first man, bashing his wrist on the top of the rail and sending the gun into the water below. Jake caught a glimpse of the red star tattooed on the man's neck, just before the man wound up to take a big swing at him. Jake slipped under it, grabbed the man by the belt, and performed a perfect *tsurikomi goshi* judo throw. The man sailed over the rail, into the water, where the mother bear was watching and waiting. After everything she had seen in this very unusual night, at least she'd finally get an unscheduled meal out of it.

"Let's get out of here," Jake said. They ran into Kate and Nick just before they reached the southern exit. Outside the gate, they found an old beat-up Honda parked in the shadows. A seasoned car thief can break into a late 1990s Honda and have it running in three minutes. It took a cold, wet, and bleeding Nick Fox less than two. When Jake was behind the wheel, Nick sat in the back with Kate and kept pressure on his leg. Quentin sat in the front passenger seat, shivering uncontrollably.

"We can't try to run tonight," Nick said. "But we have to get off the streets."

Earlier that day, they had given Professor Lewis a clean phone. Quentin called it and told Lewis to gather everything from their rooms and to head down to the ground floor using the back stairs.

"Start walking south from the hotel," Quentin said. "Stay off the main streets. We'll call you in about thirty minutes."

They found a tiny motel on Gumpendorfer Strasse. With Nick still soaking wet and bleeding, Jake went inside to the front desk. He didn't know enough German, French, Italian, or the local Romansch dialect to communicate at first, but after a little bit of sign language, he had the keys to the last two rooms. Jake gave the keys to Kate, then went back out to the car to call Professor Lewis.

He picked Lewis up a few minutes later on a dark corner near the Erholungsgebiet Wienerberg park. The professor threw the bags into the backseat, relieved not to be lugging them around anymore.

"May I inquire if the mission was a success?" Lewis asked.

"We got the next link, if that's what you mean."

Before they went back to the motel, Jake pulled up in front of a late-night drugstore. He went inside to pick up rolls of cotton batting, gauze, tape, and antibiotic ointment. He put all of those items in the bottom of his basket, then covered them with bags of snacks and bottles of water.

When Jake was back in the car, he checked behind him for the next few blocks and spotted a *Bundespolizei* vehicle on his tail. The distinctive white VW with the blue hood and the red stripes, hard to miss.

"Hold on," he said to Professor Lewis as he careened into a sudden right turn. He made another hard right, then a left, ran through a traffic light. His tail was gone.

When Jake got to the motel, he parked a block down the street and helped the professor with the bags. The two motel rooms had been turned into a small hospital ward. In the first room, Quentin had stripped off all of his wet clothes, and sat huddled near the old radiator, wrapped up in a blanket.

Jake went into the other room, where Nick was in the bathroom, with Kate waiting outside the door. The professor had taken the next map link out of the metal tube, had it spread out on the little desk in the corner, and was studying it intently while tapping away on his laptop. Jake knocked on the bathroom door and gave Nick the first aid supplies.

Nick came out a few minutes later, wearing a bathrobe and several layers of gauze and tape wrapped around his leg. Then Quentin arrived to join the party, still wrapped in his blanket.

"I feel a thousand years old," Quentin said to Jake. "How's the leg?" he asked Nick.

"I'm going to have a great scar," Nick said. "And a great story to go with it."

"We got lucky tonight," Kate said. "We all know that, right?"

Everyone else nodded in silence.

"They keep finding us," Kate said. "We've got to figure this out."

"What about Jessup?" Nick said. "Does he have anything yet?"

"I'll call him again," Kate said, "but Interpol is a huge organization. It only takes one person in the right place to keep tabs on us."

"So how do we plan on surviving this next mission?" Quentin asked. "Like Kate said, we can't get away from these guys. God knows what we'll walk into next time."

"Actually," Lewis said, turning away from his laptop, "I don't think that's going to be a problem."

"What do you mean?" Quentin asked.

"This next piece of the map," Lewis said. "It's in a place where nobody's stepped foot in years."

CHAPTER FOURTEEN

Professor Lewis had carefully unrolled the map, still curled from seventy-five years spent in a metal tube tucked behind a rock in a polar bear exhibit. Now he read aloud the banner that ran along the right side. "*Der Fels ist stabil, während sich die Welt dreht.*"

"What does that mean?" Quentin asked.

"It means, 'The rock is steady while the world turns,'" Lewis said. "It was the official dedication given to this monastery in the Alps." He turned his laptop around and showed them a picture of a snowcapped mountain.

Nick bent down to look more closely at the screen. "This is the rock?"

"It's a mountain called Furggen in the Swiss Alps, on the border with Italy, halfway between the Matterhorn and Testa Grigia. Elevation well over ten thousand feet."

"I don't see a monastery," Nick said.

The professor switched to another image, an old black-and-white photograph of a crude wooden building. "This is the Furggen Monastery, built around the turn of the century. The only access was a set of cable cars, one running from the town of Breuil-Cervinia to a midway station named Plan Maison, then another car from Plan Maison to the top of Furggen."

"So if we take the cable cars up to Furggen," Nick said, "how many Swiss police officers will be waiting for us? Or the Brotherhood's men? Or maybe this time it will be both."

"The monastery was abandoned shortly after the war," Lewis said. "A few years after that, an ice storm brought down the cable lines. So the *good* news is, for once there won't be anybody else waiting for you when you get up there."

"I have a feeling there's going to be some bad news now," Nick said.

Professor Lewis brought up another image, a more recent photo of the abandoned building. In several spots, the roof had caved in from the weight of the ice and snow. He kept scrolling through more photos, wider aerial shots of the upper sections of the mountain. The towers where the cables once ran were now empty. There was nothing else surrounding the monastery but sheer walls of rock and ice.

"The bad news is," Lewis said, "there's no way to get up there."

Early the next morning, they all gathered outside the motel. There was a cold edge to the predawn air. All five members of the team packed into the stolen Honda, a tight fit with Professor

Lewis wedged into the back with Nick and Kate. The drive would be ten hours, across Austria, through the tiny nation of Liechtenstein, into Switzerland, then finally through a pass in the Alps to the Italian border. Even though the monastery itself was on Swiss soil, or rather on Swiss rock, the cable car leading halfway up Furggen was based in the town of Breuil-Cervinia in the Aosta Valley, the very northwest corner of Italy.

When they were safely out of Vienna, and with the sun coming up behind them from the east, the team stopped in the Austrian city of St. Pölten. They abandoned the stolen car in the center of town, leaving a couple hundred euros in the glove compartment, and Nick used one of his fake passports and many more euros to rent a much larger and more comfortable Peugeot 5008. Then they settled in for eight more hours of driving.

"I don't understand why this next link is in such a remote place," Kate said when they stopped for a quick lunch. "Everywhere else has been such a major landmark."

"You raise an interesting point," Lewis said, a man who clearly *lived* for discussing interesting points. "Of course, these links were hidden seventy-five years ago, so perhaps you're looking at this through a different cultural filter."

Kate just looked at him.

"It may have seemed like more of a major landmark back then," he continued.

"A monastery hidden away on the top of a mountain?"

"Or, I have another theory," Lewis said. "You realize that every place we've been so far has been in the former Axis-occupied nations of Europe."

"Well, we started in the Vatican."

"Which is in the middle of Rome," Lewis said. "But let's not split hairs."

"Fair enough," Kate said. "Go on."

"Whoever hid these clues couldn't have done so in the middle of Switzerland, because that country was of course neutral. Although let's be clear about that. Hitler absolutely despised Switzerland, and if the plans for Operation Tannenbaum had ever been executed, Germany and Italy would have invaded and they would have broken Switzerland into two pieces. It's actually a fascinating story, how Hitler and Mussolini met in secret to draw up—"

"Professor," Kate said, "your theory?"

"Of course," he said. "My theory is that there may have been an extra-special reason to pick such a remote place for this link, in a country where technically the person hiding it was not even officially allowed to go. What I'm trying to say is that, in all the years I've been doing academic research, I've learned to trust this little voice in my head. In fact, my entire doctoral thesis was based on an idea I had when I was in the shower and it occurred to me that—"

"And that little voice is saying something to you now?"

"Yes. That voice is telling me that this may be the last link in the chain."

Everyone absorbed this. Quentin nodded and pursed his lips in a grim smile. "That's good to hear, Professor Lewis."

"But that same voice is also telling me that this link was meant to be the hardest of all. If you think about it, it's on the top of a mountain, with a group of monks who back then were probably not all that accommodating to strangers."

"Unlike the polar bears," Quentin said. "They were quite welcoming."

"Hey, they invited us in for dinner, didn't they?" Nick broke in. "We just happened to be on the menu."

The professor pressed on. "I don't know what could be more dangerous than polar bears. But I'm afraid that, if you insist on going up there, you might find out."

———

Six hours and three countries later, they reached the town of Breuil-Cervinia. It had originally been known by the French name of Breuil, then was renamed Cervinia in 1939 when the Fascists were "Italianizing" all of the town names in the Aosta Valley. Now it went by both names joined together, the ultimate alpine ski resort town, a place that would have taken Kate's breath away if she wasn't there on such dead-serious business.

The town would have been bustling during the winter, but was still half full in the late summer with the more dedicated year-round skiers hitting the nearby Plateau Rosa Glacier. The sun was just starting to touch the mountaintops as they got out of the car and stretched their legs, looking up at the vast peaks of the Matterhorn and Testa Grigia, and between them, like a forgotten middle child, Furggen.

"I don't see any extra police here," Nick said, looking all around him at the shops and lodging places. "Doesn't mean we're still not being watched."

"Let's take the gondola," Kate said. "See what it looks like up there."

The gondola from Breuil-Cervinia led up to the Plan Maison station, where it connected to other cars leading farther into the mountains, one to Theodul Pass, another to the Plateau Rosa Glacier and Testa Grigia. Most of the traffic at this time of day was summer skiers on their way down. Going up, the team had a car to themselves. It was a slow, eight-minute ride, a rough trip with the car bouncing up and down on the cable. Kate went over to stand with her father as he looked out at the rocks and snow passing beneath them.

"I parachuted into a monastery once," Kate said to her father. "Remember?"

"Of course. I arranged the drop for you."

It had been on the Greek island of Athos, when Nick Fox had "escaped" from custody and Kate had traveled halfway around the world to find him. That was the night she learned that Nick hadn't escaped at all, but rather had been recruited to work for the FBI. Finding him had been her test. To this day she couldn't decide if acing that test had been the best move of her life, or the worst.

"A lot has happened since then," Jake said, seeming to read her mind. "Look at the two of you now."

"Yeah, I'm still trying to stay on top of him. Not the easiest job in the world."

"Nope," he said, glancing at the scenery outside the window. "Nick's a lucky man to have you."

"I was asking about parachuting into that other monastery for a reason," Kate said.

"Forget it, Kate. That was an island. Large target area, plenty of open ground. This is a mountain with nothing on top but an abandoned building half-buried in ice. Not to mention the wind up there. A jump would be suicide. So would trying to land a helicopter."

"As opposed to what, Dad? Free-climbing the Matterhorn?"

"The Matterhorn's over there," Jake said, nodding toward the west. "But I get your point. It may be suicide either way."

"We're here," Kate said as the gondola started to grind to a halt. "Let's go see."

———

They all walked through the Plan Maison station and grabbed a quick bite to eat at the restaurant. There was also a small hotel attached to the station, accessible only by the gondola. Quentin found a north-facing window and stood there staring at the forlorn, empty towers that had once held the car leading up to Furggen. The towers looked like long-lost artifacts from another age.

Jake came to stand next to him, then Kate and Nick, and finally Professor Lewis.

"It's another thousand feet of elevation to reach the monastery," Nick said. "This isn't ladder ropes and grappling hooks anymore. This is the real thing."

"We're going to need equipment," Kate said.

"This is my favorite part of every adventure," Nick said. "Let's go shopping."

They reserved three rooms at the hotel connected to the station, figuring it would give them a head start the next morning, then took the gondola back down to Breuil-Cervinia and poked through the shops until they found one that carried serious climbing gear. The shop owner was about to close for the day, but Nick flashed an American Express black card and the man was suddenly a lot more agreeable to delaying his dinner.

The team outfitted themselves with full winter outfits, spiked mountaineering boots, harnesses, helmets, carabiners, pitons, ice screws, ice axes, and *lots* of climbing rope. Jake stood staring at a large topographical map mounted to the wall, showing the local mountain range in fine detail.

Nick came to stand next to him. "What do you see?" he asked Jake.

"I see two ways to go," Jake said, glancing over at the shop owner to make sure he was occupied with something else. "From Plan Maison, it's a straight shot up the old gondola line. We can use the old towers as waypoints."

"This way," Nick said, tracing the line up the map, from the hotel to Furggen.

"Exactly," Jake said. "The alternate is to come at it from the Swiss side. Start in Zermatt, then climb up to the ridge. Once you're up there, it's a traverse across the ridge to Furggen."

"Advantages?"

"It's an easier climb from Zermatt," Jake said, "especially once you're on the ridge, but it would take a lot longer, unless you take a snowcat. Problem is, a snowcat could be suicide on the narrow ridge. Going up on the Italian side is much steeper, but also much shorter."

Nick nodded his head, studying the map. "We're already on this side of the mountain and I just spent a small fortune on climbing gear. I say we stick to the plan. How bad could it be?"

Jake didn't have to think about it for long. "You have to ask?"

———

It was dark when they took their last ride of a very long day, back up to Plan Maison station. They met one more time in Professor Lewis's room, where he showed them the map link and the "locator" rune next to the banner.

"I know we got our wires crossed on the last one," he said. "I overthought it and sent you looking for a 'gift' when it was really just the X symbol itself. I'm sorry about that."

"No apologies," Nick said. "We couldn't have come this far without you."

"I think my grandfather is looking down on me right now and smiling," Lewis said. "He's the reason I became a Germanic literature scholar in the first place."

"Was he a professor, too?" Nick asked.

"No, he played the piano. But he was born in Germany, and moved to London with my grandmother just before the war. He helped translate messages at Bletchley Park, after the Enigma code was broken. When my grandfather died, my father gave me all of his old favorite books that he had brought over from Germany, as many as he could fit in one suitcase. Wieland, Schiller, Goethe. That's how it started for me, learning the language so I could understand why my grandfather loved those books so much, even though he hated the people who had taken over his home country."

"That's a great story," Nick said.

"It's been an honor to be a part of this," Lewis said. "And the adventure of a lifetime. But promise me you won't let me over-think things next time."

"We'll try to remember that," Nick said, "but for now, where's this next link?"

Lewis pointed to the rune on the map, which looked like a modern "less than" sign. "This rune is called *Kenaz*. You see what it looks like, but it also represents a torch, meaning either 'fire' or 'light.'"

"So maybe a fireplace?" Nick asked.

"Good place to start," Lewis said. "In an old monastery on the top of an alpine mountain, with no electricity, I'm sure there are many fireplaces."

"It'll be a piece of *torta*," Nick said.

In the gray predawn hour, four figures left the hotel grounds, heading north. An observer would have been curious to see them outfitted with climbing gear and heading in that direction. There were a handful of climbers who would take the gondolas up to the glacier, but rarely would they start here, at Plan Maison. Because where would they possibly go?

The ground here at 7,500 feet was soft snow with patches of semi-thawed ground peeking through. It was uneven and unpre-dictable, with one step that could be solid followed by another that could break an ankle by dropping a climber right through the snow. By the time they ascended another 3,000 feet, it would be nothing but solid ice, treacherous in a very different way.

"What's our risk of avalanche?" Quentin asked.

"Always a risk," Jake said. "You get powder avalanches in the winter, 'wet' avalanches in the summer when the snow itself is heavier."

Quentin looked back at Nick and Kate, trailing behind them.

"You have an amazing daughter," Quentin said. "But you already know that."

Jake nodded. "I do."

"Nick's mother has been gone for a while now, but I can't help wondering what she'd think of all this."

"Kate lost her mother, too. But I don't have to wonder what she'd think."

Quentin smiled. "Olivia would have loved seeing Nick with someone like Kate, that much I can tell you."

"I don't know how much they're 'with' each other. I don't know if they even know themselves."

They reached the first empty tower, about two hundred yards north of the station. The slope wasn't very steep yet. They kept walking to the next tower. The slope increased.

"Wait here," Jake said. "I'll set a line at the next tower."

He climbed the next two hundred yards, using the crampons on his boots for traction and occasionally breaking out his ice ax for a little more help. When he reached the tower, he tied a line, then led it back to the rest of the group.

"You can't do this all the way up," Kate said when they reached the tower. "You'll wear yourself out. Let me take the next one."

"I have the most experience with this," Jake said.

"I wasn't asking," Kate said. "I'm up."

Jake shrugged, knowing he wouldn't win the argument. He untied the line and gave it to Kate. She set off for the next tower. The sun was coming up now, even as the air was getting colder. The slope of the terrain had not begun to punish them. Kate started to wonder if the whole climb would be this easy, took a step into some deep snow and painfully "post-holed" herself, her leg going all the way through. She climbed out, shook that off, kept going, and hit an ice patch a few yards farther, losing her footing and nearly hitting her face on the ice. Okay, she thought, not so easy.

She reached the next tower and tied the line, led it back, and almost wrecked herself a couple more times on the way.

"My turn," Nick said when she rejoined the group. "You guys are hogging all the fun."

"Fine with me," Kate said, handing him the rope.

Nick headed off for the next section, digging into the ice with his spikes, swinging his ice ax and then using the leverage to lift himself up a sheer wall at least eight feet high, then scrambling up another incline until he reached the next tower. An old cable car had fallen and buried itself into the ice and frozen mud here. Nick was reasonably sure there were no skeletons trapped inside, yet he still didn't want to look through the hazy windows.

He led the line back and told the rest of the group about the eight-foot wall and the fallen car just beyond it. The climb was already getting interesting and they'd only been on the mountain for a little over an hour.

Jake wouldn't let Quentin take the next section. He was already looking ahead to the next tower and how high it had been set into the rocks above them. The real climbing was about to begin.

Jake worked his way up the steep incline, finding footholds and handholds in the rocks and ice, pounding in pitons every few yards, running the line through his harness so that if he fell, it would only be a miserable body slam and not an outright fatality. When he found the next tower, he saw that it had been damaged by an avalanche sometime over the years and was now tilting a good thirty degrees downslope. It was a good reminder that an avalanche could still happen at any moment.

Jake fed down the line. He didn't even have to walk it back, the terrain was so steep. The group made their way up, and then Kate took the next section. They all took a break after that, looking back down the mountain at the hotel far below them.

"Everybody still up for this?" Jake asked. "It's only going to get harder."

"Let's go," Kate said.

———————

Two hours later, the mountain had spiraled them away to the east, away from their sight line down to the hotel. The empty towers were their only guideposts now. There were no more bare spots on the ground. Everything was either snow, ice, or some combination of the two, with the temperature just barely warm enough to occasionally thaw patches in the direct sunlight, which would freeze at night, thaw again, then refreeze. Jake knew that this could be even more dangerous than in the dead of winter, when everything was ice and you never had to assume anything different.

He was working his way up an almost sheer wall, at least twenty feet high, chopping into the ice and setting pitons every few feet. There was an overhang of snow above him. Jake kept his eye on it, wondering how he'd work his way over it, at the same time hoping today wasn't the day it would all come down at once.

He glanced back at the others, all huddled together a hundred yards behind him at the last tower. Then he looked back up and suddenly the whole world was rushing at him. He heard somebody shout from below before everything turned into pure, white impact.

Jake grabbed the ice ax, already planted into the wall, held on to it with both hands, and tucked his head in as much as possible as the snow and debris pounded his helmet and his shoulders and the back of his neck. It thundered in his ears, filling his jacket with snow and dirt and ice as he held on. He wondered if these would be his last moments on earth, and wondered at the same time if his daughter and Nick and Quentin would be able to use the few extra seconds they had to climb up the tower. Or if that would even matter at all.

Maybe this was it, *right now*, for all of them, and someone would find their bodies a month from now. Or a year from now. Or maybe never if they were buried deep enough.

The weight kept pounding down on him, feeling like the entire mountain was pouring itself onto his head. He felt his fingers start to slip from the ax. He couldn't hold on much longer. The debris was in his mouth now, his ears, his eyes, his nose. It would suffocate him before it crushed him.

The roar somehow stopped. He was hanging by one hand, his face pressed against the ice. He spit everything out, shook his head, and turned to look down at the path of the debris. Most of it had settled down by the tower. More important, Kate, Nick, and Quentin were above it, holding on to the tower's legs.

"Are you okay?" his daughter called up to him.

He spit out more dirt and called back, "Never better!"

When he caught his breath, he continued his climb up the wall. The top was cleared of snow now and easier to crest than before it had tried to kill him. He saw the next tower ahead, another fifty yards away, with one more wall of ice to climb until he could reach his goal. For the first time on this whole trip, after everything they had been through, Jake asked himself if he was simply too old for this.

He answered his own question, *hell no*, and kept climbing.

———

Kate's hands were getting sore and blistered, even with the climbing gloves. She leaned her weight all the way back as she held on tight to the rope, using her feet to grip the ice and her legs to do most of the work. It was counterintuitive to keep herself so far from the wall instead of hugging it, but this was what her father had taught her. This is how you climb.

She took another step, feeling the ice break through, feeling the weight of her body thrown sideways. She grabbed behind her for the rope in the harness to make sure she didn't fall, and held her breath as her body slammed against the ice. It was the tenth time this had happened, or maybe the hundredth. Time had stopped. There was nothing but ice and rope and a slow but endless upward movement.

"We're almost there," Nick said, just behind her. "We've got this."

She looked down at him. Blood was running down the side of his face, from a cut on his eyebrow. He must have caught the ice the wrong way on one of his own body slams. Now he looked like a boxer who needed to be sent to a neutral corner to be checked by the doctor.

Kate regained her footing against the ice, leaned her body back again, took a step, and then another. She saw her father looking down at her from the top of this wall. That meant the tower was close. It would be another chance to rest.

When she was close enough to the top, her father reached down one hand to help her up. She brushed herself off as she stood up. Nick came up next, already pressing his glove against the cut on his eyebrow as Jake took out his first aid kit. Quentin came up last, breathing harder than all of them.

The air was so cold up here, the wind bracing their faces, and it was so *high*. They were approaching two miles above sea level. No wonder they were moving so slowly. Their lungs were starving for oxygen.

"Time for the tanks," Jake said. They had each packed a one-liter canister of 95 percent pure oxygen, and now they all took this moment to put them to their mouths and inhale.

"How much farther?" Kate asked between long breaths.

Her father nodded his head in the direction behind her. She turned and looked up. There was one more tower above them, then above that, the abandoned Furggen Monastery.

"The last leg is always the hardest," Jake reminded them. "You're tired, you're sloppy. The thin air is making you loopy. Just stay focused for a few more minutes."

They stopped to rest one more time when they reached the last tower. A bulge in the mountain was hiding the monastery from them, but they knew it was there, waiting in frozen silence. God knew how long it had been since anyone else had been up here.

Jake set the course for the last section, including one last wall of ice that seemed to tilt back past vertical. He waited at the crest, helped each of the rest of them climb over those last scary few feet when it felt like one slip would mean a fall into an endless void. As Kate stood up, she looked at her father. He had done most of the hard work on this climb and now his face was drained of color.

"You need to take the rest of my air," Kate said to him.

"I'm okay," he said. "Almost there." He turned to look up at the monastery, in plain view now that they had cleared this last wall.

Kate looked in the same direction, transfixed by the sight of the empty building. It was covered by a thick sheet of ice, even thicker than the photographs had suggested, and in some spots the roof had given way beneath the weight.

Nick came to stand next to her, then Quentin. Finally, Jake. The cold air whipped past them. They all stared at the half-ruined monastery, framed against the western sky by the sharp peak of the Matterhorn.

"Welcome to Switzerland," Jake said. "I think we crossed the border a few minutes ago."

"Looks like a good place to film a horror movie," Nick said.

"At least it's empty," Quentin said. "We had to climb a mountain to do it, but we won't have company this time." He was still breathing hard. The mountain had been tougher on him than anyone else. He took out his oxygen canister and put it to his mouth.

"Let's go find this thing," Kate said.

"I'm going to stay here with Quentin for a minute," Jake said. "You guys go ahead."

Nick and Kate left them there and walked up the last hundred feet to the monastery. The only sounds were the whistling of the wind and the crunch of their boots on the hard crust of snow and ice.

"Something associated with fire," Nick said. "Or with light. That's what we're looking for, right?"

Kate didn't respond. She was looking up at the ice on the roof as they approached the doorway. It was at least two feet thick, and it looked ready to either slide down and crush them or else bring down the roof and collapse the old wooden walls. Nick kicked away some of the loose snow in front of the door and tried to open it, but it wouldn't budge.

"Be careful," she said.

Nick gathered himself and then rammed his shoulder into the door. Kate closed her eyes and held her breath as it crashed open, but the ice stayed on the roof.

She followed Nick inside the building, into what appeared to have been the kitchen. After all of the brilliant white snow that had surrounded them outside, it was dark here and Kate's eyes took a moment to adjust. As they did, she saw two windows, one on either side of the room, but they were fogged with age and half-covered with ice.

"Not exactly the Ritz-Carlton," Nick said, taking out his flashlight.

A high wooden work table stood in the center of the room. Along one wall was an ancient metal sink with no faucet. Next to that was a larder that had once kept food, now holding only dust and an old flour bag, then cupboards and a few drawers containing tarnished silverware. Along another wall was an ancient woodstove.

"Fire," Nick said. "We may have something here."

He shined his light on the cast iron surface of the stove, then bent down close to examine it. Kate stepped through into the next room and saw that half of the roof had caved in here. She took a few cautious steps, feeling the cold air creeping in from above her. This room was larger than the kitchen, with a great table and at least twenty chairs. It was hard to say for sure because the table itself had been destroyed by the great slab of ice and most of the chairs had been reduced to kindling.

There was a stone fireplace in the corner of the room. The hole in the roof gave her enough light to see by, but she took out her flashlight anyway so she could closely scan every inch of every stone. The cold air kept creeping in and it seemed to wrap itself around her neck. She had this strange, impossible feeling that someone was watching her.

"Kate, come see this!"

When she went into the kitchen, she saw that Nick had pulled open a large trapdoor in the wooden floor.

"This place must be built on a ledge," Nick said, shining his flashlight down a rough wooden stairway. "It's two stories high on the back."

"What do you think they kept down there?" she asked.

"Just a few boxes, far as I can see," Nick said. "They might have kept their food down here. Maybe wine, you know, for communion or big parties on the weekend."

The cold air from the other room had seemed to follow Kate, was still wrapping itself around her neck.

"Are you getting a strange feeling?" she asked quietly.

Nick had already taken his first tentative step down the rickety stairway. "So it's not just me?"

"No. It's not just you."

———

Quentin was sitting on a mound of hard ice, drawing in one breath after another from his oxygen canister. Jake stood next to him, one hand on one knee, the other hand holding his own canister against his mouth. With the kids gone, he didn't have to pretend not to be feeling this through every inch of his body.

"I've been on mountains before," Quentin said when he was done with his oxygen. "I don't remember it being this hard."

"When was the last time you were two miles up?"

"Two miles of elevation? Damn, probably twenty years ago?"

"There's your problem," Jake said. "They took out most of the oxygen since then."

Both men started laughing. Quentin reached up a hand. Jake took it and helped him up. After brushing themselves off, they headed toward the building.

Nick and Kate had split off to the right side of the building's exterior, so Jake and Quentin went left. They found another door, pushed it open, and turned on their flashlights. It was a large room with bunk beds lined up in two rows, as in an army barracks, but now most of the beds had fallen apart.

"I'm having flashbacks to Recruit Training," Jake said, kicking a board out of his way. "Although I'd take Parris Island over this place right now."

Another great stone fireplace was centered on one wall. Both men stepped closer to run their hands over the stones.

"Probably a fireplace in every room," Jake said.

Quentin nodded, then both men looked up as they heard the distinctive sounds of wood cracking.

"Lot of weight up there," Quentin said, eyeing the ceiling.

"I'm surprised the stone fireplaces aren't the only things left standing."

"It's been abandoned for what, seventy years? I'm sure it'll hold for one more day."

Quentin left Jake at the fireplace and walked through the rest of the sleeping quarters to the next room. Here the roof had partially collapsed along one wall, but without giving way completely to the outside elements. He had to duck as he stepped around the bowed-in ceiling.

The room was filled with two dozen old pews, many of them toppled over. An elaborately carved wooden lectern stood at the opposite end, the focal point of everyone who had once sat in the pews. Quentin approached the lectern and ran his gloved fingers over the carvings. There was a cross in the center, no surprise in a monastery, and yet it wasn't elongated like most Christian crosses. It was squared off, more like a plus sign, and it was fixed inside a circle. A vague sense of unease had been growing in Quentin ever since he had entered this structure. Now that feeling was even more pervasive than the cold air.

"What was this place?" he asked out loud.

Quentin spotted a door leading to another room. He went to the door, pushed it open, and looked inside.

———

Kate watched Nick negotiate the wooden stairs to the room below, then turned on her own flashlight and followed him. The stairs creaked and groaned as she took each step, until suddenly she felt herself plunge through. Nick barely caught her, wrapping his hands around her torso and holding her there, suspended over an eight-foot drop. As they caught their breath, they were both aware of how close together their faces were.

"Another romantic moment," Nick said. "We do know how to find them."

They got down the rest of the stairs without incident, coming to rest on a rough stone floor. With no windows on this floor, their flashlight beams barely pierced the darkness.

"There's the ledge this thing is built on," Nick said, playing his flashlight across the exposed rock that formed one wall of the room. Somehow it made this lower level feel even colder, like the mountain itself was draining any last heat from the air.

"It's like a charming split-level ranch," Nick said. "With a great view. I'm thinking of putting in an offer."

Nick's flashlight settled on an old wooden crate with barely visible German words written across it. He went over to the crate and pushed it a few inches. It was empty. Kate found a similar crate, then another. Each was empty, and another two were smashed open.

"Time out," Nick said as he kicked another crate. This one didn't feel hollow. He dragged the crate across the rough stones, then shined his light along the top edges. He took out his knife and tried to work it around the edges.

"You got a better knife on you?"

"You're not using my Ontario knife as a crowbar," she said. "I'll go find something in the kitchen."

She went back to the stairs and climbed out of the trapdoor. When she opened the old cupboards and drawers, the best tool she could find was an old paring knife with a wooden handle. As she was sliding the drawer shut, she stopped dead. I'm being watched, she thought. She whirled around to see nothing but an empty ancient kitchen.

Almost as if to prove something to herself, she went to one window and rubbed it with her sleeve until she could look out. She saw only the ice and snow on the front side of the building, with her own footprints mixed in with those of her father, Nick, and Quentin. She went to the back window, rubbed it with her sleeve as she had done with the first, then peered through the window.

It took her a full five seconds to process what she was seeing.

"Oh my God."

———

Jake caught up to Quentin and stood next to him in the doorway.

"What are we looking at here?" Jake asked.

"I'm going to say it was once a library," Quentin said. He took a step into the room, immediately putting both boots on old paper. The shelves that lined every wall had once held thousands of books, but now every single one of them had been thrown to the floor, and most of them were torn into pieces. He picked up one page to read it. The words were German.

In the corner was yet another stone fireplace. Jake moved closer and shined his flashlight on the stones. Quentin went to the small writing desk that had been built into one of the bookshelves. The chair had been smashed into pieces. Quentin opened a drawer and found letters that were now little more than faded ink on brittle paper. At the top of one sheet of paper was a letterhead with the same symbol he had seen on the lectern in the other room, a square cross over a circle.

"What kind of monastery was this?" he asked.

"Maybe it wasn't," Jake said. "Just because they called it a monastery doesn't mean they were up here saying their Vespers. Who knows what they were doing?"

"I'm getting a bad feeling about this place," Quentin said.

"You and me both, brother."

"How about we find the next link so we can get the hell out of here?"

Quentin came over to the fireplace, nearly falling when the remains of a book he stepped on slid from under him. He caught himself, kicking at the papers under his feet.

"What is this?" He got down on one knee and moved more of the paper aside with his hand. There was a pattern built into the wooden floor, like spokes emanating from the hub of a wheel.

Jake came over and helped him clear more of the floor. There were twelve spokes in all, and each took a sharp jag to the right before it reached the outer circle.

"You ever seen something like this before?"

"Yes," Quentin said. "I have. It's called the *Black Sun*. I saw one like this at a gallery in Wewelsburg. They held an auction for some old SS artifacts there. Which I decided I couldn't be a part of, no matter how much I was being paid."

"SS as in Heinrich Himmler's old gang?"

"One and the same. So what is this doing *here*?"

The two men looked at each other, sharing the same chill down their spines. They both stood up and were about to leave the room when Quentin put a hand on Jake's arm. "Wait a minute," he said. "Fire. Light."

"What about it?"

"Name the one thing that's hot *and* bright. More than anything else."

"The sun," Jake said, looking at the design at his feet.

"The *Black Sun*," Quentin said.

They both got back on their knees, pushing the debris away. Jake trained his flashlight on the floor as Quentin used two fingers to brush away the last shreds of paper from the very axis point of the black sun design. Both men bent down even farther to peer at the symbol that was uncovered. A tiny swastika.

The symbol was centered in a circle of wood embedded in the floor, about two feet in diameter. Jake started to feel around for the edge, and was about to take out his knife when Quentin stopped him.

"I've seen something like this before," Quentin said. "See how those spokes jag to the right?"

"Yes?"

"Watch," Quentin said, putting both hands on the disk and pushing clockwise. It took a moment and a little more muscle to get it moving, but then the disk broke free. Quentin pushed down on one side to get the other to rise, worked his fingers underneath, and lifted it from the floor. There was a round chamber underneath, just a few inches in depth. Plenty deep enough to hold a single piece of paper, facing up.

It was the last link in the map.

———

It took Kate a full five seconds to process what she was seeing out the back window. Vehicles. Large, green, boxy vehicles with treads instead of wheels. *Snowcats.*

She was looking down on top of them, here on the back side of the building where the window was higher. The vehicles looked vintage. They must be old, she told herself, must have been abandoned here for decades.

Her mind *demanded* this, because nothing else would make sense. But no, they were in the open area behind the monastery, unsheltered, with no snow or ice covering them. Behind the vehicles, she spotted the fresh tracks leading away to the northwest.

She was sure she would have heard these snowcats arriving, but she hadn't. They were already here, she thought, waiting for us.

———

Quentin held the paper as Jake shined his flashlight on it. It was the same basic design as the others, with vague topographic lines marked with a dozen ancient runes. To the right of those, in a separate banner, was another string of words in German. *Der Zug fährt auf halber Strecke zum Bahnhof Štrbské Pleso.* The words meant nothing to Jake or Quentin. They'd have to take this back down to Professor Lewis.

"Lewis told us that this link was different from the others," Jake said.

"He did."

"Are you starting to get the feeling that this one's different because, how do I even say this? Because it brought us *here*?"

"This monastery feels like it must have belonged to the Brotherhood," Quentin said. "Is that what you're saying?"

"Yes," Jake said. "Which means that the map may have been created here, so that the different links would lead *back* here."

"'There's no place like home,'" Quentin said. "Although this sure as hell isn't Kansas."

A voice came from behind them. "No, we're a long way from Kansas, Toto."

Jake and Quentin both stood up. In the doorway was a man wearing a fur-lined parka. He had thin blond hair, almost white, with intense blue eyes behind rimless glasses. Beside him stood Franz, the giant they had thrown from the train. Franz had a patch over one of his eyes and bruises of every color all over his face, but he was very much alive, and he was currently holding a Heckler & Koch MP7 submachine gun, which looked like a toy in the man's giant hands.

"Did I get that right?" the man in the glasses asked, with a pronounced German accent. "I don't watch many American films."

"Who are you?" Quentin asked, even though he could take a good guess.

"My name is Klaus Egger," the man said. "You've already met my lieutenant, Franz."

"You're the leader of the Brotherhood," Quentin said.

"At your service," Egger said, as Franz leveled the barrel of the submachine at Quentin's chest. "Now, if you'll hand me that last link, and all of the others, please."

CHAPTER FIFTEEN

"How did you know we'd be here?" Quentin asked.

"I always knew the map would lead back here eventually," Egger said. "Back to my grandfather's mountain, where the Brotherhood began. Everything you said about the map being *born* here, it is true."

Quentin glanced at Jake. They were both thinking the same thing. Where are Nick and Kate? Are they safe?

"Your grandfather's mountain," Jake said. "Is that what you called it? I knew this place felt like pure evil."

Egger allowed a thin smile. "Of course, you've been programmed to think that way. 'The victor will always be the judge, and the vanquished the accused.'"

"Joseph Goebbels," Quentin said. "Let me guess, your grandfather worked for him?"

"Goebbels poisoned the Führer's mind and betrayed his nation. My grandfather answered only to Hermann Göring."

"My mistake," Quentin said. "Didn't mean to offend. How did you get up here, anyway? Did your father put in a hidden elevator?"

"He came up the Swiss side," Jake said.

Egger nodded. "A brave man can drive a snowcat from Zermatt," he said. "One slip of your treads and it's over. But it's considerably less taxing than traversing a mountain without one. Now, if you don't mind, the map."

Egger held out one hand, like a teacher impatiently waiting to collect homework. Quentin glanced at Jake, then at the submachine gun barrel leveled at his own chest. He took a few steps forward with the map section they'd just retrieved from the floor, handed it to Egger. He stayed directly in front of Egger, looking him in the eye.

"The rest of it," Egger said.

"I don't have it."

"You don't strike me as the kind of man who'd trust anyone else to keep it."

"Everybody else leaves this place," Quentin said. "Safely. Then I'll give it to you."

Egger frowned and nodded like he was actually thinking this over, then said, "Here's my counteroffer. Franz will shoot your friend in exactly five seconds."

Franz redirected the gun from Quentin to Jake.

Quentin's mind raced through the tactical possibilities. Egger may be armed, he thought, but he'd have to reach for his gun. Can I get to Franz before he shoots Jake?

In the end, he didn't see any scenario that didn't end up with Jake dead on the floor. He unzipped his jacket, lifted up his shirt, and took off the money belt wrapped around his waist. He didn't bother opening it. He just handed it to Egger.

Egger unzipped it, took out the other four pieces. His whole demeanor changed once he was holding the five map pieces together, as if they were the most precious objects in the world. Which they were. Put them together and they would lead the holder to $30 billion in gold.

"*Mein Gott*," he said, slowly shaking his head. "See, Franz, these are the other pieces that form the whole. Even if I *knew* the last piece would be here on the mountain, it would have meant nothing to me without the others."

As Egger flipped through the map pieces, Franz gave Quentin a shove, pushing him away from the door and back toward Jake.

"*Auf dem Turm, Deutschland Siegt Auf Allen Fronten*," Egger said, reading the banners on the map links one by one. "To the tower, of course. *Der verrückte König würdigt den Schwanenritter*. The castle. *Der Eisbär dient dem Erzherzog von Österreich und dem Heiligen Römischen Kaiser*. The polar bears. *Der Fels ist stabil, während sich die Welt dreht*. Which brings us here, of course. To this place where my grandfather once stood. The rock that doesn't turn. This map is his *life*, Franz. He helped create it, and then he disappeared forever. Nobody ever saw him again. I believe wherever the gold is, that's where my grandfather is, too.

I believe he's been personally watching over the wealth of the Reich for seventy-five years."

"The wealth *stolen* by the Reich," Jake said, unable to resist. "And if your grandfather is with the gold, he's just a pile of bones by now."

Egger gave him another thin smile, shook his head, then returned to the last section of the map. "*Der Zug fährt auf halber Strecke zum Bahnhof Štrbské Pleso.* The train stops halfway to where? Štrbské Pleso? That's a small town in Slovakia. I don't understand this."

He flipped through all five pieces of the map again, came back to the end, and stared at the last link. "I see how these have come together," he said, "but how do you use this map once you have all of the pieces? What do all of these other symbols mean?"

Quentin and Jake exchanged a quick look. They were thinking exactly the same thing. If all he needed was the map, we'd already be dead. We'll stay alive only as long as he thinks we can still help him.

Nick found another full crate not far from the first. On this one, the top was less tightly nailed down and he was able to pry it open. When he shined his light inside the crate, he saw nothing but old straw. He moved some aside to see what was underneath and heard the clank of metal on metal. He reached down and pulled out a pipe. No, a pipe with a wider section on one end.

No, Nick realized, it was not a pipe at all. It was a *Stielhandgranate.*

A vintage German hand grenade. What kind of monastery keeps a box of hand grenades next to their potatoes?

Nick placed the grenade back into the straw, very carefully, taking note of the pull cord, making sure that everything he did was the exact opposite of pulling or touching or even looking at that cord for too long. As soon as he had backed away from the crate, he heard two separate sets of footsteps coming down the stairs.

Kate was first, taking each step with her hands raised. "It's me," she said. "We have company."

Nick was frozen to the spot as he saw the man coming down behind her. The man's winter parka was covering his neck, but Nick would have bet anything on a red star tattoo. More important, he was holding some kind of submachine gun, with the barrel trained at the center of Kate's back.

"Take it easy," Nick said to him, raising his hands. "I'm not armed." Not unless you count old German hand grenades, he thought. And I don't think that would be a great option right now.

As Kate took another step, Nick realized what was about to happen. And what *could* happen if the next few seconds turned out the right way. He saw her intentionally keeping her flashlight above the line of the stairs, saw her pause just as she was about to reach the broken step.

"No need to do anything stupid," Nick said to the man, hoping to distract him just a little bit further from where his next step would be. "We'll do whatever you want."

Kate waited until the man was behind her. He gave her a little jab in the back with the barrel of his gun. Then as Kate took the long step to avoid the gaping hole, Nick held his breath for one half beat, until the man's foot reached for the next step and found nothing but air. The man tried to catch himself, but it was too late, especially with both hands on the gun. He hit his head on the way down and landed flat on his back on the stone floor.

Nick moved quickly to take the man's gun away. The man moaned, rolled over, and tried to get up. Kate gave the man a kick to put him back on the floor, then went up the stairs to grab some rope. She came back down, rolled the man onto his stomach, and tied his hands behind his back. He was getting his wind back and started talking to her in German.

Kate trained the submachine gun on him. The man stopped talking.

"Where's your father?" Nick asked her. "And my father?"

"We need to find them."

"Hold on," Nick said, eyeing the rough wooden ceiling. He led her toward the opposite end of the room.

As they passed the open crate, Kate looked in at the straw and asked, "What did you find inside here?"

"Just some old hand grenades."

"Some *what*?"

Nick put a finger to his lips, then pointed up to the ceiling. When they both stopped moving and went silent, they heard the thin sound of a voice somewhere above them. "*Der Zug fährt auf halber Strecke zum Bahnhof Štrbské Pleso.* The train stops halfway to where? Štrbské Pleso? That's a small town in Slovakia. I don't understand this."

Kate motioned for Nick to turn his light off.

The same voice went on. "I see how these come together, but how do you use this map once you have all of the pieces? What do all of these other symbols mean?"

Nick's and Kate's eyes adjusted to the darkness. A thin stream of light came through the floor.

"Let's move one of those crates over," Kate whispered. "Maybe we can see through the cracks."

They lifted an empty crate so that it wouldn't make noise against the stone floor and moved it into position. Kate stepped up onto the top of the crate and peered through a gap in the floorboards. She saw her father, then shifted to see Nick's father. They were standing together in the center of the room above her.

She heard Nick's father speak. "I just found the last link a minute ago. I haven't even had the chance to examine it yet."

"I will give you one minute to examine it," the first voice said. She still didn't know who this was, but the heavy German accent was unmistakable. "But do not touch them."

Kate shifted her position again to track the man as he crossed the room. She strained to catch a glimpse of his face, then bent down for a moment to put her mouth close to Nick's ear. "Remember when we were in Vitali's briefing, watching his slide show? He showed that photo of the man whose grandfather was part of the original Brotherhood?"

"Klaus Egger," Nick said. "The man who tried to hire my father."

"I'm pretty sure the man up there right now, with the German accent, is Egger."

Nick's eyes went wide. "Who else is in the room?"

She stood back up, shifting her head to scan the room. "The big guy, from the train."

"You're kidding me."

"We have to get up there, Nick."

"I would use your minute well, Mr. Fox," they heard Egger say. The floorboards groaned as Egger paced back and forth a few times, finally stopping next to Franz in the doorway. Kate watched her father move close to Quentin.

"What are you doing?" Egger asked.

"I'm helping him."

"If you see either man touch the map," Egger said, "shoot them immediately. If they don't have answers for us in thirty more seconds, then you should also shoot them."

Kate slipped quietly off the crate. "Let's go," she whispered to Nick.

"Show me where the doorway is," Nick said, scanning the ceiling.

Kate paced off five steps. "Right about here."

"Don't move," Nick said.

He went back to the crate with the grenades, took one out, came back, and then dragged the crate over to a few feet away from where Kate was standing. It was a point that would be behind Franz and Egger, putting them between the grenade and their fathers. Jumping up onto the crate, he shined his light on the underside of the floorboards, finding a place where he could tuck the thin end of a grenade through a knothole.

"No wonder my dad loves you," Kate said.

"Everything I learned about mass destruction, I learned from him. Just get ready to move. In fact, start now."

"Those things are so old, what if it doesn't explode?"

"Then we'll take our chances in a shoot-out. You're in charge of the machine gun. Go!"

Nick gave Kate a few seconds to move to the other end of the room. He pulled the cord, jumped off the crate, and followed, grabbing two more grenades on his way past the open crate, one in each hand. Never know when we could use these, he thought. When he got to the stairs, he saw that Kate had picked up the submachine gun and was waiting for him. They both went up the stairs, waiting for the grenade to explode.

"Nothing is happening," Kate said.

"You were right, maybe they're—"

He was cut off by the blast.

———

Quentin looked at Jake as he came closer, while Egger, standing in the doorway with Franz, consulted his watch and told them they had thirty more seconds.

Jake was about to charge Franz when he thought he heard a faint scraping sound. He glanced at Quentin, then over at Egger and Franz. They all heard the faint but unmistakable murmur of a human voice.

"Sounds like your children have been found," Egger said. "In German, we call the game *Versteck spiel*. You call it *hide-and-seek*, I believe. Your time is almost up, anyway."

He took a few steps toward them, just as the explosion ripped through the room and the floorboards he'd been standing on were blown to pieces.

————

To Nick's and Kate's ears, it was louder than a gunshot but not quite as loud as the end of the world. Through their feet they felt the impact against the wooden floor on the other side of the building. They looked at each other, hoping that the bad guys were hurting and the good guys were getting away, but before they could do anything else, the kitchen door was kicked open and another submachine-gun-toting man burst into the room. He needed a moment to orient himself, coming from the light outside into the relative darkness.

It had been years since Kate last handled a submachine gun like the MP7, but she instinctively swung it into firing position. There was no need for it as Nick had already redirected the man's stumbling momentum, guiding away the barrel of the gun with one hand, grabbing the back of the man's parka with the other. He led the man into the gaping mouth of the trapdoor, threw him down the stairs, and slammed the trapdoor shut.

————

In the library, Jake, Quentin, and Egger all went down to the floor, covering their heads. When they looked up, there was nothing left of the doorway but a great hole in the floor. The body of Franz was lying on the rough stones ten feet below them.

Quentin grabbed the map pieces, Egger went for the gun in

his jacket, and Jake went for Egger. One hard shove backward and Egger fell through the great hole in the floor, landing hard on Franz. Quentin took a piece of a broken chair and smashed open the one window in the room.

Both men climbed out and made their way through knee deep snowdrifts, around to the other side of the monastery.

"Over here!" Kate called.

Jake had never been happier to hear his daughter's voice. She was standing next to one of the two snowcats with Nick.

"Crazy bastards rode those up," Jake said, "along the ridge."

"Sounds like the best way down," Quentin said, looking back at the building. "We need to move."

"Hold on," Nick said. "No need to take both snowcats down the mountain." He took out one of the hand grenades he had brought up from the basement.

"Now I understand the hole in the floor!" Jake said. "But be careful! They can't be stable after all these years."

Jake climbed up the front tread of one of the snowcats, opened up the door, and got in behind the wheel. It took him a few seconds to figure out the controls, then he pressed down the clutch and turned the key. The machine roared to life.

The cab itself was basically a big box, with plenty of room for Kate and Quentin to get in. Nick stood by outside, waiting for the last moment. When the snowcat was ready to go, he opened the door to the other vehicle, pulled the cord on the grenade, and threw it inside. He hustled back and jumped in beside Jake, who was already engaging the clutch. Jake hit the gas, the snowcat's treads whined on the ice for a second before finding purchase, and they were off. Two seconds later, Egger and Franz came out of the building.

"What is that goon made of?" Kate asked. "He's unkillable!"

"Think so? Just watch."

Jake had to keep his eyes on the old tracks in the snow as he drove away from the building, but everyone else was watching the two men get into the other snowcat. Egger was behind the wheel, while Franz had to squeeze himself in through the other door.

"Come on," Nick said. "Blow!"

The other snowcat roared to life. Franz was still trying to get his huge body inside the cab.

"Blow already!"

With Franz finally in, even before he could close the door, Egger put the vehicle in gear and it jumped forward.

"Damn!" Nick said. "Why didn't it blow up?"

"You pull that cord, it's like dragging a seventy-five-year-old match to light the fuse," Jake said, still focused on keeping the treads within the old tracks. "I'm surprised that first one worked at all."

"I got one left," Nick said. "Maybe this one's still good."

"I wouldn't count on it," Jake said.

Jake grimaced as they left the relatively flat ground on which the monastery had been built. The other snowcat was barely a hundred yards behind them, but the ridge suddenly got perilously thin, so thin that the treads on the snowcat could barely straddle it. When he slipped off the line for just one second, they all felt the impact of rock and ice against the undercarriage.

"I can't go any faster!" Jake said. The gunfire erupted from behind them, strafing the back of the vehicle with bullets from Franz's submachine gun.

"Everybody down!" Kate said, as the back window was shattered by the next round of fire.

They were moving east, away from the Matterhorn, toward a smaller peak called Furgghorn. Jake kept fighting to keep the snowcat on its narrow line, feeling the vehicle threatening to tip over whenever he veered even a few inches in either direction. The wind kicked up, rocking the cab and making his job even harder. The back of the cab was hit by another round of bullets from the submachine gun.

Kate picked up the submachine gun she'd brought with her, pointed it out the back of the vehicle, and returned fire. But it was like shooting while riding a bucking bronco.

"Everybody hold on!" Jake said. He knew he couldn't keep following the old tracks, not while being shot at from behind. He had to get off this ridge. When he threw the wheel to the left, the vehicle dove, heading straight down at a precipitous angle and already starting to slide.

Jake kept the nose pointed forward, steering into the slide. He knew if the snowcat went sideways it would go into a roll and probably turn a few hundred times before finally reaching the bottom several minutes later.

Kate tried to hold on to a handle mounted into the inside of the cab. She turned to look behind her through the shattered rear window and saw the second snowcat making the same turn. "They're still on our tail!" she said.

Jake kept fighting, looking ahead to a slightly more level area about a hundred yards ahead of them. But then they started to spin and Jake couldn't fight it any longer. He lost all control as they turned all the way around, sliding backward and looking straight up at the other snowcat, until they hit yet another ice patch and completed the turn, coming around a full 360 degrees and re-gaining their bearings. The ground leveled, the ice softened, and the treads finally gripped, slowing the vehicle down and nearly throwing them all through the windshield.

The snow got deeper here as they lost elevation. The treads worked harder and harder to churn through it, slowing them down. On top of that, Jake saw that they would be entering a nar-row canyon between two great rock outcroppings, and he knew he'd have to keep the snowcat away from the walls. As they came over a crest, he saw a deep crevice running down the center of the canyon. He had to slow down even more so he could carefully ne-gotiate either left or right of it. He pumped at the brakes, feeling the treads sinking in the snow.

"They're gaining on us!" Kate said from behind him.

Nick took the last grenade from his coat, pulled the cord, leaned out the window, and threw it as far as he could, directly behind them. The grenade landed in the deep snow and disappeared. The other snowcat churned over the spot and kept coming.

"Another dud!" Nick said. "I demand a refund."

Three more seconds passed, then this grenade exploded. The other vehicle was well past it, beyond danger of any damage, but then the snow started moving. It was like a gentle white wave at first, then it got bigger, and bigger, feeding on the new snow it picked up as it rushed down the slope, faster and faster.

"We're going to get buried!" Quentin said.

"No, we're not," Jake said, pushing the vehicle onto the left edge of the crevice, hugging the rock wall until it gave way to a wider spot that created a safe haven, a snow break against the coming avalanche. Jake stopped the vehicle to ride out whatever would come next.

Behind them, Egger struggled to follow the same line, but the tidal wave of snow was already building against the back of his snowcat, pushing him toward the great crevice.

Jake, Quentin, Nick, and Kate all watched as Egger's door flew open and he jumped out of the vehicle, rolling in the snow and coming to a stop against the rock wall. The other door was open and Franz was fighting his way out, but it was too late. The snowcat went over the edge of the crevice, falling a hundred feet to the bare rocks below. It landed with a sickening crash and the avalanche flowed over the crevice, filling it completely with snow.

With its volume and speed reduced, the last of the avalanche flowed past the first snowcat, pushing snow up to the bottom of the cab, but rising no farther. When it was all done, there was nothing to see but a new expanse of snow in the canyon that had erased the crevice.

Surely, this time Franz was dead. But what about Egger? They spotted him clinging to the rock wall, having found a slight snow break, just as they had. He was stranded on the mountain in deep snow, but still alive.

Nick leaned out of his window to give Egger a proper salute, then added to that another hand gesture entirely. Jake put the vehicle back in gear and headed down toward the Swiss town of Zermatt.

———

They parked the snowcat next to the gondola station in Zermatt and quietly slipped away into the town. Quentin had cell reception again, so he called Professor Lewis back on the other side of the mountain, and asked him to load everything into the Peugeot and drive through the pass into Switzerland.

They waited in a café, looking like four exhausted climbers recovering after a hard day on the mountain. They ordered food and hot coffee. It felt good to be breathing air with adequate oxygen again.

"Do you have it?" Kate finally asked Quentin.

Quentin gave her a tired smile and patted the money belt around his waist.

"Was that really the last link? Are we really done?"

"I don't know. We'll have to let the professor look at it. I hope so."

An hour later, Professor Lewis showed up in Zermatt. He was excited to see the last link in the map, but they didn't want to stay here in this town, not right at the base of the mountain. Instead, they drove north into the interior of Switzerland, stopping in the town of Brig and finding another low-profile inn for the night. They got three rooms and gathered in one as Professor Lewis pored over the five links they hoped would constitute a complete treasure map, leading them finally to the *Raubgold*.

The polar bear scrapes on Nick's leg had been redressed. The new cut on his eyebrow was taped shut with a butterfly bandage. Jake's reaggravated swollen ankle was soaking in a bucket of ice. Quentin was still recovering from a long day without enough oxygen, wrapped up in a blanket and trying to get warm. Kate was just tired as hell.

They all watched Professor Lewis going through the pieces of the map, one by one. First, he ran them in a line across the desk, left to right, then he switched it to top to bottom.

"The good news is," he finally said, "there's a rune here, called *Jera*, at the bottom of the banner. It means *harvest*. A task fulfilled. That would suggest that this map is complete, and all we have to do is follow this last banner to find the treasure."

"What does that banner say again?" Quentin asked.

"It says, *Der Zug fährt auf halber Strecke zum Bahnhof Štrbské Pleso*. The train stops halfway to Štrbské Pleso, which I believe is a town in Slovakia, in the High Tatra Mountains."

"Okay, so we go halfway to that station, but halfway from where?"

"That's a good question," Lewis said. "Here's where I was expecting the rest of the map to help us. All of these topographical lines, and all of the symbols."

He held up the last link.

"Here's *Fehu*," he said, pointing to a symbol near the center. "It means *wealth*, and it doesn't appear anywhere else on any of these other links. This must be where the gold is."

"Okay, so how do we get there?"

Professor Lewis shook his head in frustration. "I don't know! It's almost like you have to start over on this first page, with one of these symbols, and follow that to the next one. Then the next one and the next one."

He kept staring at the map. He didn't move. He didn't make a sound. Nick and Kate sat on one of the beds, waiting. Quentin stayed wrapped up on the other bed. Jake rattled the ice in his bucket. Lewis looked up from the map and stared at Jake.

"Sorry," Jake said.

A few more minutes passed. Having four people watching him so intently was too much for Professor Lewis, and he stacked the pieces into a pile so he could take them back to his own room.

He paused, staring at the map pieces stacked on top of each other. He flipped from the first to the second, all the way to the fifth. "They're layers," he exclaimed. "This is how the runes line up! It all makes sense now!" He traced how the seemingly random lines actually formed one complete trail, with matching runes leading from one layer of the map to the layer below it, all the way to the bottom, where *Fehu*, the treasure, was waiting. "The map is three-dimensional," he said, "leading underground!"

When he looked up, four sets of eyes were staring at him.

"I believe we need to start planning our trip to Štrbské Pleso," Lewis said.

"Are you telling us," Nick said, "that you figured out the map?"

"That is what I am telling you, yes."

"We're going to need to be extra careful on this one," Nick said. "If Egger made it off the mountain and is still alive, he knows this last piece leads in the direction of Štrbské Pleso."

"So by the time we get there," Kate said, "or maybe soon after, Egger's men will be there, too."

CHAPTER SIXTEEN

It was yet another departure made in the cold, gray hours before dawn. The team gathered wordlessly at the vehicle, everyone operating on reserves of strength they didn't know they had. At least today there was a grim determination in the air, the knowledge that this really might be the last leg of the journey.

They knew the trains were not safe. Boarding a commercial airline would have been laughable. That left an eleven-hour journey by car to Slovakia, in what felt like a retracing of their steps, from Switzerland through northern Italy, across the width of Austria to the Slovakian capital of Bratislava. The big question hanging in the air for all of them was how long would it take Egger to get himself off that mountain, and then send forces to Slovakia?

"I've never been to the High Tatras," Lewis said as they passed through the capital. "I hear they're quite beautiful."

"Explain it again," Kate said. "We're looking for a tunnel *under* a mountain?"

Professor Lewis nodded. "We need to go to a town called Štrba, on the main train line that runs across the country. From there we can take what they call a 'rack railway,' which is a special kind of train with gears built into the tracks, for going up mountains where the grade is too steep for regular trains. At the very top of this railway is the town of Štrbské Pleso. It's the highest point of elevation for a train station in the world."

"So 'Halfway to Štrbské Pleso,'" Nick said, "like the map said."

"I think that's the idea," Lewis said. "It's roughly three miles up the mountain, so half that."

"A mile and a half," Nick said. "Is the entrance to the tunnel going to be obvious?"

"Has anything else been that easy so far?" Lewis asked.

"Yeah, I didn't think so," Nick said. "But assuming we find it, these rune symbols will guide us through the tunnels somehow?"

Lewis nodded again. "You'll have to consult the map at every turn. It will be your only hope to find the gold."

"We're talking about four hundred tons of it," Kate said. "How did they move that into a tunnel without anyone noticing?"

"Great question," Lewis said. "As it happens, the railway was closed down in 1936, so the tracks were sitting empty when they used them to hide the gold. I looked it up and a modern railcar can carry over a hundred tons. Figure a little less than that for the 1940s, but that's still only a few cars. On a totally empty track? That would have been fairly easy to keep out of sight."

"Are the tracks still empty?" Kate asked.

"No, they rebuilt them in 1970, so I don't know what it's going to look like now. Or if that old tunnel is even findable."

It was another three hours of driving to cross most of the country, heading northeast from Bratislava, finally reaching the High Tatras, the rugged border between Slovakia and Poland. Still an hour away, they could all see the jagged summit of Mount Kriváň? in the distance.

"If you talk to some of the old-timers around here," Lewis said, "they'll tell you that it's their national duty to climb Mount Kriváň at least once in their lifetime."

"You promised," Quentin said. "No more climbing."

They passed through the towns of Ružomberok and Liptovský Michal, places with old souls, old streets, and buildings that looked almost exactly the same as they did a century ago. It felt like they were driving back through time, and it brought home the reality of what they were really doing, of what they were trying to find and who had been responsible for collecting it and hiding it. Everyone in the vehicle was quiet now, alone with their own thoughts.

They reached the town of Štrba as the sun went down on another long day. They found another small inn, away from the main road, and paid for three rooms with cash euros. After a quick bite and some coffee, they located the train station from which the rack railway ran up to Štrbské Pleso.

They watched the station carefully before approaching, looking for any sign of the Brotherhood's men. Just like the gondola in Breuil-Cervinia, the traffic on the rack railway was mostly people on their way home, regular local Slovaks who'd gone up to visit the famously beautiful lake near the Štrbské Pleso station to enjoy a day in the mountains.

Nick, Kate, Quentin, Jake, and Professor Lewis all entered the station and boarded the red and white train, sitting by the windows so they could look out both sides. The train took off slowly, powered by the electric wires that ran above the tracks. It clattered along, its wheels grabbing the cogs to climb the slope. Three miles up the mountain, the forest on either side of the tracks was getting thicker by the minute. They had no exact idea what they were looking for, but there was nothing to see anyway except trees on either side, with occasional concrete embankments built against the slope to stabilize the ground.

"What kind of tunnel are we looking for?" Nick whispered to Kate. "A railway tunnel? A pedestrian tunnel? A gopher hole?"

Kate shrugged, and shook her head.

When they reached the top, they turned around and came back down. This time, because Jake had timed the slow ride up, he knew when they'd reach the midway point.

"Right about now," he said, as the train ground its way back down to Štrba, but there was nothing to see in the fading light except the dark silhouettes of the trees.

As they got off the train, Kate scanned the station, feeling like danger was a moment away. I don't know if this just a healthy surveillance instinct, she thought. Or do these guys have me spooked now? I can't even tell anymore.

"Do we look for the tunnel now?" Quentin asked everyone. "Or do we wait for daylight?"

"I want to find it as much as anyone," Nick answered, "but if we stumble around in the dark up there, we'll just be burning our energy."

They all agreed. They would get a few hours of sleep, then start looking for the tunnel at first light.

———

Nick found Kate alone in her room. She'd just ended a call with Jessup and she still had the burner phone in her hand.

"What's the good word?" Nick asked.

"I'm afraid there isn't any," Kate said. "Jessup still hasn't found the leak at Interpol. I'm really hoping we don't strike out tomorrow. I'd like to find the gold and put an end to all of this."

"I hear you," Nick said, nodding. "It's been fun, but it's time to move on. What are you going to do with your share of the gold when we find it?"

Kate's eyes narrowed to slits and she jabbed her finger into Nick's chest. "There are no shares. The gold goes back to its owners or to a righteous cause. I swear, if I find out you've taken so much as a speck of gold dust, I'll drop-kick you from here to eternity."

Nick nodded again. "Gotcha. No shares. What are you going to do with your finder's fee? I have a number of ideas."

If anyone else had said this, Kate would have smiled at the joke, but this was Nick. She knew he might not be joking. In the not-so-distant past, he had had a cavalier attitude about helping himself to other people's fortunes. She looked to the heavens for help, and groaned.

Nick took a step closer and tucked a strand of stray hair behind Kate's ear. "You're sexy when you're exasperated," he said.

"I'm not exasperated," Kate said. "I'm hungry."

"Maybe this will help," Nick said. He pulled out what looked like a candy bar wrapper and opened it.

"What is that?"

"It's called a *Horalky*. They've been making them here in Slovakia for a hundred years."

"It looks like one of those wafer cookies that taste like cardboard," Kate said. "Don't you have any of that good chocolate from Paris?"

"Try it," he said, putting it to her mouth.

She took a small, skeptical bite. There was a delicate peanut butter cream sandwiched between the wafers, and the edges had been dipped in fine dark chocolate. "Oh my God," she said. "I have a new favorite thing in the world."

The Big Bad Wolf would have been envious of the smile Nick flashed Kate. "I might have some more," he said. "Maybe you can help me remember."

She locked eyes with him. "Like how?"

"Surprise me," Nick said.

Kate grabbed Nick by his shirt and pulled him in for a kiss she was pretty sure he'd consider *Horalky*-worthy.

There was a knock on the door, and two seconds later Jake came into the room.

"Sorry," Jake said, looking at both of them. "Did I interrupt something?"

"No," Nick said, handing Kate two more packages of *Horalky*. "We were talking about tomorrow."

"The professor has a few ideas for finding the tunnel," Jake said. "In the meantime, we should all get some rest."

"Good idea," Nick said. "Because we always strike at dawn."

———

The next morning, just before the sun came up, Nick, Kate, Quentin, and Jake rode the railway up to Štrbské Pleso. They didn't try to jump off the train midway, because it was a small two-car train and getting noticed wasn't worth the risk. Plus, by starting at the top, it would be an easy mile and a half coming downhill, instead of a harder mile and a half going *up*.

The professor was back in the inn, waiting by his phone in case they called. Assuming they *could* call. Once they were in the tunnels, God knew what would happen to their cell signal. Quentin had the map with him, but now there was one particular symbol on the first page that they were focused on, the *Berkano* rune. It was shaped like a rough *B*, but with two sharp points instead of rounded mounds. It generally meant birth, or new life. Or sometimes a *starting point*. That was what they would be looking for in the woods surrounding the railway.

They got off at the upper station and waited for the people going down to board the train. The station was empty. They slipped outside and scanned the surroundings. Looking down the tracks, they saw nothing but trees and the back of the train as it rounded a bend and disappeared from view.

"Everybody be careful," Nick said. "Keep talking to each other."

They were all wearing earpieces again. For as long as they were in relatively close proximity to each other, at least, they could stay in constant contact.

"Thank you for being here," Quentin said. "No matter what happens, I'll never forget it."

"*Veľa šťastia*," Kate said. "It's Slovak for good luck. I looked it up."

"*Veľa šťastia*," everyone else said together. Then they were off to find the four hundred tons of gold that had been hidden for three-quarters of a century.

———

After a few minutes of walking, they came to a sign next to the track. It was modern, reading "1K" on one side, meaning one kilometer traveled in that direction. They knew they were looking for something a lot older. A few minutes later, they heard a rumbling noise and ducked off the tracks, into the dense forest. It was the same two-car train, which would keep going up and down all day.

When they reached the halfway point, they split up. Nick and Kate took one side of the tracks while Jake and Quentin took the other. Their earpieces kept them all connected. There was no sign of anyone else near the tracks. It was even a beautiful morning to wander around on the side of a Slovakian mountain, especially as the sun rose high enough above the trees. Unfortunately, there was no tunnel entrance to be found.

They went farther and farther away from the exact midpoint of the railway, wondering if the original line could have run on a slightly different course than the version modified in 1970.

"If you're redoing this train line," Kate said, "and you see the entrance to a tunnel, why wouldn't you go in and check it out?"

"I think we would have heard about it if they found four hundred tons of Nazi gold in 1970," Nick said.

Kate stopped, looked down at the foliage that was all around her legs. "Does poison ivy grow in this part of Europe?" she asked.

"No," Nick said, startling her as he pushed through a heavy wall of vines. "But they do have something called *aconite* around here. Also known as *wolfsbane*, or the *devil's helmet*, I think."

"Yeah? What does it look like?"

"Couldn't tell you," Nick said. "You may be standing in it."

He smiled, she glared at him, but then she stopped dead. She was staring at something directly behind him.

"What is it?" he asked, turning to see what she was looking at. About thirty yards away was one of the many fortified embankments that were dotted all up and down the mountain, whenever the ground needed to be stabilized to protect the tracks. This was one of the older embankments, not concrete like the newer ones, but made by setting a row of railroad ties directly into the slope.

"That's it," she said.

"Where? I don't see it."

"*Right there.*"

Nick zeroed in on how the railroad ties set into the slope started short, got longer and longer until they reached a peak, receded to short again, then back to longer, then back to short. It was the *Berkano* rune, the rough *B* with sharp points. It just happened to be set on its side with the points going up.

"Guys," Nick said into his earpiece, "I think Kate found it."

———

A few minutes later, Jake and Quentin were standing next to them, looking at the shape formed by the ties.

"Before we do anything else," Jake said, "let's decide how we want to play this. I've circled our perimeter. If someone else is here, they're not close. But that doesn't mean they're not watching us."

"They may have gotten smarter," Quentin said. "They may be waiting for us to do the hard work this time, then move in if they think we've found something."

There was a rumbling sound in the distance. It resolved into nothing more than another train going by. They waited, and when it passed they heard nothing but the silence of the forest again, broken only by the buzzing of insects and a slight breeze through the leaves.

"For all we know, Egger's still stuck in the snow," Nick said. "If we've really found the tunnel, I don't see why we should wait."

Kate did a slow 360, scanning the forest as far as she could see in every direction, waiting for her *I'm being watched* sensor to fire. Finally, she added her agreement and the team moved toward the railroad ties.

The ties were set firmly into the slope, the bottom ends sunk at least three feet into the ground. Kate took out her flashlight and shined it through the narrow gaps between the ties. As she moved toward the center, the light seemed to reach farther. She found one spot where the gap was slightly larger, foraged around on the ground for a long stick, and worked it into the gap. As far as she inserted the stick, it hit nothing but air.

Nick and Jake climbed up the slope to the top of the ties. When they tested the center, it didn't budge. They started rocking it back and forth. After a minute of this, it started to move. They worked it more and more, until Kate could see a black *nothingness* behind it.

"You've got it," she said. "Keep going."

They worked at the tie, until finally it came all the way down. Kate shined her light into the gap.

They had found the tunnel.

Nick turned on his flashlight and squeezed his way in through the narrow opening. He was barely able to fit. The floor of the tunnel was packed dirt. Trusses made from railroad ties held up the walls and ceiling, placed roughly every ten feet. The tunnel led off into the darkness, farther than Nick's flashlight beam could penetrate.

"Come on in, guys," he said, putting his face in the gap. "It's like a Disney ride, but with no lights. And probably lots of rats."

"And maybe some gold," Kate said. It was easy for her to squeeze through the gap.

Quentin slipped through next. That left Jake, who stood outside looking at the gap, thinking, No way in hell.

"Exhale," Nick said. "Think thin."

"Hold on a second," Jake said. He went to the other end of the tie they had pulled off to create the opening, grabbed the free end, lifted, and then tilted it back toward the opening.

"What are you doing?" Nick asked. "Walling us in now? *Think thin*, that was just a joke."

"I'm hiding our tracks," Jake said.

He leaned the tie against the embankment, lining it up at the top. Now it was less likely that someone coming by would notice it. He stepped back, took a breath, and prepared himself mentally to squeeze through an opening that he *might* have fit through thirty years ago.

Quentin and Nick grabbed the arm that came through first. They each put a foot on either side of the opening for leverage. With one final wrench, Jake came through and they all fell down.

"That was graceful," Kate said.

They brushed themselves off and started walking down the tunnel, quickly leaving the sunlight behind them. The air got heavier, the smell of damp earth got stronger, and the overall closed-in feeling grew more acute. Nick shined his light on what passed for the ceiling. Thin boards ran lengthwise from one truss to the next, but most of these boards were cracked. Some were broken off completely and lay in pieces on the dirt floor.

"They either made this on the cheap or in a hurry," Nick said. "Or both."

"How far do we have to go?" Kate asked.

"Good question."

About a hundred yards later, they came to the first fork in the road. Quentin took out the map and shined his light on the first page. "I think we're here," he said, running one finger on the line leading away from the initial *Berkano* rune. "That means we go, what, right now?"

"No, I think it's left," Nick said, looking over his shoulder. "See how that other line cuts over this way?"

"I think that's a different tunnel," Quentin said. "This one goes *this* way."

"It's this way," Kate said, nodding toward the right-hand tunnel.

"How do you know?" Nick asked.

"Look." She put her light on the wooden beams over their heads. On one was carved a symbol in the shape of a diamond. On the other was a symbol that resembled a rough capital *Y*.

"I'll be damned," Nick said. "I wonder what happens if you go the wrong way?"

"How about we don't find out?"

They kept going down the next segment of the tunnel until they came to another juncture. Once again, they stopped, looked carefully at the map, found the symbols carved into the railroad ties that spanned across the rough ceiling, then chose what they believed to be the right direction.

When they reached the last symbol on the first page of the map, they matched up the same symbol on the second page. With each step, they could feel the floor of the tunnel sloping down-ward. They were heading to the bottom of the mountain.

When they stopped to rest, they all coughed out the dirt that had been collecting in their throats and lungs.

"Everybody okay?" Nick asked.

Before anyone could answer, they all felt a low rumble.

"What is that?" Kate asked. "A train?"

Nick shook his head, looking back up the tunnel they had just come down. "I don't think that's a train. I think they're here."

"We were wondering what happens when you take a wrong turn," Jake said. "There must be a tripwire, or maybe a plate set into the dirt floor. Dynamite might leak a little nitroglycerin over the years, but it'll still have a kick to it."

"This is why you don't leave home without your treasure map," Nick said. "The question is, did that blast take out all of them? Or are they still coming?"

The question was answered a minute later with another rumble, louder to the ear, with a harder kick that they could not only feel but *see* as a cloud of dirt came drifting down from the ceiling. They kept going, even as they still had to carefully pause at each junction, to remember exactly where they were, what the last symbol had been, and where the next symbol was pointing them.

The next rumble wasn't just louder. Through the white noise of the explosion they could also hear the sound of several men yelling at once.

"They're right over us," Nick said.

"We have to stay careful," Jake said. "No need to rush. We're the ones with the map."

"What happens when it's time to get back out?" Kate asked.

"Maybe they'll make enough wrong turns," Nick said, "that we won't even have to worry about them anymore."

The question hung in the air as they kept moving, even as the explosions continued and each one seemed to get closer and closer. Even between the explosions, the voices drifted down the tunnels, as harsh and threatening as the barks of vicious dogs.

"Concentrate," Nick said, as the team almost misread the map on the next junction. "We make a mistake, they won't even have to catch up to us."

They made it to the last page of the map. There were seven more symbols to negotiate, seven more junctions in this impossibly complex labyrinth of tunnels. They heard the voices close behind them, closer than ever. Jake took out his SIG Sauer and positioned himself behind the team. A figure appeared at the far end of a straightaway. Jake fired and was answered with a spray of bullets from a submachine gun. "Get to the next turn!" Jake said. "I'll hold them off!"

"We're not leaving you!" Kate said. She took out her own Beretta and started firing down the same straightaway.

"It's right here!" Quentin said. "A hundred more feet!"

Nick hurried to the next junction and quickly checked the map. There was no time to double-check. "To the right!" Nick yelled. "This way. *To the right!*"

As Jake and Kate caught up to him, he motioned to the *left*, where Quentin was already waiting. "*To the right!*" Nick yelled again, hoping that someone behind them could hear him. Someone who knew enough English to understand "right" versus "left."

They disappeared down the left tunnel, moving quickly but quietly. The voices could be heard in the other tunnel. Nick counted it down in his head. *Five, four, three, two, one.* The explosion reverberated down the narrow tunnel, almost blowing them over with heat and sound and a wave of concussed air.

"That was a dirty trick," Quentin said.

"Yeah, well done," Kate said.

They had six more symbols left, then five, then four. They didn't hear any more sounds behind them. They let themselves slow down. Three left, then two, until they reached the last test. Here the tunnel branched off into two last tunnels, placed very close together, but there were no symbols carved into the wood bracing up the ceiling.

"What's the symbol we're looking for?" Nick asked.

"Professor called it *Fehu*, meaning wealth," Quentin said. "Which is how he knew it was the last one. But I don't see it."

Nick examined the entrance to the last two tunnels, without daring to step foot into either one. Jake pulled out his burner phone, tried to call Professor Lewis, but he was underneath a mountain. If the phone could have laughed in his face, it would have.

"Let's think about this," Nick said. "We can't blow this last one."

They heard the sounds of voices again, and with heavy pounding footsteps. Whoever was still alive, they were right behind them.

"We don't have much time," Jake said, drawing his gun and getting ready to fire. "Somebody better make a decision."

The voices and the footsteps got louder. Kate, Nick, and Quentin stared at the last page of the map, waiting for the answer to reach up and grab them.

"Right about now would be great," Jake said, getting ready to fire at the first man he saw come around that last corner.

"This way!" Kate said. She didn't wait for anyone else to come with her. She just headed straight into the right-hand tunnel, holding her breath and waiting for the explosion. It didn't come.

Nick and Quentin ran in behind her, followed by Jake. They made it down the tunnel and barely out of sight, just as the men behind them reached the same junction.

"How did you know to go *that* way?" Nick asked.

"I didn't," Kate said. "Not for sure. But look."

She showed them the last page of the map, where the *Fehu*

rune was created with two lines coming off a single vertical line, like two branches on a tree, but both on the right side. "So I just figured, go right," she said.

She was cut off by another explosion, the biggest and loudest of all. This one really did knock Jake, Quentin, Nick, and Kate off their feet.

They all lay on their backs for a long time. It was completely dark. Kate fumbled around on the ground for her flashlight, found it, and shined it on the men. "Is everybody okay?"

"You'll have to speak up," Nick said. "I think my eardrums are broken."

When they were all on their feet again, they shook their heads clear and walked a few yards back up the tunnel. Jake led with the barrel of his gun, but it was a pointless gesture. The tunnel behind them was completely closed off by a cave-in.

"So there's another way out of here, right?" Nick asked. "I'm sure that's on the map, too. Right?"

They walked down the last hundred yards of the tunnel, until it opened up into a larger space. How much larger, it was impossible to say, but the air suddenly *felt* different all around them and the beams of their flashlights were lost in the darkness.

"Watch where you're walking," Nick said. "God knows what other booby traps got set around here."

They moved forward slowly, until their flashlights reflected against a hard, black surface. As they got closer, the huge object in front of them took form.

It was a locomotive.

"Are we really seeing this?" Nick asked. "How did this get here?"

"On these tracks," Quentin said, kicking at the metal rail beneath one of the train's great wheels.

Jake found the ladder to the cab of the locomotive and hoisted himself up. A few moments later, a miracle happened. There was *light*. He jumped back down to the ground, holding a lantern.

"I'm a little surprised the oil still burns," he said. "But I'll take it."

He handed a second lantern to Quentin, took a match from an ancient box of matches, and lit it. Now there were two glowing lights and they were able to make out just how big the space was that they had found. It was a railway tunnel with high vaulted ceilings, not like the cramped, barely propped-up passageways they had been walking in. The tracks led into the darkness, farther than they could see.

"Maybe that's the way out," Nick said, shining his light on the tracks.

But Quentin wasn't listening to anyone else now. He was facing in the opposite direction, not at all interested in what was ahead of the locomotive, but in what was behind it. A half-dozen boxcars.

"Do you realize what this is?" he asked, turning to look at them. "Do you know how many people have been looking for this? For seventy-five years? There have been so many rumors about where this was hidden. Most treasure hunters, the ones who are still looking, they think it's in Poland somewhere, probably between

Breslau and Waldenburg. But it's *not*. It's *here*, across the border in Slovakia."

He turned back to stare at the train.

"This is it," he said. "This is what we've been looking for. *We found it.*"

Jake came forward to put a hand on Quentin's shoulder. Nick and Kate stood on the other side of him. After everything they'd been through, even if they still had to face the problem of finding a way back out of here, Quentin was right. *They had found the treasure.*

"I know we still have work to do," Quentin said, snapping back to reality. "But we have to check inside first. What does four hundred tons of gold even look like?"

They all went back to the first car behind the locomotive, a box-car with a big sliding door on the side. Jake and Quentin worked together to pull the door open. Nick and Kate moved closer and shined in their flashlights, expecting to see it piled high with gold bars. They couldn't quite make out what they were seeing at first. Old tattered cloth, and something else, scattered all over the floor. Pale in the glare of the light.

Bones. They were looking at the skeletons of a dozen men.

"Holy God," Quentin said, playing his flashlight across the skulls. "These must have been the men who brought this train down here."

"Dead men tell no tales," Jake said.

They all knew he was right. These were the mainline grunt soldiers who had helped hide this gold, men who could never be trusted again.

"Let's check out the next one," Quentin said.

They went to the next boxcar. When the door slid open, there was nothing inside. They continued to the next car, and the next, and the next. Aside from the bones of the men who had brought it here, the "gold train" was completely empty.

CHAPTER SEVENTEEN

They followed the track backward from the last car. It disappeared quickly into a massive wall of rock, what had once been another section of the tunnel but was now essentially part of the mountain itself.

"No way out here," Quentin said, stating the obvious.

They walked back up the length of the train, past the nose, following the tracks to the opposite end. As they neared the rock wall, they saw the faintest glow of sunlight, filtered through the rocks that blocked this end of the tunnel.

"It's caved in," Quentin said, "but not nearly as much as the other side."

"At least we have air," Jake said. "We won't suffocate."

As they got closer, they saw something else on the tracks. It was a classic handcar, half-buried in the rubble that had sealed off this end of the tunnel, the kind of car with the seesaw handle to make it run, right out of an old cartoon. What *wasn't* right out of an old cartoon was the remains of the man on the car.

He was mostly a skeleton at this point, almost but not quite as desiccated as the dead men they had found in the boxcar. Dried skin and a few locks of hair clung to his skull. His clothes were rat-eaten rags. They could only see him from the waist up, because everything below that was covered by the rubble.

"What is this?" Quentin stepped closer, dusted off the dirt from the deck of the handcar, and picked up an old book that had been lying close to the man's head. He opened the pages gently.

"It's an old logbook of some kind," he said. "Dates, numbers. But wait."

There was writing on the last page. German words that Quentin couldn't understand, but at the bottom of the page was a signature. He closed the book and looked back at Jake, Kate, and Nick.

"I think we just found Egger's grandfather."

———

It might have been one hour that passed. Time was already starting to lose its meaning. They were all thirsty now. They were all hungry. Everyone was doing their absolute best not to accept the feeling of panic and despair.

Jake climbed up on the rubble that filled the tunnel exit, trying to find a cell phone signal. There was none. He started moving some of the rubble by hand. Nick and Kate joined him, shoveling the dirt and sand with their fingers. All they needed was one slim gap to climb through, but every time they cleared a small hole in the wall it would immediately get filled up with even more debris.

It made them more thirsty, more hungry. It made it even harder to keep the fear at bay.

"I think I know what happened here," Quentin said, standing over the remains of Egger's grandfather.

Jake, Kate, and Nick stopped working and sat down on three of the larger rocks in the pile.

"They drove this train into this section of the tunnel, near the exit. Grandpop here was in charge of the operation. He worked directly for Göring. Egger told us that himself."

Jake nodded. "He did."

"Göring was the number two man in the Reich," Quentin went on. "It makes sense he'd be directing this. Once the train was here, they blew up one tunnel behind it." Quentin nodded toward the opposite end of the train. "They already had their secret passageways built, full of booby traps, leading down here." Quentin paused again, nodding to the narrow passageway that had brought them here. "So now all they had to do was blow up this end, right? Seal the train in for good?"

"Right," Nick said, "but—"

"But he didn't!" Quentin said. "He killed the men, left this end open. At least for a time."

"Why would he do that?" Nick asked.

"Because it was a double cross," Quentin said. "The oldest story in the world. This was a perfect opportunity to move the gold out, one load at a time, on this handcar. The railway was empty then, remember? I bet it was just Göring and Egger's grandfather at that point. Save it for themselves instead of sharing it with everyone else in the Reich. Göring was a straight rat bastard, don't forget."

Quentin looked back toward the train. "It explains why the train is empty. And why he's *here.*" Quentin kicked the handcar, then looked up and down the tracks like he was playing the movie in his head. "Göring and Egger's grandfather are taking the last load out. They're going to blow the tunnel when they're done. That's when Göring decides that having it all for himself is even better than sharing it with *anybody.* All Göring has to do is get out and then blow the tunnel on top of Egger's grandfather here. Who now knows he's trapped in this rubble, knows he only has a few minutes to live. He writes these last words in his book."

"If that was true," Nick said, "then he'd be lying in a pile of gold. That last load he never got to take out."

Quentin kicked at the dirt beneath the handcar. Then he bent down, picked up a handful of coins, and brushed them off. He tossed one to Jake, one to Nick, one to Kate. As Kate shined her light on it, she saw the bright gold finish, the eagle stamped into the face, holding the wreath, and in the center of the wreath a swastika.

"This is all fascinating," Nick said to his father. "But it's not going to help us get out of here."

"You're right," Quentin said. "We're just as trapped as Herr Egger."

Each one of them took their own moment of silence to consider that fact, until Nick looked up at the train.

"Maybe we're not," Nick said. "Come on, I may have a crazy idea."

He led them back to the train and climbed up into the cab.

"What are you thinking?" Quentin asked, looking up at him from the ground.

"See if the tank has any water in it," Nick said.

Quentin climbed up the side of the locomotive to check the tank. "I think it does," he said.

"Are you telling me this is a *steam* engine?" Jake asked. "They were still using those in the 1940s?"

"Yes," Quentin said as he hopped down from the tank into the cab and leaned his head out the window. "The Germans made a lot more steam engines during the war. The price of diesel fuel was killing them, but steam was still cheap and easy."

"You actually think you can get this thing running?" Jake asked.

"It's possible," Quentin said. "If this was a diesel engine, we wouldn't have a chance. The fuel would be dead by now. But the tank is closed so the water never evaporated. And coal never goes bad."

Quentin turned to see Nick staring at the controls. He touched the big lever set into the floor, then the two levers on the bar that ran from the floor to the ceiling of the cab. Finally, he grabbed hold of the largest lever of all, extending horizontally in front of the conductor's chair.

"You took me to that train museum," Nick said. "Do you re-member?"

"You were just a kid," Quentin said. "I didn't think you were paying attention."

"Maybe I was. More than you think."

"Are you telling me you really did enjoy all the trains?"

"Just don't tell anyone I'm a big train nerd," Nick said, smiling. "It'll be bad for my image."

"But even if you get this thing running," Quentin said, looking out the dusty front window, "we've got, what, five hundred yards? You really think we can build up enough speed?"

"Only one way to find out," Nick said. "Unless you've got a better idea."

"I don't. What can I do to help?"

"We need some of that lantern oil to start a fire in the box," Nick said. "Whatever wood we can find. Then I'll probably need help shoveling the coal."

Quentin leaned out of the cab window and asked Jake and Kate to go find some wood.

"I know where to go," Kate said to her father. He followed her back to what was left of the passageway, to collect some of the slats that ran between the ceiling trusses. As they approached the site of the explosion, they both heard muffled scraping sounds. Jake moved closer to the cave-in, listening carefully.

"They're digging," Jake said. "Who knows how long it will take them to get in here?"

"We can ambush them," Kate said. "Mow 'em down as soon as they break through."

"They're still using submachine guns," Jake said. "We're out-manned and outgunned."

They both took armfuls of broken wooden slats back to the train and handed them up to Quentin. Nick threw them into the box to feed the fire. He knew he had to get the water boiling, and that the water gauge next to the firebox would start to fill when that happened. Then it would be time to ramp up the fire's temperature with the coal. After that, well, he was still trying to remember what to do.

"Should we uncouple from the cars?" Quentin asked.

"Yes," Nick said. "We need to get the engine up to speed as fast as we can."

Quentin opened the door to climb down. Nick stopped him.

"Remember how to do it?" Nick asked.

"You pull the two pins on the knuckle coupler," Quentin said. He smiled at his son, then jumped down to go uncouple the locomotive.

Nick wiped the grime off the water gauge. It was filled halfway, meaning that the water was boiling in the tank. Or so Nick thought. He opened up the door to the firebox and started shoveling in coal.

Kate and Jake went down the passageway again. This time Jake had his SIG Sauer drawn and Kate had pulled out her Beretta. The sounds of the men working on the other side of the cave-in were getting louder and louder.

"They're close," she said.

"We don't want to be standing here if they break through," Jake said, surveying the meager pile of rocks at their feet. "There's not much cover."

Nick kept feeding the fire. The coal embers were glowing a furious bright red and the heat coming through the door was already making him sweat through his shirt. I hope to hell I remember the rest of this, he thought. There were a dozen other steps in the middle that were all about protecting the engine parts. Greasing, lubricating, heating up oil and feeding it to the cylinders. None of which I give a damn about because if this thing actually moves, it will be for the last time ever.

As Quentin made his way back to the cab, he saw the steam starting to billow out of the locomotive's stack. Nick is actually doing this, he thought. He's starting up a steam train.

Kate and Jake saw a small rock fall to the ground. Then a light shined through the hole. Kate opened fire and the light was extinguished, followed immediately by the sound of a man in excruciating pain.

"Get down!" Kate said, knowing what was about to happen next. The barrel of a submachine gun came through the hole and several dozen rounds were fired, chipping away at the rocks all around them.

Nick heard the gunfire and realized it was about time to try to get the locomotive moving, ready or not. He stepped up to the driver's console and looked at the various levers again, one by one. This is the Johnson bar, he thought. Then there's the brakes. Then there's the throttle. That's the order you go in. I think.

Behind him, the fire was roaring, and somewhere in the engine a high-pitched scream was starting to build. Some valve that probably had to be released, but he had no idea where or how.

"Here goes nothing," he said out loud. He squeezed the handle on the large lever on the floor, felt it release, then pushed it forward. The train bucked a few inches down the tracks. The high-pitched scream grew louder, pierced by more gunfire.

"Let's go!" he yelled out the window. The whistle chain was

right above him. He didn't know if it would work, but he pulled it anyway. The sound reverberated off the tunnel walls.

"I'll cover you," Kate said to her father. "Go!"

Kate fired at the widening gap in the wall as Jake got up and ran toward the train. She kept firing until her gun was empty. The submachine gun fire chased her as she turned and followed her father.

Quentin climbed into the cab. Nick pulled back on one of the brake levers. The locomotive bucked forward another few inches. Jake reached the ladder and pulled himself up. Kate was right behind him.

"Hurry!" Quentin yelled.

Kate reached for the ladder just as Nick released the second brake lever, then pulled back on the big throttle bar with both hands. Jake tried to say something, but the engine's screaming was loud enough to drown everything else out. The locomotive was moving.

Kate finally got herself into the cab, pulled inside by Quentin as Jake leaned out and fired at the men who even now were entering the train tunnel. A spray of submachine gun fire raked against the metal sides of the locomotive.

Nick pulled back even farther on the throttle bar. The locomotive kept accelerating, faster than any of them would have guessed. It wobbled on the old tracks, the engine screaming louder and louder, but they were *moving*, picking up speed and momentum with every yard, and they were heading directly toward the wall of rubble blocking the exit.

Another round of submachine gun fire hit the engine. The

wall was getting closer. They all seemed to realize at once that this was going to be a hell of an impact and that they'd better get themselves ready. Jake, Quentin, and Kate all found something solid to hold on to. Nick was too busy holding back the throttle bar with both hands.

The front of the locomotive hit the old wooden handcar first, reducing it to splinters. The remains of Egger's grandfather were swept up in the next fraction of a second and crushed into the rocks. As the full weight of the locomotive slammed into the wall, everyone in the cab was thrown violently forward as 400,000 pounds of irresistible force met the immovable object.

Every circuit in Kate's mind was suddenly turned off.

When she came to, the high-pitched scream of the train's engine was all she could hear, the only sound that existed in the world. She felt strong hands pulling her up, and looked into the face of her father. Blood was streaming down between his eyes.

She couldn't understand why everything was suddenly so bright it made her head hurt. Nick was half-pulling, half-carrying his father out the twisted door of the cab.

Jake returned to her. "Can you walk?" His voice sounded like it came from far away, but she nodded.

When her eyes were adjusted to the glare of sunlight, she looked back and saw the front half of the locomotive sticking out of a great pile of rocks and debris. The front wheels were dug into the ground, but as she looked down she saw that there were no longer any tracks here anyway. It was just gravel and weeds on a long-forgotten shoulder next to a modern railway line. She felt like she had taken a trip on a time machine and had just been thrown back into her own world.

"We've got to get out of here," Nick said. He took out his knife, cut off a piece of his shirt, and used it to wipe away the blood from Jake's forehead. Quentin was woozy on his feet, but Nick helped him take a few steps and he seemed to come back to himself.

"Which way?" Quentin asked.

"This way," Jake said, holding the cloth to his forehead with one hand and pointing down the track with the other.

They were maybe a hundred feet down the tracks when the steam engine on the locomotive exploded. Thankfully, most of the force seemed to blow backward, back into the tunnel and not outward onto the tracks.

"I hope that took out a dozen of them," Nick said.

A minute later, they heard a train approaching. It must have been the strangest sight of the engineer's career, seeing the four filthy stragglers, one bleeding from his forehead, walking down the tracks and then a few seconds later, the nose of a World War II–era steam engine locomotive sticking out of the mountainside.

They followed the tracks all the way back to the lower station, where this whole day's adventure had begun. They climbed into their vehicle and just sat there for several minutes. Nobody said a word.

Jake flipped down the mirror on the visor and looked at the

cut on his forehead. Quentin took out the logbook he had found on the handcar and opened it. He flipped through the old pages like he might find something there that would make sense of everything that had happened.

Jake started up the vehicle and drove them back to the inn. They stumbled upstairs to shower and find clean clothes. Nick knocked on the professor's door as he passed.

The door was ajar. Everyone stopped in the hallway.

Nick pushed the door all the way open. The professor's laptop was on the floor. The desk chair was lying on its side. The bed-spread was half-pulled off. Nick checked the bathroom. It was empty.

A cell phone rang. It was Professor Lewis's phone, on the desk. Nick picked it up and answered the call.

"Who am I speaking to?" the caller asked. Nick recognized the diamond-hard voice immediately. *Egger.*

"This is Nick Fox. Where is Professor Lewis?"

"He is safe. Where is the gold?"

"There is no gold."

"That's a lie."

"Do you think we brought it all back here in our pockets?" Nick asked. "*There is no gold.*"

"If that's really true, then I have no reason to keep this man alive. He is now worthless to me."

As Nick held his breath and closed his eyes, he heard Egger giving instructions to someone else, hard words in German that were probably not good for Professor Lewis.

"We have something else," Nick said.

"What do you have?"

"We found a logbook that once belonged to your grandfather. It records all of his movements as the gold was taken from the train. Including his last words before he died. This book is your only chance to find out where that gold was moved."

There was a pause on the line as Egger absorbed this. "What does he say? Read it to me now."

"You can read it for yourself, as soon as you give us the professor."

"You will bring it to me."

Nick hesitated. "Fine. I'll come alone."

"No. All of you. I will see you tomorrow."

"Not tomorrow," Nick said. "Now. Tell us where to meet you."

"I'll send the instructions over this phone," Egger said. "You will bring this book you claim you have, and you will lay it at my feet."

The call ended. Nick just stood there, staring at the phone.

The phone beeped to indicate it was receiving a text message. Nick read the text with the exact directions they needed to follow, then read it again, because he couldn't believe it the first time.

CHAPTER EIGHTEEN

"Tell me again why we're going to *Casablanca*," Kate said. "He could have waited and gotten to us here in the inn, just like he got to Professor Lewis."

"Because Morocco may be just across the Straits of Gibraltar," Quentin said, "but it's the best place in the world to disappear. Or to *make* people disappear."

"That may be his plan," Nick said. "Doesn't mean it's going to work."

"What's our plan?" Jake asked. "We can't just walk into Egger's trap. We'll never leave."

"I'm working on an angle," Nick said. "In the meantime, we better get going. I don't imagine the professor's enjoying his little vacation."

"This is not the way I wanted to go to Casablanca," Kate said. "I'd rather walk into Rick's Café, see if Sam is playing the piano."

They all piled into the van and drove back across Slovakia, through Bratislava, and into Austria. As they were approaching the Vienna airport, Kate took out her passport and looked at it.

"As soon as they scan this," she said, "I'm going to be detained. We're *all* going to be detained."

"It's not going to be a problem," Nick said. He'd been texting on his phone for most of the drive.

"There was already an Interpol Red Notice on Quentin," she said. "By now, there might be one on all of us."

"I have it covered," Nick said.

When they arrived at the airport, Nick asked Jake to pull over so he could drive. With Nick behind the wheel, they drove past the commercial terminals, to a special security gate. Nick gave the guard a name that nobody else in the vehicle recognized.

"I haven't used that name in years," Nick said as he drove onto the tarmac, heading toward a Dassault Falcon jet. The door to the jet pivoted open and Captain Duckworth came down the stairs.

"How the hell did you get here?" Quentin asked, giving him a bro hug.

"Easy on the ribs," Duckworth said. "I'm still on the mend. But when your son sent me an SOS, I figured I needed to come myself."

"Thanks, Captain," Nick said, shaking his head. "I didn't know who else we could trust right now."

"I've already met Kate," Duckworth said, taking her hand. "She came to give me a hard time in the hospital."

"Sorry about that," Kate said.

"Don't be," Duckworth said. "It was the highlight of my week."

"Are you sure you should be out of that bed already?" she asked.

"It's not exactly the recovery plan my surgeon recommended," Duckworth said. "But as long as I don't get shot again, I should be all right."

"This is my father," she said. "Jake O'Hare."

Duckworth looked Jake up and down as he shook his hand. "Former Marine, am I right?"

"Nothing *former* about Semper Fi," Jake said.

"Man after my own heart. I'm glad to meet you."

"Let's get on that plane," Nick said to Duckworth. "We have to get to Casablanca, and do we have a few stories to tell you on the way."

———

It was a three-hour flight from Vienna to Casablanca, on a private jet that under any other circumstances would have felt like luxury. Kate stared out the window as they passed over northern Italy and then the blue water of the Mediterranean. Nick sat next to her, as Quentin told Duckworth about everything that had happened to them, and Jake bonded with Duckworth over a lifetime of military and extra-military adventures.

"We were so preoccupied with finding that gold," Kate said to Nick. "I admit it, I got caught up in the search as much as anyone. But right now I only care about two things."

"What's that?" Nick asked.

"Getting the professor back," Kate said. "And taking down Egger."

Nick nodded. "Sounds like a plan."

"And then we can all go home."

Nick nodded again, thought about it, and said, "Unless that book really can lead us to where the gold is now."

They both looked over at Quentin, who had the logbook out. The three older men were poring over each page.

"It's just dates and amounts," Duckworth said, wearing reading glasses and carefully examining each page. When he got to the last page, he picked up the book and read the words carefully, angling the page for better light. "My German isn't great, and this handwriting is pretty rough. But the very first word here is *Verrat*. Betrayal."

"I knew it," Quentin said. "Göring trapped him in that tunnel."

"The next couple of sentences," Duckworth went on, "he's got something here about *die Karte*, the map, and the *überlegener Intellekt*, the superior intellect, of the man who might follow it. Then what's this?" Duckworth looked over his glasses at the faded words that came next. "Is this *Tiefbrunnen*? I'm not sure what that means. *Brunnen* is like a fountain or a well. Something that holds water. But all the rest of this, it's basically just him feeling sorry for himself because he's trapped in a tunnel and he'll never get to see the Third Reich become what it's supposed to be. *Ein Land der Verheißung und Erfüllung*. Land of promise and fulfillment. The usual Nazi twaddle we fought a war to bury forever."

"Amen to that," Jake said. "My own grandfather fought that war. His destroyer went down in the Java Sea."

"Mine, too," Duckworth said, looking up at him. "Shot down over Berlin. My grandmother gave birth to my father the day after she got the telegram."

Duckworth paused a moment, looking at the handwriting in

the book. "The man you're going to see today," he finally said, "he's the grandson of this Nazi?"

"He is."

"Do me a favor and kick in his teeth for me."

———

The sun was still high in the afternoon sky when they landed in Casablanca. Duckworth slipped some money into one official's waiting palm at the airport, then two more, and then they were out of the airport through the private exit, having never shown a passport to anyone.

"They may already be watching you," Duckworth said. "I'm going to leave you on your own now. Where did they say to meet you?"

"Southeastern side of town," Quentin said. "A place called Moulay Rachid."

Duckworth winced. "I'll try to watch your back, but this is a tough city to keep tabs on someone."

They stood on the sidewalk for a minute, drawing stares. Jake raised a hand to hail a taxi and a car screeched to a sudden halt. It was too small, too loud, and the tires could barely be called round anymore. Everyone squeezed in and Quentin gave the driver the address, written down on a piece of paper. The driver gave the paper back, shaking his head and saying something emphatic that nobody could understand. Quentin returned the paper with twenty euros on top. It went back and forth like this for a few more beats until finally the money was enough and the driver pulled out into the heavy afternoon traffic.

"Just how big a favor did Captain Duckworth owe you?" Jake asked Quentin.

Quentin shrugged. "I may have saved his life once."

The conversation was cut off when the taxi driver nearly ran over a man on a scooter. Many harsh words were exchanged in Arabic, then the driver went another hundred yards before nearly committing another vehicular homicide.

The taxi worked its way slowly through the heart of the city. Carts on crowded sidewalks sold food, clothing, and knockoff American movies. Kate started to feel a little sick, sitting in the middle of the brick-hard backseat as the car hit every pothole in the streets.

The buildings got smaller and the streets got even rougher. Finally the taxi stopped and they all piled out. Kate's feet were barely on the ground when the taxi spun its wheels and fishtailed away from them.

They were in a small market square. It was empty, but the smell of fried fish hung thick in the air. Dogs barked. Faces looked at them through open windows and then the shutters were loudly slammed shut.

Nick looked up and down the deserted street. "This place could use a Starbucks."

A man dressed in desert camo approached them. On his head was a classic German officer's hat with goggles on the brim, like something Field Marshal Rommel would have worn. Standing next to him was Franz. His left eye was still hidden behind a black patch, but now he was also missing part of his right ear.

"My name is Rolf," the first man said. "If you will all come with me, your transport is waiting."

"Where's Professor Lewis?" Nick asked.

"You will see him soon," Rolf said.

"I want to see him now," Nick said. "Or else speak to him on the phone."

"You are wasting time, when we could already be on our way."

Nick looked at the rest of the team. "Guess we're taking a road trip," he said.

Rolf gestured toward a nearby alley. The team approached it, warily. When they turned the corner, they saw a windowless panel truck with the rear door open.

"We're not getting in that thing," Nick said.

Rolf drew an H&K semiautomatic from his belt, put the barrel in Kate's back.

"I believe you are."

———

The outside world slipped away, replaced by the two simple elements of heat and motion. Nick, Kate, Jake, and Quentin sat on the hard metal floor, drawing breath inside a furnace as it bounced its way down the roads of Morocco. The sounds of the city grew quieter and finally faded away, the air became a slightly less punishing degree of hot, and the thin bands of light running across the imperfect seams in the metal grew dimmer.

Kate and Nick slept for a while, their heads leaning together against the wall of the truck. They were jarred awake when the truck came to an abrupt stop. The rear door was thrown open and cool air rushed in. It was one of the best things Kate had ever felt.

They all climbed out of the truck and looked around at a small desert outpost, just a gas station and two other buildings. There was nothing else but the open desert all around them, a mostly dark sky, and a billion stars starting to shine.

Franz unfolded himself from the cab, stretched his muscles, and went to pump the gas.

"Two at a time," Rolf said, nodding toward the building. "Use the bathroom, drink some water. Do anything else and the two people left behind will die."

Kate drank as much water as she could, breathed in the cool air until it was time to go back into the truck. The warmth of the day had vanished and now she started to shiver.

"The sun went down to our right," Quentin said. "We're heading south."

———

Time went into limbo again. The gaps in the truck's metallic sides started to glow with light again. The air quickly got warmer. They felt the truck come to a stop, then they heard muffled voices arguing. The truck started moving again.

"I don't think we're in Morocco anymore," Quentin said. "We've come so far south. That was probably the border."

"The border to where?" Kate asked.

"Essentially *nowhere*," Quentin said. "The biggest no-man's-land in the world."

Jake nodded. "Western Sahara."

"That's right," Quentin said. "Morocco has claimed it ever since it was a Spanish colony. But the local desert nomads are called the Sahrawi. They've been here for centuries, and they're claiming the land for their own independent country."

"How do you know so much about it?" Nick asked.

"It was on the Agency's radar for a while," Quentin said. "If there was oil involved, or really anything at all except empty sand dunes, they might have cared a little more."

The road beneath the truck's wheels turned into hard, rutted ground. They bounced up and down like popcorn in a popper for at least another hour until finally everything stopped. The door was thrown open. Kate winced at the sudden glare of morning sunlight.

"Welcome to *Die Zitadelle*," Rolf said. "Herr Egger is anxious to see you."

"Where's Professor Lewis?" Nick asked.

"He is inside. Come."

They got out, all stumbling as they found their legs again after so many hours in the truck. As they blinked away the glare, they saw a compound made up of white single-story buildings. Each one looked like it had been baking in the sun for centuries. Beyond the buildings, as far as the eye could see in any direction, was nothing but endless sand, swept into dunes by the wind.

Aside from the beat-up panel truck, there were a handful of other large vehicles, all equipped with large tires for desert travel. A dozen men, all wearing desert camo, stood watching as Rolf led his hostages into the largest of the buildings. These men are different, Nick thought. They're dressed in real uniforms. They look sharper, more disciplined. And I haven't seen one red star tattoo yet. Which means this isn't a bunch of hired goons. This is the real thing. The Brotherhood.

"This way," Rolf said. He opened two hulking doors that looked like they'd come off Noah's Ark, leading to a large, mostly empty hall. High windows ran down both long walls in the hall. The floor was once intricate tiles, now cracked with age and covered with a light dusting of sand. At the opposite end was a great wooden table, also probably from the Ark, set upon a dais, which was shared by a pair of camo-wearing, submachine-gun-toting guards who served as bookends to the table. Seated behind the center of the table, like a desert king receiving visitors, was Klaus Egger.

"How was the journey?" Egger asked.

"The nuts weren't warm and the champagne was flat," Nick said. "I want to see Professor Lewis."

"We've had some interesting conversations, your professor and I. It's amazing how much he knows about German literature. And yet so little about the German soul."

"I'm not sure your soul represents the best of modern-day Germany," Nick said. "Where is the professor?"

Egger just smiled. Franz, who'd been standing at the back of the room with Rolf, came up behind Quentin and picked him up by the back of his neck. Jake aimed a kick at Franz's knee. It would have folded any other man in half. But Franz just looked down at Jake as if to say, *you're next.*

"The book," Egger said.

Holding Quentin in the air with one hand, Franz searched him with the other. The logbook was tucked into Quentin's belt. Franz took it, dropped Quentin to the hard floor, and brought the book to Egger.

"Thank you, Franz," Egger said.

Franz nodded without saying a word. Jake and Nick helped Quentin get to his feet as Egger paged through the book.

"Just to be clear," Egger said. "Adolf Hitler was a drug-addled fool, easily manipulated by men like Heinrich Himmler."

"Hitler, Himmler, Göring," Jake said. "Nobody cares about them anymore, Egger. They all hanged, at least the ones who didn't kill themselves to avoid it. The world's got bigger problems right now, and it doesn't need you running around here playing Nazi dress-up, trying to find some gold your grandfather helped steal."

Franz took a step toward Jake.

"Stop!" Egger said. "Silence!"

Franz froze in his tracks. Everybody looked at Egger as he put the book down on the table and bent over to carefully read the last page.

"He wrote this," Egger said, transfixed. "With his own hand. These are the last words of Gerhard Egger."

"Hate to tell you," Nick said, "but your grandpa Gerhard had a pretty rough exit."

"I said *silence!*"

Egger looked carefully at the page, saying the first word out loud. "*Verrat!*" Betrayal. He took a moment to absorb this, then kept reading, mouthing each word to himself as he went down the page.

261

"What does this mean?" he said. "*Tiefbrunnen vom Eisenmann. Tiefbrunnen vom Eisenmann.*" He kept saying it to himself, over and over again, like a man in a trance. Until at last, Egger looked up at the ceiling, raising his hands as if receiving a benediction from God Himself.

"*Danke, mein Gerhard,*" he said. "*Danke!*"

"We kept our end of the bargain," Kate said. "Now give us back Professor Lewis."

When Egger came back to earth, he looked down at Kate as if she were a child interrupting serious grown-up business.

"You're going to watch your professor die now," Egger said. "Along with the rest of these men. Then I'm going to let my brothers use you for their own amusement."

Jake and Nick both took two steps toward Egger, and were stopped only when the guards pointed their guns at Kate.

"Take them to the box," Egger said. "I want to watch how they die. Every minute of it. Don't start until I'm there."

As they were all led outside, Kate squinted in the harsh light, then looked one by one at Nick, Quentin, and finally her father. Behind them were the two guards with their submachine guns, Rolf with his semiautomatic, and Franz, who never really needed a gun at all.

"If anybody's got a great idea," Kate said, "now would be the perfect time to share it."

CHAPTER NINETEEN

As soon as the door to the "box" was opened, they saw Professor Lewis, a man having the worst day of his life. "Oh, thank God above," he said, rushing toward them. "I never thought I'd get out of here."

"You're not," Rolf said. "But at least you'll have some company now."

Quentin, Jake, Nick, and Kate were all pushed forward into the center of the room. It wasn't hard to see how the room got its name. It was a perfect cube, with the same high windows they'd seen in Egger's hall, six feet off the ground to keep out the blowing sand. But these particular windows all featured three metal bars, like a jail cell from the Old West.

"We'll be back as soon as Herr Egger is ready," Rolf said. "In the meantime, you can all decide who goes first."

"Just hold on," Nick said, coming back to stand next to Rolf. "Can we talk about this for a minute?"

"There's nothing to talk about, Mr. Fox."

Nick draped his arm around Rolf's shoulder and leaned toward his ear. "See, here's the thing, Rolf. We haven't even signed our contracts yet. And this dressing room is just not going to cut it. We're going to need a full buffet table. With a wet bar."

Rolf smiled at him. "You no longer have to worry about who goes first. It's going to be you, my friend."

"Oh, and a big bowl of M&Ms," Nick said, "with all of the brown ones taken out."

Franz stepped forward, picked up Nick, and threw him back into the middle of the room. The door slammed shut behind them.

"If I find any brown ones in there," Nick called after them, "I'm going to be pissed!"

Nick turned around and showed everyone the black Iridium satellite phone he'd just picked from Rolf's pocket, then tossed it to his father. "You better hurry up and call Duckie," he said, "before Rolf notices this is missing."

When Quentin was done with the call, he handed the phone back to Nick. "He tried to follow us in Morocco," Quentin said, "but he lost us when we crossed the border."

"How soon can he get here?" Nick asked.

"He's tracing our signal. He'll be here as soon as he can."

"I need something a little better than that," Nick said. "Did you hear what Rolf said? I'm first."

Jake glanced over and noticed that Professor Lewis had gone over to sit in the corner by himself. He went over to him and kneeled down next to him. "Professor Lewis, are you okay?"

"I tried to fight them off," Lewis said. "I really did. But there were three of them, including the big one! The worst part was sitting next to Egger on the plane. He's quite brilliant, you know, but also quite barking mad."

"That's one way to put it," Jake said.

Nick went over to the door and inspected the lock. "I could probably open this," Nick said. "But then what?"

"We could steal one of the vehicles," Kate said.

"Those are on the opposite end of the compound," Nick said, "but you're right, that might be our only shot if Duckie doesn't get here in time."

A full hour passed. Nick and Kate were sitting together against a wall. Quentin and Professor Lewis were sitting against the opposite wall. Jake was pacing back and forth like a caged animal.

"He's making us wait," Kate said. "It's a power trip."

"Like an interrogation," Nick said. "Remember how long you made me wait before you finally came in to question me?"

"That seems like a lifetime ago right now," Kate said. "But yes, I remember."

Quentin got to his feet and went to stand next to Jake, who was staring at one of the high windows. "I don't think we're getting out that way," he said.

A low, half-whispered voice from outside answered. "You always were a pessimist, Quentin."

"Duckie! How did you get here so fast?"

"You wouldn't believe me if I told you. You'll have to see for yourself."

They all watched as a hand appeared at the window. It grabbed one of the bars and rocked it back and forth. The bar moved slightly in the old masonry. The hand disappeared for a moment and a thick rope was fed through one side of the window, looped across all three bars, then back out the other side. There was a low guttural sound as the rope was suddenly pulled taut. Something not human.

"Easy!" Duckworth said, in a hushed voice. The rope went slack again, then taut, then it started to pull, *hard*, on the bars. One bar snapped free, then the second, then the third. The window was open.

At the same time, they heard footsteps outside the door.

"You first," Nick said, putting his hands down to make a step for Kate.

She grabbed the edge, lifted herself up, and climbed through. Nick did the same for the professor, leaving Jake and Quentin to debate who would go next.

"We could all just stay here and get killed," Nick said. "Let's go! Dad, you first!"

Quentin took the step from Jake's hand, climbed through the window. Jake followed.

The noises outside the door were getting louder. Someone was about to enter the room. Nick looked up at the window, jumped, caught the edge of the window, and pulled himself through, just as the door opened behind him. A submachine gun strafed the wall.

Nick jumped to the ground. When he stood up, he saw six camels. On top of each was a local Sahrawi, dressed in a brightly colored, long-flowing djellaba. Duckworth, Quentin, Jake, Kate, and Professor Lewis were already on board five of them, holding on tight behind the drivers. That left one for Nick.

"Jump on!" Quentin said. "Let's go!"

Nick ran and jumped again, grabbing the Sahrawi's hand to help himself up, and then they were off. The camels headed south, away from the compound, moving surprisingly fast.

A minute later, Kate heard the sound of gas-powered vehicles. As she looked back, she saw the first of the Desert Patrol Vehicles, or DPVs. They were essentially souped-up dune buggies that often carried heavy armament. As the DPVs got closer, Kate was relieved not to see any .50-caliber guns riding on top, but the man in the passenger seat of the lead vehicle leaned out and tried to spray them with his submachine gun. The DPV was bouncing up and down on the rough terrain, enough to keep his fire wildly erratic, but one smooth stretch of sand and they'd all be sitting ducks. Or rather sitting camels.

"They put the bombs in the sand," the man driving Kate's camel said, with remarkable calm. "What do you call them?"

"Land mines?"

"Yes, the land mines. They put them in our ground. They hide them in the night. But we watch them."

On cue, the man turned his camel hard to the right, at the same moment that every other driver made the same maneuver. The animal responded with more dexterity than anything weighing over a thousand pounds should have, and Kate had to grab the driver's waist to avoid falling off. As she looked back, the DPV kept on a straight line for another few yards, until, with an ear-splitting bang, the sand erupted beneath the wheels, sending the vehicle twenty feet in the air.

The camels picked up speed, spooked by the loud noise behind them. Kate saw Duckworth grimacing in pain as he held on tight to his driver. This wasn't great therapy for a man just out of the hospital.

"Hold on!" Kate's driver said, cutting hard to the left, again at the exact instant that every other camel made the same move.

Another DPV roared past on their right. This time Kate could see the driver's face as he realized what was about to happen, his last moment on earth before the land mine exploded.

When Kate looked back one more time, she saw no other vehicles behind them. Her relief was cut short when one more DPV appeared on the horizon. As it quickly closed the gap, she saw that it was being driven by Franz, who made the vehicle look like a toy, his body cramped into the cab and his head sticking out above the windshield. The driving sand whipped against his face, so hard it was probably already drawing blood, but he kept coming at top speed.

As Franz neared the camels, his strategy became clear to Kate. He hadn't even bothered to bring a gun with him. He was going to knock them all down like bowling pins.

Kate looked around desperately, trying to find some way to

stop him. Then she spotted the knife in the belt of the driver. "I'll pay for this," Kate said, as she pulled it from his belt. It was sharp and heavy, with a six-inch blade. She weighed it carefully in her hand, turning her body as much as she could without falling off.

Kate waited for Franz to get closer, then she threw the knife. It lodged into Franz's right arm. Franz looked at it like it was a mild inconvenience, pulled it out with his left, and threw it into the sand. He picked up speed and approached the last two camels in the pack.

"*Wahid!*" the driver of one of the two lead camels yelled. "*Athnan! Thlatht! Ainqisam!*"

The camel drivers split off at exactly the same time, three camels going left, three going right. It created a moment of indecision for Franz. One moment too many.

He tried to pull right, quickly changed his mind, then went left, but it was too late. The explosion of the land mine threw him from the vehicle, catapulting him *Mad Max*–style as he turned end over end in the open space between the camels. For a split second, he caught Kate's eye. A moment of recognition, maybe even a good-bye, and then his body hit the sand, where he slid a good forty yards. As soon as he stopped sliding, he tried to raise his head, but then his airborne vehicle landed on top of him and burst into flames.

The camels finally slowed down. Kate's driver patted his on the neck. "*Batal,*" he said, one of the few Arabic words that Kate knew. It meant *hero*.

Kate rubbed the camel on his rump, said the same word. "*Batal.*"

After another thirty minutes in the desert, they reached the small oasis town of Bir Lehlou. There were many more of the same simple, single-story buildings like Egger had claimed for his *Zitadelle*, but instead of sociopaths pacing around in desert camo, here were Sahrawi of both genders, all dressed in their djellabas of every color, and children running around chasing a soccer ball.

"Those bastards thought they were being clever," Duckworth said to the group, "picking a spot in the no-man's-land between Morocco's territory and the Sahrawi's. They didn't realize, it works both ways. I could have rolled a tank into that place, and nobody would have noticed. Or cared."

"Instead you chose camels," Nick said.

"When in Rome. But seriously, these good folks did *not* care for those men coming in here, taking one of their old outposts and planting land mines. They were quite eager to help me. Which reminds me, by the way, you're all going to help pay for a new wing on the school."

"Glad to do it," Nick said. "But how do we get out of here?"

"There's an airstrip half a kilometer away," Duckworth said, "with the jet waiting for us. Will that do?"

They all thanked the Sahrawi one more time and headed over to the airstrip, a simple ribbon of pavement laid out on the flat desert floor. Food and cold beverages were waiting for them.

Kate sat next to Nick as the jet took off, and looked out at the vast open expanse below. "We got the professor back," she said. "But that was only Item One on my list."

"Now we return to the hunt," Nick said, nodding to their fathers. They were on the other side of the plane, strapped in on either side of the table.

"Tell me about this logbook," Lewis said. "Every detail you can remember. Especially that last page."

"I can do better than that," Duckworth said, taking out a piece of paper. "I didn't understand half of it, but I did write it all down."

"Brilliant!" The professor took the paper and studied it carefully.

"I understood the part about the betrayal," Duckworth said, "but then I got lost right around here. What's *Tiefbrunnen vom Eisenmann*?"

"That's the part that got Egger excited," Quentin said. "He acted like his grandfather had sent down a message from heaven."

The professor wasn't listening to them anymore. He was staring at the words on the page, mouthing them to himself over and over, just as Egger had done. *Tiefbrunnen vom Eisenmann, Tiefbrunnen vom Eisenmann.*

"*Brunnen* is 'well,'" he finally said. "*Tief* is 'deep.' And of course the Germans will always make a compound noun by joining the words together. *Tiefbrunnen,* deep well. But *vom Eisenmann.* Of the iron man?"

They all thought about it for a moment, until Professor Lewis slapped his own head. "The iron man!" he said. "That was Göring's nickname!"

"The same man he worked for," Quentin said. "The man who betrayed him."

"That's right," Lewis said. "Which tells me exactly where we have to go next!"

CHAPTER TWENTY

After everything they'd been through in the past twenty-four hours, including a trip on a jet from Austria to Northern Africa, their next step, ironically, would be flying the same jet back to Austria.

"It's called Lake Toplitz," Lewis said. He was using Duckworth's laptop, connected to the jet's onboard Internet. "The closest airport is Salzburg."

Duckworth got up to tell the pilot about the next destination. Nick and Kate came over to join the conversation.

"I've heard of Lake Toplitz," Nick said.

"There was a Nazi naval station there during the war," Lewis said. "It's a very deep lake, very secluded. They tested depth charges there. Maybe torpedoes, too. They also used it as a sort of dumping station, like when they printed a hundred thousand pounds' worth of counterfeit notes for Operation Bernhard. When they scuttled that plan, they dumped all of the notes in the lake. Some people think you can even find sunken aircraft if you go all the way to the bottom. There's even a legend that there's a flying saucer down there."

"And gold?" Nick asked.

Lewis nodded. "All part of the legend. Maybe we're about to prove it's really true. At least the gold part."

"But what makes this lake the *deep well of the iron man*?" Kate asked.

"Göring had a villa nearby," Lewis said. "It was his favorite place in the world, and he spent as much of his free time there as he could. Out of all the Nazi leaders, he was the one man most surprised when he was found guilty of war crimes at Nuremberg. He must have believed he would just retire to Lake Toplitz, live out the rest of his life there."

"With his own personal stash of gold," Nick said. "After he sold out everyone else."

"You can leave gold in water forever," Lewis said. "It never degrades. And Toplitz is still very isolated. Even today, the nearest public road is a mile away from the lake."

"Well, we still have one problem," Nick said. "Once again, Egger knows the same thing we know. It's going to be a race to get there first."

"He thought he was untouchable in the western Sahara," Jake said. "But if he comes to Austria, we can take him, hold him for Interpol."

Kate shook her head. "If we tell Interpol that we think the

gold's at the bottom of the lake, they'll do whatever they want when they find it."

"What are you suggesting?" Jake asked. "Bring the gold up ourselves? That's impossible."

"We don't have to bring it up," Nick said. "We just have to *find* it. Take photos, send word to every news service. Let everyone in the world know what's down there."

"I've done a little diving in the Caribbean," Quentin said. "But this is a serious, technical mission you're talking about. We don't have the gear, even if we were crazy enough to try it."

"Scuba gear?" Duckworth had just come back from the cockpit to catch the end of the conversation. "I can probably scare up something by the time we're on the ground."

"I haven't been under sixty meters in a long time," Jake said, "but I'm up for it. Fortunately, we have one of the best divers I've ever known, here on this plane."

They all looked at Kate. She smiled and nodded, already getting herself psyched up for the greatest dive of her life.

They landed in Salzburg, Austria. They had to wait for an hour on the ground while one of Duckworth's contacts rounded up the necessary scuba gear and delivered it to them.

"I don't like this waiting," Nick said. "Who knows how long it'll take Egger to get here?"

When they finally had the gear they needed, they started driving east. With the professor and Duckworth along, it was now a team of six.

This time, it really did feel like the last leg of the journey. Ninety kilometers on the winding roads that led into the heavy forests of the Austrian Alps. One more time into the mountains, but this time the mission would end up underwater. They couldn't imagine the existence of another clue that would lead them anywhere else.

"They call these the *Totes Gebirge*," Lewis said as the vehicle started to climb. "The Dead Mountains. Did you know there's no oxygen in this lake under twenty meters?"

"Doesn't matter," Kate said, "as long as you have your own air strapped to your back."

"If it's all right with everyone," Lewis said, "I think I'd like to write a book about this adventure when it's all done. My last book was a survey of *Minnesänger* lyric poetry in the twelfth to fourteenth centuries. I think this one might sell a few more copies."

"Can't wait to read it," Kate said.

"Especially the happy ending," Nick said, "where we find the gold and get medals of honor and go on talk shows."

"I know you're going to," Lewis said. "All of those things and more. I can feel it in my bones."

———

When they arrived in the Salzkammergut lake district, they parked the vehicle in the area between the two largest lakes, Grundlsee to the west and Toplitzsee, as it was called locally, to the east. They put on their wet suits, because regardless of the surface temperature, it would be dangerously cold when they reached the lower depths of the lake. They slung everything else over their shoulders and started walking. Duckworth and the professor came along.

No matter how dangerous this last mission might turn out to be, Kate felt no nerves at all, because today she would be going into the water, not into the air. In her brief history as a SEAL, it was the diving that had come most naturally to her. No matter how much noise and chaos were taking place above the surface, as soon as she rolled over the edge of that boat and plunged into the water, it was like a return to her own private sanctuary. A place of peace and utter silence. It had been a while since Kate had been back to that place, but as she walked down the forest road, air tank on her back, she could already feel the same sense of calm settling over her.

The lake was a mile-long oval, just over a thousand feet across at its widest, nestled between the high cliffs of the Totes Gebirge. "The deepest part of the lake is on the eastern end," Lewis said. "The *Tief*-est part of the *Brunnen*. I'd say that's your best place to start."

The equipment was already getting heavy after they had walked a mile, but they summoned their second wind and hiked around the rough path that led to the opposite end of the lake. When they reached a small clearing, they put down their equipment, caught their breath, and got ready to dive.

"I don't see anyone," Nick said, surveying the stone cliffs and trees that surrounded the lake. "Did we actually beat him here this time?"

"We still have to be careful," Kate said. "We thought the same thing when we found the tunnel."

"Quentin and Nick," Jake said. "Go down as deep as you're comfortable, but I wouldn't recommend anything over sixty meters. If you see something interesting, let us know and we'll go deeper."

"Same for you, Dad," Kate said. "If it's under sixty, give me the sign."

He was about to argue, but Kate cut him off. She was the dive master. She was the boss.

Kate put on her buoyancy control vest, then her flippers. Finally, she put her mask over her face. It was a modern low-volume mask, not the old-school cylinder type she preferred, but she'd manage. The foursome waded out into the water, each one of them with underwater lanterns strapped to their wrists to help them see in the inky depths, along with a waterproof camera attached to a lanyard. Even with the wet suits, the water was an icy shock, but the suits would let their bodies warm up quickly and keep their body heat from escaping. Kate put her respirator in her mouth and submerged, then lifted her mask and blew out air to clear it. She swam out several yards, watching the floor of the lake quickly drop below her. She let air out of her vest to become heavier, then started to sink, holding her nose and blowing out through her ears to equalize the pressure.

She saw a few fish swimming around near the surface, but nothing when she got below twenty meters, where the water became starved of oxygen. A few more meters and the sunlight faded into a distant memory. She turned on her lantern.

The sense of peace and calm she was expecting somehow didn't come to her. Instead she felt a strange sense of eerie disquiet, as if, for the first time in her life as a diver, this underwater world did not welcome her.

Kate looked around for the other three divers and saw faint glows in the distance, all slightly above her own depth. Kate looked at the gauge on her wrist. She was just shy of sixty meters. If anyone was going deeper, it would be her. She steeled herself, put her head down and kicked with her flippers, clearing her ears as fast as she could. The water became darker and colder, until the beam from her light reached barely three feet in front of her.

Finally, something emerged in Kate's vision. With one more kick she leveled off just above it, shining her light on its contours. It was a huge log, slowly disintegrating in the water. Next to it was another log, then another, randomly crisscrossed over each other. She tried to shine her wrist lantern through the gaps, peering through to see if there was anything underneath this layer other than the rocky bottom floor of the lake itself. She gave another kick to move laterally over the layer of logs, but still couldn't see past them. Slow down, she told herself, don't kick up sediment or it'll be even harder to see down here.

The strange, eerie feeling was growing stronger inside her.

As she continued to move laterally, she sensed something vertical that was about to stop her. It was a wall of rock, like an underwater cliff. She moved along its face, wondering how high it was. There was no way to see, but then, just as she was deciding whether to retreat and continue scanning the logs, or to rise up along the wall, she saw something else. There was an opening in the layer of logs that otherwise acted like an impenetrable barrier to the lower depths. She paused for a few seconds, staying at neutral buoyancy, then she made up her mind and let out more air to descend through the opening.

She followed along the wall of the cliff, until the surface of the rock abruptly ended. As she drifted down a few more meters, clearing her ears, she realized that she had found the entrance to an underwater cave. It wasn't the first time she'd seen one, not by a long shot. The first time she'd ever ventured into a cave, it was only twenty meters down, on one of her very first dives, but she remembered the feeling of claustrophobia when she went inside and lost visual contact with the surface. She'd dealt with it then. She would deal with a different underwater cave now. They found $7 million worth of gold in that underwater cave in the Catskills, she thought. Is it possible this cave could hold a lot more?

With the almost useless lantern on her wrist shining in front of her, she advanced slowly into the cave. She knew she had to be careful. *Keep your sense of direction*, she reminded herself, playing back her first dive master's instructions in her head. *Know exactly where you came in, exactly how to get yourself back out. Even if you're blindfolded, which is essentially what you are right now.*

Kate didn't see any contours emerging. No floor, ceiling, or walls. She had no idea how big the space was, until finally she saw something just above her. She moved up slowly, saw dull metal.

She moved her light closer and saw something even more unexpected. On the metal surface was a symbol. Just a few days ago, it would have meant nothing to her, but now she recognized the single vertical line with two smaller lines angling off it on one side. It was the same symbol she'd found in the tunnels, the symbol that made her decide to go right instead of left. She even remembered the name. *Fehu*, the symbol for wealth. I found it, she thought. I think I just found the gold!

But then two more thoughts came to her. First, this dull metal object shaped like a barrel obviously wasn't gold. Was the gold stored inside it? If so, there must be a thousand other barrels down here.

Then the second thought, a small one but something that ran a chill down Kate's wet suit. Why is this *Fehu* rune upside down?

She moved the light above the barrel, saw the links of a chain attached to the top. It went up to a point somewhere above her, apparently holding the barrel in place. She moved to her left, came upon another barrel, another chain, and another upside-down *Fehu* rune. The chill in her wet suit turned into a full arctic cold front. These aren't barrels of gold, she said to herself. They look more like depth charges.

She willed herself to remain totally calm and in control, the first rule of handling any crisis underwater. As she turned to leave, a hand grabbed her arm. She whirled around, expecting to see her father, but Kate didn't recognize the wet suit. She shined her light through the other diver's mask, into the ice-blue eyes of Klaus Egger.

This was the man who had sent an army of hired soldiers to chase them across Europe. This was the man who would have let his soldiers do unspeakable things to her in the desert. Now she was alone with him in an underwater cave, and Kate felt nothing but a calm resolve. You don't have your gun, Kate thought. You don't have any leverage to use your size or strength. You're in my world now.

Egger drew out a large diving knife, a thick, eight-inch blade that on land would have struck fear into anyone on the wrong end of it. Down here it was just a great way for Kate to concentrate her attention on what was coming next. Egger drove the knife forward, his movement so slow in the water that she easily avoided the blade, grabbing his wrist and turning it. With the bubbles streaming furiously from his respirator, the blade fell from his hand.

She gave him a little come-hither gesture with her fingers, like *bring it on, give me your next move.*

All of Kate's training came back to her in an instant, her underwater combat instructor's words ringing in her ears. *Your attacker is going to go for the easy targets. Your mask. Your respirator. When he does that, you're going to stay calm, and then you're going to win the fight.*

Egger did exactly as she expected, reaching for her mask and ripping it from her face, then grabbing her respirator. She let him have both. Kate was blind now, and unable to breathe, but that was temporary. She stayed close to him, slid around to his side, and turned off his tank.

It took him a few seconds to realize what had happened. As his eyes went wide and he gasped on his respirator, Kate calmly put her own respirator back in her mouth, cleared her mask, and put it on her face. She watched Egger as he went into a full panic, deflecting his grasping hands as he clawed at her.

Another diver appeared into the cave. He was about to go for Kate, but she pointed at Egger and he quickly realigned his priorities. He swam by her, took out his respirator to give to Egger. On his way past, she reached over and turned off his tank, too.

The two men were wildly flailing at each other's tanks now,

and as they jostled against the depth charges, Kate knew that she suddenly had a much bigger problem. She shot out of the cave, driving herself forward with her flippers. Before she could reach the entrance, she saw two more divers appear in the glow of her lantern. They were fighting each other, in a swirl of bubbles and stirred-up sediment that made it impossible to tell one from the other.

As the water cleared, Kate recognized her father's wet suit. He had the other diver wrapped up tight, his forearm locked across the man's throat. She recognized the old-school maneuver, a choke-out with pressure against the carotid artery. On land, it leaves your opponent lying on the mat. Sixty meters underwater, it's fatal.

As Jake released the other diver, Kate gave him an emphatic thumbs-up sign. In scuba language, that doesn't mean *okay*, it means *get to the surface right now*.

Together, they broke every rule on the way back to the surface. *Come up slow, no faster than your smallest bubbles. Wait at ten meters to decompress. Unless you really are determined to get decompression sickness, aka the dreaded bends.*

Kate put two fingers to her mask, letting Jake know that they had to find Nick and Quentin as quickly as possible. When they separated, Kate turned in the direction where she had last seen Nick, finally seeing the glowing light. She had to descend again to grab him, and she gave him the same signal to get to the surface immediately. That left Quentin.

When she broke to the surface and tore off her mask, Nick was there waiting for her, a few yards away.

"Where's your father?" she yelled to them.

"There!" Nick yelled back.

She looked over and saw her father helping Quentin out of the water. Quentin was coughing and spitting out water.

"We have to get out!" Kate yelled to Nick, and then she kicked frantically, driving herself faster than any swimmer could ever go without flippers. They both arrived at the shoreline together, and Jake pulled them out.

"What the hell's going on?" Jake asked.

She was still struggling to get her breath back when the explosion went off in the cave. It was an incredible sound, somehow muffled and deafening at the same time. There was an eruption of water directly over the cave. A few seconds later, the first dead fish floated to the surface, followed by another and another until there were at least a hundred they could see, because according to the basic physics of a depth charge, water cannot be compressed, but the hydraulic shock it creates will compress anything with air in it. Like the hollow shell of a submarine. Or a lung with air in it, whether fish or human.

Kate waited to see if Egger or one of his men would also float to the surface. She wasn't surprised when they didn't, because a diver panicking inside a dark underwater cave has little chance of getting out, and the third diver her father choked out had no chance at all.

"Are you telling me there were *depth charges* down there?" Jake asked.

"That is what I am telling you," Kate said.

As she glanced behind her, she saw yet another of Egger's men, lying with his face on the ground and Duckworth's foot on his back.

"This one tried to detain the professor and me," Duckworth said. "It didn't go so well for him."

———————

They all walked back up the trail together, lugging their tanks, nobody saying a word. The four divers dried off as well as they could, then they all got in the vehicle and just sat there for a while in total silence.

"If the gold was really down there," Kate said, "then it's buried under tons of rock at the bottom of the lake now."

"This isn't the ending you wanted for your book," Nick said to the professor.

Lewis shook his head. "I can't believe it's all over. Am I supposed to just go back and teach my classes now? What do I tell the dean when he asks what I did on my unannounced vacation?"

And what do I tell Jessup, Kate thought, when I fly back to Los Angeles and both of us have to face the deputy director? I know we broke into a half-dozen landmarks all over Europe, sir, but the gold is down there somewhere, we promise!

Jake started up the vehicle, put it in gear, and pulled out onto the road. "Hey, we all got out," Quentin said. "And Egger didn't. I call that a success."

"Damned straight," Jake said.

"You actually saw *depth charges* down there," Quentin said, turning to look over the seat at Kate. "You must have been scared out of your head."

"You could say that, yes."

"Extraordinary."

"They had the *Fehu* rune on them," she said. "Can you believe that?"

"Pardon," Lewis said, "are you saying that the *depth charges* had a *Fehu* rune printed on them?"

"Printed, drawn, whatever it was."

"I find that quite twisted," Lewis said.

Another minute passed.

"The runes were upside down," Kate said.

"Pardon again?" Lewis asked.

"The runes," she said to the professor. "They were drawn upside down. On both depth charges I saw."

The professor's mind was churning.

"Is that significant?" she asked.

"When a rune is upside down, the meaning is reversed. Up becomes down, love becomes hate. In this case, *wealth* becomes—" He paused to think about it. "*Wealth* becomes *greed*. It becomes slavery to the *pursuit* of wealth, instead of the value of the wealth itself."

The words hung in the air. Nobody knew quite what they meant.

"So it was like a final message," Kate said. "Here's your reward for being so greedy, for chasing wealth all the way down to the bottom of a lake."

"I suppose that's the best way to look at it," Lewis said. "What a strange message to send to someone who at that point is about to die. But it must have felt poetic to whoever set that trap. And perhaps, for us, it's just as fitting a note to end on."

Jake kept driving. Everyone stayed lost somewhere deep in their own thoughts.

"Professor," Kate said, "do you remember when you told us to not let you overthink things next time?"

"I do remember that, yes."

"I'm just thinking out loud here," Kate said, "and feel free to tell me I'm completely off base, but tell me again, why did you call the lake 'Göring's deep well'?"

"Because he had a villa overlooking it. And this lake is about as deep a well as you can find."

"Okay, I get that," she said. "But what if the lake was just a misdirection? A death trap meant to catch anyone who came looking for the gold? Like you said, a poetic message to someone who was about to die because of their own greed."

"I don't understand," Lewis said. "What are you asking me?"

"I'm just saying, this villa of his."

Another long pause.

"Wouldn't it have had an actual *well* on the property, don't you think?"

Three seconds later, the vehicle skidded to a stop, did a quick U-turn, and then kicked up gravel with its squealing tires as it headed back toward the lake.

CHAPTER TWENTY-ONE

They drove back to the Salzkammergut lake district and found the one restaurant nearest to Lake Toplitz. The woman at the door looked up with alarm when all six of them stampeded inside.

"Pardon me," Quentin said to her. "I know this is a strange question, but is there someone here who might know where Göring's old villa was located?"

She tilted her head in confusion as she tried to decipher what she was being asked. The professor stepped up and asked the question again in perfect German.

"*Ah, die Villa, das ist lange her,*" she said. "*Wir versuchen zu vergessen.*"

"It was a long time ago," the professor translated for everyone else. "We try to forget."

"Tell her we understand how she feels," Quentin said. "But it's very important."

The professor talked to the woman again, this time a more extended conversation that he didn't bother to translate.

"She and her husband have owned this restaurant for almost forty years," the professor finally said to the others. "They've never heard anyone ask about Göring's villa. But her mother grew up around here, and if there's anyone who would know, it would be her."

"Where is she?" Quentin asked. "Can we talk to her?"

"We're about to," Lewis said. "But we should know that her mother *hated* Göring. We've been warned."

The owner took the whole crew to the back of the restaurant, where an old woman was sitting at a corner table by herself, cutting into a Viennese *apfelstrudel*. The woman looked up demurely at the half-dozen strangers who were interrupting her meal, until the owner whispered something into her ear. The mother's demeanor changed instantly. She said the single word "Göring!" looking like she would have spit if she was sitting anywhere else but in her daughter's restaurant.

Nick nudged Lewis forward. "Do your thing, Prof."

The professor bowed to the old woman, then started apologizing in German. His sincerity seemed to cut through the hostility and, after a few more proclamations and dramatic hand gestures, she appeared to tell him something useful. He thanked her profusely.

"I think I learned a few new German profanities," he said on their way back to the vehicle. "That's a very colorful woman."

"Did you happen to learn anything else?" Nick asked.

"Yes, I also learned where to find Göring's old villa."

They took the access road back to what passed for a small town between the two lakes, and then took another narrow, winding road up into the hills overlooking Toplitz.

"I should have written this down," Lewis said, looking out his window at the occasional farms and outbuildings.

They finally came to what looked like an old stone fence and the professor told them to turn. The vehicle rumbled down an overgrown dirt driveway that probably hadn't been used in decades, until they came to a stop at what might once have been called a villa. It would now more accurately be called a pile of rotting lumber and a half-fallen-over stone fireplace.

They all got out to look around. With the van turned off, it was eerily quiet. Kate walked down what was once the front walk, stones set into the ground, now cracked and barely visible through the thick weeds. Nick came up next to her and stood looking at the piles of rotten wood.

"It's like time is trying to erase the memory," he said. "How would anyone even know that a man like Göring lived here?"

"They sure didn't turn it into a museum, did they?" Kate said.

"I read somewhere that Hitler's bunker got plowed over and they intentionally kept the location as secret as possible. They didn't want certain people to turn it into a shrine."

Kate nodded. There wasn't much else to say. "I don't see a well around here, do you?" she asked.

"No," he said. "But there *must* have been one. How else would you get water to the building?"

Jake and Quentin had split off to search the rest of the cleared area around the villa site. Duckworth and the professor were doing the same, in the opposite direction.

"There's no gravity feed up here on the cliff," Kate said, looking around at the weeds and the wreckage. "How far could they pump water back then?"

Nick and Kate circled the pile of wood, then started picking through the old boards, on the off chance that the well had been dug *inside* the villa.

"I found something here," Nick said, kicking at several planks that were imbedded into the ground. Kate came over and together they pried them up, but found nothing underneath but the stony ground.

"You couldn't dig a well here," she said. "Even if you wanted to."

"You're right."

"No, listen to what I'm saying. You can't dig a well *right here*."

She looked around at the dense forest that surrounded the villa site.

"Come on," she said.

Nick followed her as she walked a wide circle around the clearing, peering into the dense underbrush. When he understood what she was doing, he started advancing into the brush, moving aside the vines and stinging nettles. A few minutes later, Nick pushed away a thick mound of leaves and saw something that made him stop.

"I think we might have something," he said to Kate.

"Over here!" she yelled to the others.

A minute later, they had all made their way through the brush and were looking down at another pile of rotting wood.

"There was a structure here," Nick said. "This big beam has some old hardware on it." He bent down and pushed aside the vines to reveal a rusted old bracket and a massive chain. "Look at this thing. Do you really need something this massive to bring up a bucket of water?"

They all started clearing the area. Under any other circumstances, they would all be swearing at the thorns and stickers that jabbed at their hands. They'd stop and insist on sturdy work gloves before touching another vine, but today, in this moment, on the top of a hill in northern Austria, five men and one woman did not care about thorns so sharp they drew blood.

"There's a platform down here," Nick said. Together they lifted off the great crossbeam and put it aside, then pulled up the center board of the platform.

"Careful," Jake said. "This thing could collapse at any moment."

Nick took out his flashlight and shined it down into the hole. The well was maybe thirty feet deep. It was lined with stones, and it was dry. There was no gold to see.

"We should go get some rope," Jake said.

"This chain looks sturdy enough," Nick said. "Help me tie it to something."

The two men untangled the great chain, wrapped one end around the nearest sturdy tree, and fed the other end down into the well. There was just enough play to reach the bottom.

"I don't know about this," Quentin said to Nick. "There might be one last booby trap down there."

"I'll be careful," Nick said. He grabbed on tight to the chain and lowered himself into the well. There were countless spiderwebs all around him, but he brushed those aside. One hand over another, he descended to the bottom.

Kate leaned over to look down at him. "What do you see?"

Nick was busy sweeping the dirt away from something on the bottom of the well. "There's a pair of iron rails," he said. "Like railroad tracks. And an old wooden door."

There was a long silence as they absorbed what they had just heard.

"Can you open the door?" Kate asked.

Nick took a deep breath, grabbed the old iron latch on the door, and pulled. It came off right in his hand. He looked at it for a moment, then at the door, and then he said, "What the hell," and gave it a good kick. The old wood cracked where it was joined to the hinges and the whole thing fell over with a crash.

"Nick!" Kate yelled. "What happened?"

There was a long beat of silence as Nick turned on his flashlight and took a few steps through the doorway. When he reappeared, he looked up toward the mouth of the well, brushing dirt from his face. "You all need to come down here," he said. "I think it's safe."

Kate climbed down the chain first. When she hit the bottom of the well, Nick wrapped his arms around her. "What's inside?" she asked, peering through the doorway, into the darkness.

"We're all going to find out together."

Quentin came down next. Then Duckworth, further trashing his doctor's orders. That left Jake and the professor on top.

"I'll give you a hand," Jake said.

"Are you serious?"

"You were kidnapped and taken into the desert," Jake said. "This is nothing. And besides, think how much better the book will be."

"Quite right."

Lewis took Jake's hand and carefully lowered himself onto the chain. Nick and Quentin were waiting at the bottom for him. There was barely enough room for the five of them to stand, but a minute later, Jake climbed down and they all had to squeeze against the filthy walls. But Nick was right, there was no other way to do this.

Leading with their flashlights, the whole team stepped inside.

It was hard to make out the exact dimensions of the space they were in, but it was immense. The floor sloped downward immediately, the rails leading down to the rest of the cavern. They followed the rails down to the lower level and found the railcar resting there, like something out of an old mine. They kept shining their lights in every direction around them, until the beams all came together, revealing the same thing.

Gold bars. Rows and rows of countless gold bars, stacked onto wooden pallets.

"Oh my God," Quentin said, looking all around him. "Oh my God."

Those were the only words said for a full minute, as every member of this team stood transfixed, shaking their heads in absolute wonder.

Their reverie was shattered by the sound of two great boots landing on the stone bottom of the well. A large body wedged itself through the doorway. They all turned to shine their lights on Franz. He was wearing the burned remnants of his desert camo. All of his hair and his eyebrows had been singed off. It accentuated the partial right ear, the scar visible across his left eye now that his eye patch had been burned off, and as he smiled, his missing two front teeth.

Franz wasn't carrying a firearm, but neither was any member of the team at the moment. All they had were knives and well-trained fighting skills and a six-to-one numerical advantage. Not nearly enough.

"Franz," Kate said, stepping forward.

"What are you doing?" Nick whispered to her.

Kate put up a hand to hush him, took another step closer to the behemoth. "That's your name, right? Franz?"

Franz nodded.

"Egger is dead."

Franz didn't react.

"The Brotherhood is dead. And all of this gold—" She gestured to the rows behind her. "It belongs to the people it was taken from."

Still nothing from Franz.

"I'm sorry we threw you out of a train," she said. "And buried you in an avalanche. And made you flip a burning dune buggy on yourself."

"And made you fall off the Eiffel Tower," Nick said.

Kate waved a hand at him.

"You shot him, too," he said to Kate. "Plus that hand grenade we tried to blow him up with."

Kate turned around and glared at him. *Really, Nick?*

"You shouldn't have done those things," Franz said, in perfect English.

Kate turned back to him, shocked.

"But I understand," Franz said. "I was trying to kill you."

"Yes," Kate said, tentatively. "But now—"

"You said Egger is dead?"

"He is."

"May I see his body?"

Kate hesitated. "That's going to be difficult."

"He blew himself up in the lake," Nick said. "The fish would be eating the pieces right now if the fish weren't all dead, too."

Kate closed her eyes. *So help me God, Nick.*

"Egger is dead," Franz said, mostly to himself. "Egger is dead."

They all waited to see what would happen next, and what happened was the same moment experienced by the guards at the castle when Dorothy melted the Wicked Witch of the West.

"Egger is dead," Franz said once more, and this time he smiled a big gap-toothed smile.

He looked around at the vast quantity of gold and said, "There is much work to be done here. I am very strong, and I will help you."

CHAPTER TWENTY-TWO

When Kate, Nick, and crew arrived at St.-Exupéry Airport in Lyon, France, they soon discovered that interest in the discovery of the *Raubgold*, the greatest treasure the world had ever known, had already grown large enough that there was a throng of international media personnel waiting for them. Television reporters stood in front of cameras, speaking into their microphones, and photographers flashed their cameras at anyone who happened to walk through the baggage claim area. Interpol had scheduled a big press conference for that evening, to announce the creation of a special commission to help distribute the proceeds from the *Raubgold* recovery. This is why the team had been flown to Lyon, home of Interpol headquarters.

Special Agent in Charge Jessup was waiting for them near the gate, inside the security zone and away from any of the press. Kate hadn't known what to expect from him. Anything from a medal to another tongue-lashing seemed possible, but she had been utterly shocked when Jessup wrapped her up in a hug.

"I'm sorry," he said, breaking away. "I didn't mean to do that."

"Yes, you did," she said. "And that's okay."

Jessup shook Nick's hand and was still all smiles when he spotted the two fathers. He had already met Jake O'Hare on previous occasions, but he hadn't yet seen Quentin Fox in person.

"This is Quentin Fox," Nick said. "My father."

"Very happy to meet you," Jessup said, shaking his hand.

Nick continued with the introductions, Professor Lewis and Captain Duckworth, and then Nick finally stepped back to introduce Jessup to the newest, and biggest, member of their team. "Sir, I'd like you to meet Franz Gruber."

Jessup's eyes traveled upward until he reached Franz's face, then he stood there speechless until Franz extended a massive hand.

"I've been looking forward to meeting you," Franz said, with a slight whistle through his two missing front teeth. "We have a lot to talk about."

"Do we?" Jessup looked back and forth between Nick and Kate, waiting for any of this to make sense.

"You remember that leak at Interpol?" Kate asked. "The one you were supposed to be finding for us?"

"That got a little complicated," Jessup said. "You have to remember, there are 194 member countries. Any one of them could have had an officer on loan at the headquarters, and if just one agent happens to see the wrong information at the wrong time, it would have been so easy to—"

"To communicate with the wrong person," Kate said. "We understand. But if that wrong person happened to share that information with one of his lieutenants, is that something you might be interested in?"

"Especially if that person wants to make a deal?" Nick asked. "Like the deal I made with you not so long ago."

"We would need to be very careful about this," Jessup said, looking back up at Franz. "If anyone else interrogates him, the information could end up tipping off our leak."

"Which is why he's with us," Kate said. "I think the two of you should go talk somewhere, and we'll catch up to you later."

Jessup nodded and walked away with Franz, still looking a little unsure about what was happening, and why he was being left alone with a man big enough to stuff him through a basketball hoop.

As Nick, Kate, Jake, Quentin, Duckworth, and Professor Lewis approached the baggage claim area and saw the throng of media waiting on the other side of the ropes, that was Nick's cue to make his own separate exit. He didn't want his own working relationship with the FBI to be compromised with a sudden, huge amount of public exposure.

"You guys got this," Nick said before he slipped away. "You all know how shy I am in front of strangers."

When he was a hundred yards away, he turned to see Kate behind him.

"What are you doing?" he asked. "Don't you want your fifteen minutes of fame?"

"That's not for me," she said. "I was just doing my job."

The two of them went to the far end of the airport and found a quiet door they could slip through without being seen.

———

Two hours later, Agent Jessup called Kate at the hotel. "Did you know that Franz speaks seven languages fluently?" he asked her.

"I didn't know he spoke *one* until yesterday," she said.

"He's going to bust this thing wide open, Kate. It's not just one leak to some psycho Nazi who wanted to find some gold. There's an entire criminal organization that has infiltrated Interpol at the highest level. With Franz's help, we're going to bring the whole thing down. It's going to make our careers."

"Which 'we' are you talking about right now, sir?"

"I understand you're still just catching your breath right now," Jessup said. "You've been through a lot, so by all means, take a few days off to recharge your batteries. But then we can all meet to talk about how you and Nick and Franz are going to tackle this new assignment."

"Sounds like a plan," Kate said. I'm not even surprised, she thought. First they teamed me up with Nick, now with Franz. Next will be those polar bears from the zoo.

"I'll see you tonight, Agent O'Hare. I'll save you and Nick a spot at the back of the room. I'm sure you'll want to be there to see your fathers."

"Of course," she said. "I'll see you tonight."

———

As Kate walked down the streets of Lyon, France, it felt strange to be truly alone for the first time in days. She didn't have to run anymore, because there were no new clues to find. She didn't have to watch over her shoulder, because nobody was chasing her.

They had all worked together to bring some of the gold up from the cavern, into the daylight. They had taken photographs of several bars, each one with the gleaming eagle and the wreath and the words stamped into the metal, "1 Kilo Feingold," along with the unique serial number below that. They had taken even more photographs underground, but it was hard to generate much light down there, so whoever saw the photographs would have to imagine just how large the cavern was, just how many one-kilo bars it would take to equal four hundred tons, and just how amazing it would feel to walk down the endless aisles between the pallets.

They had worked together to create a carefully worded press release on Professor Lewis's laptop, and then they had transmitted that press release, along with the photos, to every major news organization in the world. The one piece of information they did not include was the location of the well.

When they were done with this, they took the gold they had brought up and returned it to the cavern, where it had been placed seventy-five years before. They covered the top of the well and erased every sign that anyone had set foot on that parcel of ground above Lake Toplitz.

———

Kate went back to the hotel and opened her door with her key card. Nick Fox was standing in front of the full-length mirror, wearing a new Armani suit and looking something better than perfect.

"Nice suit," she said, "but I think you're in the wrong room."

Nick took his jacket off and draped it over the back of a chair. "I disagree," he said. "I'm here to discuss our next adventure."

"Did you talk to Jessup? Do we have a new project?"

"No," Nick said. "I was thinking more along the lines of a private, personal adventure."

"How private are we talking?"

"Private villa in the Seychelles, complete with private dining and a private beach. So private you won't even need to pack a swimsuit."

"And how are we going to afford all of this private?"

Nick smiled. "Funny story. Before we left the lake, while everyone else was packing up their gear, I happened to find a large duffel bag hidden near the shore. You'll never guess what was inside."

"Please don't say a bar of gold."

"That would be silly," Nick said. "The answer is pants. You know, from the men who came after us in the water. There were some other pieces of clothing, too, but it's the pants that are important."

"Please don't tell me there was a bar of gold in the pants."

"No, but there were wallets in the pants. Between all of the wallets, there was a considerable sum of cash. I was stuffing all this cash into my pockets when the ghost of Egger appeared to me."

Kate rolled her eyes.

" 'Sorry I tried to kill you so many times,' the ghost said. 'Take the money and use it for something righteous.' "

Kate groaned. "Booking a vacation in the Seychelles is righteous?"

Nick pulled her close to him. "Believe me, I've been having all kinds of ideas about things I'd like to do to you, and I promise they will all feel righteous."

Kate closed her eyes and leaned her head back a bit. "Or maybe a couple of them could be a little 'wrongeous.' "

His lips brushed against hers and then moved to her neck. "That's my girl."

The Lyon traffic was far below them, the sounds barely audible. The whole world, finally, had faded into the background.

"In this whole adventure," he said, "how much time did we have alone together?"

"We were kind of busy," she said, "you know, finding the biggest treasure in the history of the world."

"No," he said, "the biggest treasure in the world is *you*."

"You really think a corny line like that is going to work on me?"

Nick moved back to Kate's mouth. "Yes. I do."

Damned if he wasn't right.

ACKNOWLEDGMENTS

The authors would like to recognize the contribution of Peter Evanovich for the original story idea.

Here's a sneak peek at Janet Evanovich's next irresistible thriller, *The Recovery Agent*, coming in July 2021.

Gabriela Rose was standing in a small clearing that led to a rope and board footbridge, which was swaying in the wind. The narrow bridge spanned a gorge that was a hundred feet deep and almost as wide. Rapids rushed over enormous boulders at the bottom of the gorge, but Gabriela couldn't see the water, because it was raining buckets and she could barely make out the far side.

She was celebrating her thirtieth birthday deep in the Ecuadorian rainforest. The birthday wasn't important to her. She was all about the job. Her long dark brown hair was hidden under her Australian safari hat, its brim shading her exotic almond-shaped brown eyes. She was 5'6" and slim. She kept in shape for the job but also because she liked pretty clothes. And pretty clothes didn't always come in size fourteen.

She was with two local guides, Jorge and Cuckoo. She guessed they were somewhere between forty and sixty years old, and she was pretty sure that they thought she was an idiot.

"Is this bridge safe?" Gabriela asked.

"Yes, sometimes safe," Jorge said.

"And it's the only way?"

Jorge shrugged.

She looked at Cuckoo.

Cuckoo shrugged.

"You first," she said to Jorge.

Jorge did another shrug and murmured something in Spanish that Gabriela was pretty sure translated to "chickenshit woman." *Let it slide*, Gabriela thought. Sometimes it gave you an advantage to be underestimated. If things turned ugly, she was almost certain she could kick his ass. And if that didn't work out, she could shoot him. Nothing fatal. Maybe take off a toe.

It had been raining when she landed in Quito two days ago. It was still raining when she took the twenty-five-minute flight to Caco and boarded a Napo River ferry to Nuevo Rocfuerte. And it was raining when she met her guides at daybreak and settled into their motorized canoe for the six-hour trip down a narrow, winding river with no name. Just before noon, they'd pulled up at a crude campground hacked out of the jungle. Four hours on foot after that, following a trail that barely existed. All in the pouring rain.

She'd been hired to find Henry Dodge and retrieve a ring he was carrying. Not a lot of information on the ring or Dodge. Just that he couldn't leave his job site, and he'd requested that someone come to get the ring. Seemed reasonable, since Dodge was an archeologist doing research on a lost civilization in a previously unexplored part of the Amazon rainforest. The payoff for Gabriela was a big bag of money, but that wasn't what convinced her to take the job. She was a treasure hunter. For profit and for pleasure. She was an amateur anthropologist, a descendant of Blackbeard, a history buff, and a collector of pirate plunder. The opportunity to visit a lost-cities site was irresistible.

"How much further?" she asked Jorge.

"Not far," he said. "Just on the other side of the bridge."

Ten minutes later, Gabriela set foot on the dig site. She'd been on other digs, and this wasn't what she'd expected. There was some partially exposed rubble that might have been a wall at one time. A couple of tables with benches under a tarp. A kitchen area that was also under a tarp. A stack of wooden crates. A trampled area that suggested several tents had been recently used and recently abandoned. Only one small tent was left standing.

There were no people to see except for one waterlogged and slightly bloated dead man lying on the ground by the rubble, and a weary-looking man sitting nearby on a camp chair.

"This is not good," Jorge said. "One of these men is very dead, and something has eaten his leg."

"Panther," the man in the chair said. "You can hear them prowling past your tent at night. This site is a hellhole. Were you folks just out for a stroll in the rain?"

"I was sent to get a ring from Henry Dodge," Gabriela said. "I believe I was expected."

The man nodded to the corpse. "That's Henry. Had some bad luck."

"What happened?"

"He was checking on an excavation in the rain first thing this morning, fell off the wall and smashed his head on the rocks. Then a panther came and ate his leg before we could scare it away. Everyone packed up and left after that. Too many bad things happening here."

"But you stayed," Gabriela said.

"They couldn't carry everything out in one trip. I stayed with some of the remaining crates and the body. Cameron said he would be back with help before it got dark."

"Do you know where Henry kept the ring?" Gabriela asked.

"It's on his finger," the man said. "He felt it was the safest place."

Gabriela looked at the dead man's hand. It was grotesquely swollen and clenched in a fist. The ring was barely visible.

"Someone needs to get the ring off his finger," Gabriela said.

No one volunteered.

Gabriela flicked a centipede off her sleeve. Could the day get any worse? She was wet clear through to her La Perla panties, her boots and camo cargo pants were covered with mud, and she had bug bites everywhere. *All part of the jungle experience*, she told herself. The dead man with the swollen hand was not. The question now was, how bad did she want the ring? The lost-cities site had turned out to be a bust, but there was still a payday attached to the ring. So, the answer to the question was that she wanted the ring pretty damn bad. Without the ring, there would be no big bag of money. And she needed the money to finance her own treasure hunt. She'd recently found a three-hundred-year-old map that had been lost in her family for fifteen generations. It was a treasure map signed by Blackbeard, and she had it on good authority that it was real.

"I've come this far," she said. "I'm not going back without the ring." She looked at the man in the chair. "I need to pry Dodge's hand open and work the ring off his finger. I need gloves and a baggie. I know all archeological sites have them."

The man shrugged his shoulders as an apology. "They were all packed out. Truth is, we were shutting down before Henry happened. Henry was the holdout. He found the ring, and he thought there was more here. The rest of us didn't care."

"We need to leave now," Jorge said. "It will be bad to be in this jungle after sunset. Hard to find the way, and panthers will be hunting at night. We have maybe five hours of daylight left."

"I'm not leaving without the ring," Gabriela said.

Cuckoo took his machete out of its sheath and whack! He chopped Henry Dodge's hand off at the wrist.

"I suppose that's one way to go," Gabriela said. "I would have preferred to try my way first."

"He's dead," Cuckoo said. "He doesn't need the hand."

He picked the hand up by the thumb, grabbed Gabriela's daypack and dropped the hand in.

"Problem is solved," Jorge said.